A BODY
IN A
CORNISH
VILLAGE

BOOKS BY DEE MACDONALD

A BODY
IN A
CORNISH
VILLAGE

DEE MACDONALD

bookouture

Published by Bookouture in 2023

An imprint of Storyfire Ltd.
Carmelite House
50 Victoria Embankment
London EC4Y 0DZ

www.bookouture.com

ISBN: 978-1-83790-744-1
eBook ISBN: 978-1-83790-743-4

ONE

There wasn't a cloud in the August sky. The sea was sparkling, and the sun was highlighting every ledge and crevice on the dramatic cliffs bordering the little beach. After two days of rain, and a great deal of sighing from the crew, Cornwall had finally come up trumps. Filming could commence at last.

But Kate Palmer, clad in a coarse, scratchy, canvas-like brown shift, was already rueing the day she'd been persuaded to be an extra in this stupid film in Port Petroc. She felt fat and frumpy, and every one of her sixty-two years. The brilliant hairdo that Guy had created yesterday, with its highlights and lowlights, was now covered in a grubby white mob cap, and what was visible was dangling sadly round her ears. She could only console herself with the fact that eighteenth-century peasants would not have had highlights and lowlights. Anyway, she was too far away from the action for anyone to notice. Life as a film extra was certainly not as glamorous as she'd imagined, and she was much happier with her role as a nurse in the Tinworthy Medical Centre. But she had to admit that she was happiest of all when acting as an amateur sleuth, and was quite proud of the name she had made for herself locally with her detecting skills.

'Everyone in position? Silence now – action!'

Filming was not going well. Sonia Somerfield, the director, was becoming increasingly frustrated by a series of mishaps and hitches, all causing delays to an already tight schedule.

'This bloody thing is jinxed,' Kate had heard one cameraman murmur to another when she'd arrived on set.

The Limelight Films setting was idyllic: the secluded cove, the white sand and the aforementioned cliffs on the dramatic coast of North Cornwall. Then there was the two-masted brigantine out in the bay – the quintessence of an eighteenth-century smuggling drama for television – and a dozen or so extras on the beach, ready for action, a couple of them already complaining about the sand being hot beneath their bare feet. And the weather forecast was good for the coming week. What could go wrong?

When, earlier in the day, the bus from Tinworthy had disgorged its load of passengers, all eager to be extras in the Cornish smuggling drama, the casting director had sighed audibly and said, 'They'll *all* have to be peasants.'

All, that was, except for Angie, Kate's errant sister, who was to blame for getting her involved in this entire event.

At some time in the distant past, in her acting career, Kate realised that Angie had presumably slept with Crispin Wyngarde, the producer and writer of *Pengorran's Revenge*, who had also insisted on having a cameo part in the production himself. Not only was Angie still on Wyngarde's Christmas card list, but she'd actually got herself a small cameo part too, and had volunteered to produce a busload of extras from the local area as well. Angie was telling anyone who would listen that it was thanks to *her* that they were all here as extras – or 'supporting artists', as Angie liked to call them – in the first place, and in a location so close to Tinworthy, just along the coast, where they all lived.

She had suggested the location to Crispin in a Christmas card note, she told Kate, because he'd mentioned that he'd written a Cornish smuggling drama and was eager to get it filmed. Angie had maintained her Equity card because, up until they made the move to Cornwall, she'd still been getting the odd part in minor productions and the occasional advertisement. She was not, of course, playing the part of a peasant like the others, but was now strutting around in satin and lace and lording it over everyone.

Kate looked round to where her husband, Woody Forrest, was standing nearby, looking extremely bored. He looked very fetching though, in some sort of leather tabard, plainly a more upmarket peasant than she was. Then again, Woody, even at sixty-five, still managed to look fetching in pretty much anything.

It was the moment of Angie's big scene. Her *only* scene really. As the mother of Mark Pengorran (an ex-merchant navy captain turned smuggler), she was begging Crispin, who was playing her on-screen lover, not to shoot Mark. He was paying no attention, and so Angie's character was required to grab the blunderbuss from him, accidentally pressing the trigger and killing Crispin's character. The big worry, from the director's point of view, had been: would Crispin drop to the ground at the *exact* moment the blunderbuss fired the gunpowder, which was to make a dramatic explosion with smoke and a flash? It had to be timed perfectly.

Kate, trying hard to resist the urge to scratch, due to the coarse fabric, yearned for the scene to be over. But as long as the cameras were rolling, she had to continue being a peasant, halfway up a cliff, drawing (non-existent) water from a (plastic) well.

Angie's big line: 'Please, please, darling, don't shoot my son!'

– which she'd been rehearsing for weeks – was said, but Crispin's character ignored her and began to point the blunderbuss at his target. Then, as Angie wrestled the gun from him, she pulled the trigger, the blunderbuss fired and Crispin, a true trooper, fell dramatically to the ground. This was followed by Angie cradling the body with much weeping and wailing.

'Cut!' shouted Sonia, the director. 'That was *brilliant*! The timing was perfect.'

She looked at Angie, who was becoming increasingly hysterical. 'We've got it in the can, Angie, so you can get up now!'

But Angie's cries and screams were only getting louder.

Several of the crew were now running towards the prone Crispin, and the weeping Angie, turning a tear-stained face towards the director, said, 'But he's *dead*!'

'Yes, very convincing,' Sonia agreed.

'No,' screamed Angie, 'he's *dead*! *Really dead*! He's been *shot*!'

TWO

'Well, well, well,' sighed Charlotte Martin. She had replaced Kate's husband, Woody, as detective inspector for the area two years ago. Charlotte's arrival in Cornwall had worried Kate more than a little, because she was a stunner: tall, blonde, slim, beautiful and immaculate. Kate had considered this to be extremely unfair at the time, because Woody had to familiarise this woman with the area and any dubious characters as part of the changeover. Kate, constantly battling with her weight, had been anxious that Woody might be smitten with this paragon of beauty. But she needn't have worried. Charlotte and Woody were just friends, and any competition between the two women had been diluted now that Kate had a ring on her finger!

The paragon of beauty was now ordering that the entire area be taped off. No one could enter and no one could leave. She and her team then began interrogating everyone on the set.

'I was halfway up the cliff,' Kate informed her, her wobbly legs betraying her state of shock. 'Nowhere near the shooting! And I'd never set eyes on that blunderbuss before.'

'Hmm,' said Charlotte, 'but it's interesting that it was your sister who pulled the trigger.'

'She was *supposed* to pull the trigger! She even had a day's training on how to do that scene!' Kate spoke defensively and wondered why she was being quizzed about Angie. 'There should have just been a loud bang and some smoke, but plainly the gun must have been loaded to kill.'

'That much is obvious,' Charlotte agreed, 'and I need to find out who loaded it.' She studied Kate for a moment. 'Why are you always around when there's a murder, Kate?' She gave a faint but unconvincing smile.

'I've no idea,' Kate said sadly, 'but I really wish I wasn't.'

Charlotte then turned to question Woody, who was standing anxiously nearby. As Woody had been on the beach, pretending to unload boxes of disguised contraband from small boats, brought in from the brigantine out at sea, he'd also been some distance from the crime scene.

After Charlotte had moved on, Woody asked, 'You OK?' as he hugged Kate tight.

'Well I'm as shocked as everyone else,' Kate said, leaning against his still-leather-bound chest, 'but I'm particularly bothered about Angie. After all, she pulled the trigger. I believe Charlotte's grilling her now.'

'Poor old Angie!' Woody sighed. 'I've been given clearance to change into my own clothes, although it doesn't look like we're going to be allowed to leave here any time soon.'

'Yes, I've been told I can change too, but last time I looked, Angie was being questioned in there,' Kate said, looking anxiously towards the wardrobe trailer.

When Kate saw Charlotte emerge from the trailer ten minutes later, she went in to find Angie, who, very distressed, had been photographed several times in her bloodstained yellow satin before being permitted to remove the offending garment and don her own clothes. The dress, Angie said, had been placed in a bag, which was labelled and taken away.

'I was questioned *first*!' she complained to Kate through her tears. 'I can't believe what's just happened! And that Charlotte woman was interrogating me like I was some sort of *criminal*!'

'It's her job to question everyone,' Kate soothed.

'And *now*,' spluttered Angie, 'she's giving poor Fergal the third degree! God, I wish I'd brought some gin with me because I damn well need it!' She glared at Kate. 'See how *you'd* feel collapsing onto a dead body all covered in blood!'

Fergal was Angie's black-haired, black-bearded, blue-eyed Irish partner. Theirs was a tempestuous relationship to say the least, punctuated by constant rows, followed by making-up sessions. He, too, was an extra on *Pengorran's Revenge*.

Three hours later, a still inconsolable Angie wept all the way back on the bus to Lower Tinworthy.

Kate felt exhausted. If there was anything more wearying than supposedly drawing non-existent water from a non-existent well for hours on end, it was having to then hang around for hours to be questioned by Charlotte Martin and her team.

'No,' Kate had repeated countless times. 'I had never set eyes on the blunderbuss until that scene!'

Neither had Woody, but it appeared that Fergal, Angie's partner, had.

'Sure, I went to have a look at the feckin' thing,' he told them now, stroking his black beard as the bus lurched its way up the steep slope from Port Petroc, 'because it was *real*, unlike everything else on that bloody phony set.'

Woody was looking thoughtful. 'There were plenty of people who had access to that blunderbuss,' he said, 'so the police will want to know who might have had a reason to bump off poor old Crispin.'

'Well *I* didn't!' snapped Fergal.

'But you *were* jealous of Crispin giving me a proper speaking part,' said Angie, stifling her sniffs, 'and you made it clear to everyone that I'd known Crispin for years before I ever set eyes on you. Perhaps the police could make out that you had a motive to want him out of the way.'

'Are you accusing *me* of putting lead balls or something into that gun?' Fergal shouted at her.

'What makes you think it was loaded with lead balls?' Woody asked.

'Because that's what they feckin' fired from feckin' blunderbusses!' Fergal shouted, his voice rising several decibels.

'Someone tell that Irishman to stop shouting,' a man from further back in the bus piped up, 'cos I'm trying to calm my nerves.'

'Why, did *you* kill him?' Fergal yelled back.

No chance of anyone calming their nerves with these two arguing, Kate thought.

Since she'd come to live in Cornwall, Kate had acquired a reputation as the local Miss Marple, of Agatha Christie fame, because of the several unfortunate murders she'd had a hand in solving. But she'd sworn never to get involved in any more crime-solving. Nevertheless, Kate couldn't help herself and she immediately began to wonder how many people might have had a motive to kill Crispin Wyngarde.

'*No*, Kate,' said Woody out of the blue.

'What do you mean?' Kate asked, startled.

'Don't even *begin* to think about trying to solve this one!'

'I wasn't!' Kate protested.

'Yes, you *were*.'

That was the thing about Woody: he had this ability to read her mind, which was not always an advantage, although she loved him to bits.

He wasn't wrong of course, because she was already wondering how to solve this one, if only to clear her sister's name.

THREE

Kate and Woody had been attracted to each other from the moment they met, shortly after she and Angie had left London some four years earlier for a supposedly tranquil retirement by the sea in North Cornwall. Woody, then still the local detective inspector, was American by birth, with an English father, from whom he'd inherited a calm, very logical manner, and an Italian mother, from whom he'd inherited his dark good looks and golden skin. Kate and Woody had finally married the previous year and were now happily ensconced in Lavender Cottage, on the hillside overlooking the village of Lower Tinworthy and the Atlantic Ocean.

Although she was now over sixty, Kate still worked a couple of days a week as a practice nurse at the local medical centre, which was situated up the hill in Middle Tinworthy. Since she normally only worked there on Mondays and Tuesdays, she hadn't needed to beg time off to be an extra on *Pengorran's Revenge* because they were only required to be on the set on Thursdays and Fridays. For the rest of the week, the production was filming at a local National Trust property. It would be a new, exciting experience, she'd thought. Except that there was a terrific amount of time hanging around, doing nothing, or very little. If nothing else, this real-life drama would certainly liven things up.

Angie was still wailing. 'Poor Crispin! And I was only doing what I was supposed to.'

'Well that's one less Christmas card to send,' Fergal said drily.

'Don't be so bloody heartless!' Angie shouted. 'Crispin was my *friend*!'

Kate glanced across the aisle of the bus at Guy, the hairdresser, and wondered what he must be thinking about the catastrophic damage her mob cap had done to his wonderful efforts on her hair. And then she wondered why on earth he might want to be an extra on any film when he had such a successful business in Middle Tinworthy. He was looking thoughtful but saying nothing.

Kate was very relieved when the bus finally disgorged some of its passengers in Higher and Middle Tinworthy, and headed down the road to the lower village. It stopped outside The Old Locker, which was Angie's latest project. She, with Fergal's assistance, had transformed it from a ramshackle old tearoom into a smart café and bar, and they lived in the tiny flat above. Unfortunately, Angie was frequently her own best customer, due to her long love affair with gin, and Kate knew perfectly well that the first thing her sister would do, the second she got through the door, was pour herself a mega-measure of Bombay Sapphire, with a minimum amount of tonic. The first of many, no doubt, knowing that although Charlotte had been happy to let Angie go for now, she'd be questioning her again before long.

They disembarked and, with a wave of his hand, Fergal led a still distraught Angie into The Old Locker.

Kate and Woody were the final two passengers.

'We'll walk,' Woody told the driver. 'We live just up the lane and we could do with some exercise.' He looked at Kate for confirmation, and she nodded.

Kate and Woody held hands as they made their way up the lane towards Lavender Cottage.

'Why is it,' Kate asked, 'that everywhere we go, someone comes to a sticky end?'

Woody sighed. 'I really don't know. I thought I'd left crime behind when I retired, but at least this incident isn't actually *in* Tinworthy.'

'No, but most of the extras are *from* Tinworthy,' Kate remarked.

'True, but not all the extras would necessarily have had access to the blunderbuss. And who, apart from poor old Fergal, or perhaps Angie, might have a reason to kill Crispin?'

'I don't know, but I'd really like to know why Guy, the hairdresser, wanted to be an extra,' Kate remarked.

'I expect Angie talked him into it when she was recruiting,' Woody replied.

He stopped in his tracks as they approached The Greedy Gull pub, which was halfway up the lane. 'How about we pop in for a drink? I think I could do with one!'

'Me too,' Kate confessed, suddenly feeling the need of a gin and tonic for herself.

It was only half past five and the pub was still empty.

Des Pardoe, the somewhat lugubrious landlord, looked up from *The Racing Times*, which was spread across the bar counter.

'How's our local *film stars* then?'

Kate snorted. '*Extras*, Des, only extras. But we've had a fair bit of excitement today and I have great need of a gin and tonic.'

'And I have an equally great need for a pint of best bitter,' Woody added.

As Des folded up his paper and set about getting their drinks, he asked, 'What's wrong with you two – you look a bit shook up?'

'We've had an awful day – there's been an accident on the set,' Kate said. 'Actually, it's a bit more than an accident; more of a tragedy really. One of the actors has been shot. Well I say actor, but he was actually the producer as well.'

'What, shot *dead* do you mean?' Des looked stunned for a moment.

Kate nodded.

'He's dead all right,' Woody confirmed.

'Well I never!' said Des, turning around to reach a bottle of tonic. 'So what's this film all about then?' he asked, placing the drinks on the bar.

'It's only a television film,' Kate said. 'You won't be seeing it on the big screen. It's a smuggling adventure, set in eighteenth-century Cornwall, and it's about a merchant navy sea captain called Mark Pengorran.' Kate took a sip of her gin and tonic. 'The backstory is that he came home one day to find that his wife has been shot dead by excise men and, in his sorrow and anger, he became a smuggler, to get his revenge. The film is called *Pengorran's Revenge*.'

'Sounds like a good story,' Des said. 'Plenty of smugglin' used to go on round here, that's for sure.' He winked. 'And probably still is!'

'Is that where you're getting your cheap booze from then, Des?' Woody asked.

Des shook his head. 'If only... but tell me more about this actin' you're doin'. Are you all goin' to be stars?'

'Apart from my sister, Angie, we're all just peasants in the background,' Kate explained, 'and doing the same thing hour after hour, or else hanging around, which is equally boring.'

Des lifted an eyebrow. 'So what's *her* then? Your sister?'

'She plays the part of Mark's mother, which is only a tiny part, but she does get to say a few lines,' Kate replied. 'Unfortunately, in the story, she has to snatch this blunderbuss away from her lover, who was about to shoot her son. But when she grabs the blunderbuss, it goes off and accidentally kills the lover.'

'Good actin' was it?' Des asked.

'Well it was good acting as far as we could tell, but the blunderbuss was loaded.' Woody paused and took a sip of his beer. 'And *it wasn't loaded* with blanks.'

Des stopped dead with a pint halfway to his lips. 'What are you sayin'? Are you tellin' me that your Angie killed him?'

'I'm saying that Angie shot the actor, who also happened to be the producer, *and* probably her one-time lover to boot, and killed him stone dead,' Woody said, taking another large slurp of his beer.

'What, killed proper? Proper job like?' Des's eyes were out on stalks.

'Proper job,' Woody confirmed with a grimace.

'They stopped filming when it happened this morning,' Kate said, 'and we've only just been allowed to leave because the police wanted everyone's details. It has to be said that this producer wasn't very popular and the rumour is that there might be any number of suspects.'

'Well,' said Des, 'there ain't nobody in any of the Tinworthys who'd want to kill some producer or actor or whatever he was. Who was he anyway? Did he do anythin' famous?'

'Crispin Wyngarde was his name,' Woody replied, 'but I shouldn't think you've ever heard of him. Anyway, he is no more!'

Des took a large gulp of his beer. 'He's dead then? You're certain he's dead, good and proper?'

'Yes, he is,' Kate replied. 'He's as dead as dead can be.'

'Well, well,' remarked Des, taking another large slug of his beer.

As Kate and Woody took their drinks and seated themselves at their favourite table by the inglenook, Kate could only think about Angie and how she could well be the main suspect.

FOUR

Kate had fallen in love with Lavender Cottage, in Lower Tinworthy, when she'd viewed it online, but, when she and Angie came to see it, she'd realised that the pictures really didn't do it justice. The old stone cottage, with its quirky interior and hedges of lavender, had the most magnificent panoramic views. From the front windows, Kate could see right down to the River Pol with its ancient stone bridge, all the shops and cafés, the beach and a wide stretch of the Atlantic Ocean. In the winter, this wasn't always advantageous when the gales and horizontal rain rattled relentlessly against the windowpanes.

By the time Kate had fallen in love with Woody, Angie, always a restless soul, had taken over The Locker Tearooms, and so Woody had bought her share of Lavender Cottage and moved in, letting out his own house on the other side of the valley. This arrangement suited everyone concerned.

'This case will be giving Charlotte a class-one headache,' Woody said, now back in the kitchen of Lavender Cottage, 'because, not only was this producer guy not particularly popular with the film crew, but there's now a connection with an ex-lover.'

'Meaning Angie?' Kate prompted as she put the kettle on for tea and rooted out the biscuit tin.

'It would appear so.'

Although it was slightly beyond the rules, Charlotte Martin liked to chat with Woody, and generally kept him up to date with how things were going, because she needed to call on his experience. Or, at least, that was always what he told Kate. She had to remind herself that this was only because he'd once done her job and was greatly respected in the area.

'And Fergal had shown great interest in the blunderbuss, as had one or two of the others,' Woody added.

'No one else from Tinworthy though?' Kate asked.

'Who knows?'

Even though Woody was focused on Angie and Fergal, it was Guy who was intriguing Kate. Guy wasn't only a brilliant local hairdresser, the kind you wouldn't expect to find in a small place like Tinworthy (he performed absolute miracles with her highlights and lowlights), but he'd become a friend as well. He was a tall, blonde, blue-eyed, mega-handsome man, in a steady relationship with another equally handsome man called Roly.

What Kate couldn't get her head round was the fact that Guy had told Angie, when she was on her recruitment drive for extras, that he would take a couple of weeks' holiday because he'd *love* to be an extra. Why? Kate wondered. Guy made a great deal of money in his salon, and women came from miles around to be transformed by his skills. Why would he spend his precious holiday time on a boring old film set when he could be jetting off to some exotic resort? Kate had put this question to Angie, who'd replied, 'Oh, he worked in the film industry once – didn't you know? Perhaps he's still a little starstruck.'

There followed a two-day break while the film location was sealed off and no one was allowed to enter. The police examined the blunderbuss minutely, and questioned everyone who had been anywhere near it again and again.

Then Sonia Somerfield, the director, announced that the show must go on and that she'd be replacing Crispin's character *and* Angie's character with established stand-by actors, and would the extras please come back on Thursday morning as usual?

On Wednesday morning, Kate took Barney, her springer spaniel, for a walk along the beach and, on the way back, she decided, as usual, to call in at The Old Locker for her coffee, although she suspected that Angie might not be in the best of moods.

'*Bloody woman!*' Angie shouted before Kate had shut the door behind her.

'Who's a bloody woman?' Kate asked as she clambered onto her favourite barstool.

'That director, Sonia whatever-her-name-is, *that's* who!'

'What's *she* done?' Kate asked, knowing perfectly well what was coming.

'She's replaced *me*, that's what she's done!'

'Well, Angie, perhaps that's understandable because—'

'Whose side are you *on*?' Angie bellowed.

'Yours of course,' Kate replied obediently, 'but surely it goes without saying that they were going to have to replace Crispin, doesn't it?'

'But why *me*?'

'Angie, could I have a cappuccino please?'

Angie grunted as she assaulted the coffee machine, which grunted back and hissed a bit as well.

'You know perfectly well,' Kate continued, 'that you only got that part because of Crispin. Sonia knows nothing about you and she plainly wants to resume filming with fresh stand-bys, or whatever they're called. It was only *one* scene after all.'

'There was no reason why she couldn't have kept *me*,' Angie bleated, refusing to be pacified.

Kate accepted her cappuccino from her sister and took a sip. 'Face facts, Angie, now that there's no Crispin, she can do whatever she likes.'

'Well *I'm* not going to be one of her bloody extras,' said Angie. '*I* shan't be going back to Port Petroc! And nobody seems to give a damn about my *grief*! Crispin was a *lover*!'

'Ah, I suspected as much! But that must have been a very long time ago,' Kate said.

'Not *that* long ago.' Angie gave Kate an uncharacteristically coy look.

Kate stared at her in amazement. 'You're joking!'

'No, I'm not. He was a good lover, and we met up several times in London.'

'But not since you came down here?'

'Only once or twice.' She shrugged nonchalantly.

'*What*? Are you telling me—?'

At this point, Fergal emerged from the upstairs flat. 'Is she still sounding off about that feckin' part?' he asked Kate.

Before Kate had a chance to reply, Angie shouted, 'It's all right for *you*!'

'Oh, for sure,' said Fergal, 'it's all right for me because I'm only a bloody *suspect*, all thanks to you and your late friend fawning over each other. And the fact that I showed interest in that bloody blunderbuss!'

'We were *never* fawning over each other,' Angie snapped back, 'and it's thanks to me that you got to be carrying boxes across the beach every day, in the sunshine too. Much easier than working behind the bar here.'

'If you two are going to have one of your rows,' Kate said, draining her coffee, 'then I'll be off.'

'No, no,' Angie said hastily, 'pay no attention to us; we're just a bit on edge. But who else might be a suspect, do you suppose?'

Kate shook her head. 'I still wonder why Guy was persuaded to be an extra. I mean he was the only extra from Tinworthy who really didn't need the money."

'*He* didn't need much persuasion,' Angie replied. 'He was *desperate* to be on it!'

'Why would he be desperate?'

'How would I know? Perhaps he just wanted to revisit old times or maybe, like I said before, he misses the glitz and the glamour.'

'There wasn't a great deal of glitz or glamour down at Port Petroc,' Kate remarked. 'Perhaps he's fallen out with Roly and wanted to get away?' she mused.

'You know what, Kate? I don't go around giving people the third degree! That's *your* speciality. I was just glad to have him on board, along with the other thirty or so I managed to persuade.'

Kate stood up to go. 'Nevertheless, I'd certainly like to know why Guy was so keen to be there.'

'And I've no doubt you'll find out, Miss Marple,' said Angie, just as the door opened and in walked Charlotte Martin, brief-case in hand.

'Good morning, everyone,' Charlotte said breezily, 'I just need a word with Angela Norton.'

'Me?' squeaked Angie.

'Yes, you,' confirmed Charlotte, 'so could we go somewhere private please?'

'But *I'm* not really a suspect,' said Angie, looking pointedly at Fergal.

'I'm afraid you are,' said Charlotte.

FIVE

'Do you really seriously think Angie is a credible suspect?' Kate asked Woody, who was painting the garden fence when she got home. She'd brought out two mugs of tea and sat down, looking out to sea, while Woody dealt with the fence.

He shrugged. 'She did fire the damn thing.'

'Yes, maybe, but she didn't load it with whatever it was that killed Crispin Wyngarde. That was done by the armourer behind the scenes, or so I'm told.'

'Well the armourer would have prepared the gun for firing, but that, if it was just gunpowder, would have been harmless. It could have been *anyone* on the set who put the projectiles into the gun. Charlotte may enlighten us on that,' Woody said, dipping the brush into the paint pot, 'but, if not, I've no doubt Angie will have plenty to say.'

'She's just admitted that she and Crispin Wyngarde had an ongoing relationship,' Kate added. 'I thought she hadn't set eyes on him for *years*.'

'Well she's been widowed a long time.'

Kate watched Woody painting for a minute. 'Yes, but she's not exactly been leading a nun-like existence.'

'I know you like solving things, Kate, but don't you think you might just be getting a bit carried away with all this?'

'No, I damn well don't!' Kate snapped. 'And I suppose we should be thankful that neither one of us is a suspect *this* time, but I'm really worried about Angie, who looks like being the main suspect.'

Kate knew she wouldn't rest until she could prove Angie's innocence, which meant finding who the culprit was. It wouldn't be easy, but she had to try.

'Extras will still only be required on Thursdays and Fridays from now on,' the assistant director trilled loudly as the Tinworthy extras – minus Angie – disembarked from the bus the following morning. 'And you must all be here at ten o'clock sharp. *Thank you.*' With that, she turned and marched away, clipboard under her arm.

Kate was surprised that Charlotte had permitted filming to resume so quickly, but Woody reckoned it was because she wanted to observe first-hand the interactions between everyone involved and was hoping that the killer would give themselves away.

'That's us told,' Fergal said gloomily as they headed towards the wardrobe and make-up mobile units.

Kate had been a little surprised to see him, and he'd been uncharacteristically quiet on the bus.

'I'll be damned glad when they don't need us any more,' said Woody. 'God only knows why I allowed myself to be persuaded to do this in the first place.'

'We all like new experiences now and again,' Kate said.

Woody turned to Fergal. 'I can see Kate here getting her teeth into this one – her Miss *Marple* teeth that is.'

'Well don't go looking at me,' Fergal said to Kate. 'I didn't much like the guy, but I'd never swing for him.'

'As far as I can see,' Kate reassured him, 'there are most likely going to be other suspects. I hear he wasn't too popular in the film business.'

Fergal sniffed. 'Angie's going mad, fit to be tied.'

'What's wrong with her now?' Kate asked.

'That Charlotte woman is insinuating that Angie could have loaded the gun and fired it *knowing* that it was full of shot and could kill him.'

Kate was mystified. 'But why would she *want* to kill him? They'd been friends for years, and he *did* give her a speaking part after all. What possible motive could she have?'

'Only that he chucked her over once,' Fergal said.

Kate thought it politic not to mention that the relationship appeared to have been ongoing.

The girl in the wardrobe trailer was called Jilly and she was extremely chatty. She was a tiny, cheerful little soul with a mass of blonde curls which constantly escaped from her attempts to tie them back. As she fitted Kate into her ensemble, she said, 'Adds a bit of excitement, doesn't it, having a killer on the set?'

'Yes, I suppose it does,' Kate agreed, already feeling itchy as the material made contact with her skin, 'although I think it's alarming rather than exciting, when we don't know who the murderer is.'

'We've all got a good idea who's done it though,' Jilly went on, nodding as she narrowed her eyes.

Kate, adjusting her mob cap, stopped and looked up at Jilly. 'Who do you think that might be?'

'Sonia Somerfield, more than likely.'

'And why would you think that?' Kate wondered if this girl really did have any relevant information, or was she just jumping to easy conclusions so she'd have some juicy gossip to impart?

'Sonia had a steamy affair with Crispin Wyngarde way back in the nineties! Before I was even *born*!'

'I don't suppose she was the only one,' sighed Kate, thinking of Angie.

Jilly moved closer. 'You're right there. He had affairs with everyone in a skirt, and that includes *kilts*!' She nodded knowingly.

'Kilts?'

'Yeah, Sonia's then-husband was Scottish and wore a kilt on special occasions. And do you know what? Wyngarde dumped Sonia because he fancied her *husband*!'

'I don't suppose that resulted in marital bliss?'

'No, it didn't – Sonia ditched her husband soon afterwards.' Jilly produced a pair of leather clogs. 'Try these,' she said, handing them over. 'Sonia's got a new one now – husband, I mean. But she's hated Crispin Wyngarde ever since.'

'So why would she take on directing this production if she hated him so much?' Kate asked.

Jilly lowered her voice. 'Two reasons. She hadn't worked for a while, so I don't suppose she could be choosy. And' – here she leaned closer again – 'it gave her the ideal opportunity to get her revenge on the bugger and finish him off!'

'I suppose it's a possibility,' Kate agreed, considering this new information.

'And would you believe that Wyngarde was *still* leching around after the younger girls,' said Jilly, 'the silly old goat! God, he must have been in his *sixties*! And still after *sex*! Can you *imagine*?'

Kate was amused. 'There isn't a cut-off point for having sex, you know.' She took comfort from the fact that Jilly did not appear to realise that she, too, had passed the big six-O. 'So, did the police talk to you, Jilly?'

'Oh yes, they spoke to everyone, and I told them just what I told you. In *confidence* of course.'

'And how did they react to that?'

Jilly snorted. 'They didn't react at all. But not known to get excited, are they? The police, I mean.'

Kate grinned. 'Not as a rule.'

'But, you mark my words, it was *her*. Those shoes OK?'

Kate took a few experimental steps. 'They're fine.'

Jilly grinned. 'Great. See you later.'

Now thoroughly confused by this possible increase in suspects, Kate headed back to the hill.

Kate had been 'promoted' to walking down the steep hillside carrying a pail. Each time they required another take, she had to scramble back up the hill and then set off down again. Woody, in the meantime, in his sexy leather, was down on the beach still heaving the boxes to and fro. By the end of the day, they were both exhausted.

'I'll be glad to get back to the medical centre on Monday,' Kate admitted wearily as she got back on the bus hours later. She looked around. 'Anyone seen Guy?'

There was a shaking of heads and then someone piped up, 'He refused to come back after the first day.'

'That's interesting,' Kate remarked as she sat down next to Woody. She'd honestly thought he'd been sitting further back in the bus, and she didn't normally see him during filming anyway.

'He probably prefers being a hairdresser to being a peasant,' Woody said, 'and who can blame him?'

Kate didn't reply but thought it was perhaps time to make an appointment for a shampoo and blow-dry.

SIX

Guy had space available on Saturday. While Kate was sitting in the chair, watching him perform his miracles in the mirror, she turned the conversation round to his absence from the location set.

'Well I couldn't take any more time off,' he said. 'The two weeks' leave I'd allowed myself were mostly taken up with the break in shooting.'

'Were you disappointed that you were only on the set for one day?' Kate asked.

'Not really... to be honest, I was glad,' Guy said as he brandished the hairdryer. 'When Angie first suggested I might like to be an extra, I thought that, for old times' sake, it would be nice to be back on a film set again. Did you know that I used to be employed in the film industry – briefly – not long after I first qualified?'

Kate nodded slowly, trying not to let her face give her away. 'Angie did mention something about it.'

'I was amazed,' Guy continued, 'that, when I got there, I found a few familiar faces from years ago. I'd forgotten how phony everything could be, but that blunderbuss was *not* a replica, it was the *real deal*! I have to admit I did spend some time looking at it because I was so fascinated. They're rare these days, you know.'

'It seems that everyone who went anywhere near it is now a suspect,' Kate remarked.

Guy switched off the dryer. '*I'm* not a suspect.' He held up the mirror for Kate to see her back view.

'That's great, Guy, thank you.' Kate paused. 'I was talking to one of the wardrobe girls and I gather Crispin Wyngarde wasn't a very nice man?'

'He was a good producer, well thought of in the film industry, but he upset a lot of people. Including me. But that's a long time ago, and I won't bore you with the details now.'

'Oh, Guy, you can tell *me*! I assure you I wouldn't be bored!' Kate said truthfully. 'Why were you glad that you didn't have to come back after that first day? Did it really upset you so much?'

Guy shook his head. 'It didn't upset me at all. Let me just tell you this: I was only eighteen when I was hired as an assistant hairdresser on Limelight Films. And it was on another historical costume drama, set up in Northumberland. Crispin was a good-looking man back then, and he paid me special attention. And I was *flattered*! Of course I was, and I fell for him hook, line and sinker! I honestly thought I was madly in love!' Guy rolled his eyes. 'The affair lasted for four whole months and then he fell for this wardrobe guy who suddenly appeared on set, and I was *booted out of the door*! Just like *that*! Nice knowing you – bye, bye!'

'How awful! What did you do?'

'I had a fight with the wardrobe guy; Brook something-or-other was his name. And I nearly damn well killed him! So I was bound over to keep the peace, banished from the set and Crispin assured me that he'd see to it that I'd *never* work in the film business again. I only hope the police don't check my records. He grinned. 'I can pack a fair punch, you know!'

'Sounds like you needed to,' Kate replied. 'But surely all this will come to light?'

'Well when the police questioned us, just after Wyngarde was killed, I told that woman detective that I'd worked with him once and didn't like him. I don't carry a grudge after nearly thirty years. But, of course, she's looking for suspects, so I suppose I might be a sitting duck.'

'If you had such bad memories of the film business, what on earth possessed you to become an extra?' Kate asked.

'It was a long time ago, and I was curious to see if things had changed.'

His explanation didn't ring altogether true to Kate.

As they parted company, she asked, just to see his reaction as much as anything, 'So you don't have any wish to go back as an extra then?'

'No, I don't. I'm not going back there, Kate. But,' he said, grinning, 'if you hear of any interesting titbits, you will let me know, won't you?'

'Oh, I will,' Kate assured him, patting her coiffure.

She was now thoroughly confused. Guy did indeed have a motive to kill Crispin, but he'd only been on set for one day.

The day Crispin was murdered.

'So how was your weekend?' Denise, the receptionist, asked when Kate appeared for work on Monday morning.

Denise, Kate reckoned, was well into her fifties, ash blonde (at the moment) and hell-bent on finding herself a man.

'Good, thanks,' Kate replied. 'I treated myself to a shampoo and blow-dry.'

'With Guy, at Guys 'n' Dolls?'

'Yes, with Guy. I *always* go there, Denise.'

Denise leaned forward. 'Did you know the police were

round there questioning him the other day? Wasn't he an extra on that film too?'

Kate sighed. Denise had a voracious appetite for gossip.

'Yes, he was an extra, but decided to pull out – he couldn't take any more time away from the salon. And the police have been questioning *everyone*.'

'Including your sister?'

The woman didn't miss a trick.

'*Including* my sister.'

'I can't imagine *Angie* wanting to kill anyone,' remarked Denise, looking hopefully at Kate.

'Neither can I. Like I said, Denise, *everyone* is being questioned.'

'Hmm,' replied Denise, unconvinced. 'I don't recall you saying that *you* had?'

'*Everyone*, Denise!' Kate smiled and made her escape.

It had now become public knowledge that she was an extra on a film being shot nearby, and that there had been a *murder* on the set no less, and wasn't it funny that Nurse Kate always seemed to be around when there was some crime or other being committed? Kate spent half the morning explaining that she'd never met Crispin Wyngarde before in her life, and neither had Woody.

Just before it was time to go home, Ida Tilley came shuffling in through the doorway of the treatment room. Ida was the housekeeper to Seymour Barker-Jones up at Pendorian Manor, which meant that she did very little in the way of housekeeping, because Seymour, rumoured to be a big shot in MI5, rarely came down from London. Ida had been with the family since she'd left school and was now nearing eighty years old, but Seymour obviously felt loyal to his old retainer and allowed her to rattle around, in solitary splendour, in Pendorian Manor.

'It's me knees,' said Ida.

'Yes, I thought it might be,' Kate replied, smiling. Ida, with her dodgy knees, was a regular visitor to the surgery.

'I'll soon be needin' new ones,' Ida suggested hopefully for the umpteenth time.

'Not just yet,' Kate said, also for the umpteenth time, 'but we'll renew your prescription.'

'It's scrubbin' all them stone floors,' Ida explained.

'People don't, as a rule, get down to scrub floors on their knees any more, Ida,' Kate remarked. 'They use mops, and electric floor cleaners, and things. Ask Seymour for something more up to date.'

'Don't do a proper job,' said Ida dismissively. She hesitated for a moment. 'I hear there's been a killin' down at Port Petroc?'

'I'm afraid so.' Kate carried on typing Ida's prescription.

'And I hear your sister, and her' – Ida coughed – '*companion* were questioned by the police?'

'So were lots of people, because they were *all* extras.'

'Extras to what?' Ida looked confused.

'Well there are the main stars and then there are the people in the background, you know? The extras?'

'Why were they down there in the background? Were they goin' for a walk? Couldn't they find a nice walk closer to home?'

Kate decided not to take the matter any further. 'I'm sure they wish they had. Now, Ida, here's your prescription, and I see no reason for you to be scrubbing floors when Seymour only comes down a couple of times a year.'

Ida stood up with much grunting. 'You be sure to tell that sister of yours not to go walkin' so far from home in future.'

'Oh, I will,' Kate agreed, sighing with relief as Ida finally hobbled out of the door.

SEVEN

It was with further relief that Kate completed her two shifts at the medical centre. Everyone seemed to think that she had some inside knowledge as to what was going on and were particularly interested because Angie was her sister, and Angie had *fired the gun*. No matter how many times Kate explained that the blunderbuss should not have been loaded, and that it was *meant* to go off during the scuffle, nobody really wanted to believe her.

On Thursday, Kate was back in her rags, hauling her pail down the steep hill, when Sonia Somerfield, on the beach below, began to cough, wheeze and stagger around. A couple of cameramen had helped her to sit down, and one was rubbing Sonia's back, to no avail.

Kate knew an asthma attack when she saw it and, abandoning her pail, made it down to the beach as fast as she could. When she got to Sonia, who was now coughing badly and struggling for breath, she checked the woman's pockets in the hope of finding an inhaler. Sonia, between gasps, was pointing mutely at her bag, which was lying on the sand some distance away. Kate rummaged around in the bag and finally unearthed the Ventolin inhaler, which she hurriedly applied to Sonia's mouth.

In under a minute, Sonia was showing signs of recovery and trying to stand up. She was, Kate guessed, in her late fifties, of medium height and build, with long, greying, messy hair escaping from a chignon of sorts, and pronounced crow's feet round her beady brown eyes. Her spectacles, as always, dangled from a silver chain round her neck. When working, she spent most of her time settling the glasses on her nose and then, minutes later, pulling them off again, an operation which went on all day. Kate couldn't quite work out why she just didn't keep them on all the time because it was apparent she could see little without them. Even now she was tugging at them on the chain.

'Take it easy!' Kate warned. 'You're not out of the woods yet, Miss Somerfield.'

By now, a crowd of extras, along with most of the crew, had gathered around.

'What are they all gawping at?' Sonia wheezed.

Kate looked around. 'Miss Somerfield's going to need some time to recover,' she announced loudly, 'so this could be a good time for a coffee break perhaps?'

Woody had now appeared from further down the beach. He kneeled down beside Kate. 'Don't they have a doctor on this set?' he asked.

Sonia, now recovering, shook her head. 'There's a first-aider around *somewhere*,' she said crossly, 'but God only knows where she's got to.' She looked at Kate. 'Thanks so much for your help. I should have had the inhaler in my pocket, but there's so much stuff in here...' She rummaged in her pockets and gestured aimlessly.

'Stay still,' Kate ordered, 'and get your strength back.' She pulled a bottle of water out of Sonia's bag. 'Sip some of this.'

'And where did *you* appear from?' Sonia looked genuinely puzzled.

'I'm a peasant carrying a pail of water down the hillside to the beach,' Kate replied with a grin.

'Oh, an *extra*.' Sonia digested this for a moment. 'Well I'm glad you were so clued up, and I owe you a huge thank you.'

'I'm really a nurse, you see,' Kate explained.

Sonia appeared fully recovered now. 'A nurse? Wish we had you on the set instead of the dizzy girl they sent us.' She rubbed her head and turned to Woody. 'And where have *you* come from? Don't tell me you're one of my extras too?'

'That's me,' confirmed Woody.

'I should have looked more closely at the list of extras,' said Sonia, 'because I'm sure I'd have remembered *you*.' She gave him a coy smile.

'He's my husband,' Kate got in quickly, 'and he was the local detective inspector round here at one time.'

Sonia was still gazing at him. 'Any chance you can find out who might have put that shot into Crispin then?' she asked hopefully. 'So we can all get on with filming this damn thing without the police descending on us every five minutes!'

Woody shook his head. 'No, I'm glad to be retired from all that now. I leave the detective work to Kate here because, believe it or not, she's become a dab hand at crime solving!'

'Have you indeed?' Sonia was gazing at Kate again. 'Now, what do I call *you*?' She took a swig of the water.

'I'm Kate, and this is Woody.'

'And I'm Sonia.' Her eyes swivelled back to Woody. 'Are you American?'

Woody nodded. 'Yeah, but I've been over on this side of the pond for a very long time. And my father was English.'

Sonia signalled to one of the runners standing nearby. 'Go get me a coffee, sweetie. Black, no sugar. As for Woody here, we can't have his good looks going to waste! We're going to need a few mugshots, I think.' She was openly admiring him. 'Give me the extras list before you go, would you?'

The girl obliged, handed over a file and went off in search of coffee, leaving Sonia studying what was presumably the list and peering at it closely.

'What's your name exactly?'

'Woody Forrest.'

'Hmm. A. L. Forrest is what it says here.'

'Those are just my initials. Everyone calls me Woody.'

'So, tell me, what's with the A. L.?'

Kate was trying hard not to giggle.

'It's a bit embarrassing,' Woody admitted.

Sonia chortled. 'All the better! Let's have it!'

Woody cleared his throat. 'Well, you see, my dad was very proud of his success in the States, so he gave us all historical American names.'

'And yours is?'

'Abraham Lincoln Forrest,' admitted Woody, 'but I'd prefer that did *not* become public knowledge.'

'A name to be proud of surely?' Sonia suppressed a smile before turning to Kate. 'I don't suppose you're Kate Clementine Churchill Forrest by any chance?'

'I'm afraid not; just plain old Kate Palmer! I didn't change my name when we married.'

For a brief moment, Kate wondered why she *had* hung on to her ex-husband's name for so long, when Alex Palmer had been such an unfaithful swine. Still, he was the father of her two sons, and it had been easier for them to all have the same surname, particularly when the boys were young. And, as everyone liked to point out, her surname *was* an anagram of Marple.

'I'm OK now,' Sonia said, standing up.

'Perhaps you need your medication updated?' Kate suggested. 'If you come to the surgery in Middle Tinworthy next Monday or Tuesday, I could check you out.'

Sonia grinned. 'You know what? I might just do that.'

Kate hoped she would, because Sonia just *might* provide a much-needed clue. At the moment, she was no further along with finding out who had really killed Crispin Wyngarde.

EIGHT

Kate and Woody walked Barney up Penhallion Cliff on Saturday morning. It was a cloudless summer day and the Atlantic had that 'Caribbean look': deceptively calm, blue and turquoise. The white sand sparkled on the beach below as the wet-suited surfers and bellyboarders waited hopefully for a big wave.

'I'm rather enjoying being an extra now,' Kate said, 'because I'm getting to know lots of people—'

'Which means that you can nose around the suspects,' Woody interrupted, 'and probably endanger yourself, *yet again*.'

'Well, yes,' Kate admitted, 'but I'll keep a very low profile. None of the film crew is aware of my crime-solving reputation, are they?' She hesitated. 'But *you* mentioned that fact to Sonia Somerfield, if I remember rightly.'

Woody sighed. 'And if Sonia does just happen to be the killer, then she's going to be keeping a very close eye on you.'

'She'll be keeping a very close eye on you as well, because she obviously fancied you!' Kate giggled.

'I don't fancy her,' Woody said, 'but if she wants to up my profile, and my money, that's fine by me.'

'Anyway, I don't think she's the killer,' Kate remarked.

'And how have you managed to come to that conclusion, Miss Marple?'

Kate shrugged. 'Just a feeling.' She shouted at Barney, who was digging down into a rabbit hole.

It was quite a climb and, when they reached the peak of the cliff, they sat down on the old wooden seat which looked out to sea and gave panoramic views of the North Cornwall coastline. There, to the north, was the rocky headland of Hartland Point, with the island of Lundy a mere grey smudge out in the ocean and, to the south, the cliffs and coves stretching as far as Trevose Head. Many a shipwreck lay out there, and many a tale had been written about them, including the one that was now being filmed at Port Petroc.

'There's bound to be more than one person in that film crew who harboured some kind of grudge against our friend Wyngarde,' Woody remarked. 'And what about the so-called armourer? Where was *he* when the gun was loaded?'

'Good question. What exactly does an armourer do?'

'Apparently, he has to be present to ensure the safety of the cast and crew when lethal weapons are being used, and ensure that only blanks are loaded. I'm guessing that, if he didn't load the gun himself, he wasn't keeping a close enough watch to stop whoever it was who *did*.' Woody was squinting out at the horizon, where a very long cargo container ship could be seen heading north up towards the Bristol Channel.

'Paul Bacon, the armourer, has been seen at The Gull, so perhaps Des has heard something useful from him when he was having a drink?' Kate suggested. 'Some sort of clue perhaps? Are *we* planning on having a drink there this evening?'

Woody rolled his eyes good-naturedly. 'Apparently we are.'

·   ·   ·

The first thing Kate and Woody noticed, as they approached The Greedy Gull later, was a large white caravan pitched in the car park.

'That's strange,' Woody commented, 'because I know Des worries about having enough parking. Must be a friend or something.'

Inside the bar, Des was very much his usual self.

'You plannin' on eatin' here later?' he asked as he plonked two glasses of wine on the bar-top. 'The missus is doin' a real good curry, the speciality dish for tonight.'

'No thank you,' Woody replied, 'because *I* am cooking this evening.'

Des snorted. '*You? Cookin'?*'

Woody nodded and made the sign of a halo over his head.

'His latest toy is a slow cooker,' Kate informed Des. 'He chops up everything in sight in the morning, chucks it in there and leaves it all day.'

'Well, well,' said Des, shaking his head.

'What Kate means by "everything in sight", Des, are all the wonderful fresh vegetables I've been slaving over, in my allotment, for months on end, freshly picked and chopped with my own fair hand,' explained Woody.

'I'll give you a job if the missus ever decides to pack up the cookin',' Des remarked, with one of his rare smiles.

'Whose caravan is that out there?' Woody asked, pointing towards the car park.

'Oh, a bloke on that film set of yours. Likes a drink, he does, and he's been spendin' some money in here the last few nights.'

'Do you know his name?' Kate asked, intrigued.

'Paul Somethin' – he's the bloke who deals with the guns.'

'I wonder why he's parked here instead of at The Pheasant in Port Petroc, which is a lot closer to the site?'

'Well The Pheasant was plannin' on chargin' him a fortune,' Des explained. 'And it's a tiddly little car park, so I said he could use this one so long as he bought a few drinks in here every evenin'.'

'Where is he tonight?' Woody asked.

'He's havin' a drink at The Pheasant with some of the blokes he works with. He'll be back here later.'

As they sat down near the inglenook with their glasses of wine, Kate said, 'I can't believe Bacon has parked here or, for that matter, why Des has allowed it.'

'He must be buying a fair few drinks, that's all I can say. There's always been a fair bit of rivalry between The Gull and The Pheasant, particularly at the darts matches, so Des must reckon that he'll make more money out of Paul Bacon than Sid, down at The Pheasant.'

'It's a shame that Bacon bloke isn't here at the moment,' Kate said, 'because I'd like to know why he wasn't doing his job and stopping whoever it was from spiking the gun.'

'Wouldn't we all like to know that?' said Woody.

NINE

On Monday afternoon, shortly before Kate was due to leave for home, Sonia Somerfield arrived in her treatment room.

'I asked for you,' Sonia said, 'so I hope you don't mind.'

'Not at all,' Kate replied, noting that Sonia's spectacles were today suspended at a sideways angle against a bright blue T-shirt which proclaimed: *Hollywood or Bust?*

'I decided to take you up on your offer,' Sonia said, 'because I've been having these attacks more often recently.'

Kate updated her on the latest anti-inflammatory medicines and bronchodilators, plus the steroid therapies for severe asthma. A new product was available for trial, and Kate told Sonia she'd bring it down to Port Petroc as soon as it arrived.

'That's so good of you,' said Sonia. 'I must buy you a drink. Where's the nearest pub?'

The nearest pub in Middle Tinworthy was, of course, the ancient Tinners' Arms, with its wonky stone floors, low black beams and nicotine-stained walls. And so it was that Kate found herself sitting next to Sonia and a double gin and tonic in The Tinners' pub garden, at a rickety wooden table, surrounded by tourists enjoying the late summer sun.

Sonia raised her glass. 'Thank God you were around when I had the attack the other day, because I've no idea where our so-called first-aider had disappeared to. I just wish you could be our first-aider.'

'Well thanks for the kind remarks,' Kate said, 'but, as you can see, I do have a part-time job. And I do like a day off on Wednesdays!'

Sonia's eyes twinkled. 'With that gorgeous husband of yours?'

'Yes,' Kate replied, grinning, 'with that gorgeous husband of mine!'

Sonia wanted to know how they'd met, and remarked on how funny it was that they'd both been working in London but their paths had never crossed until they'd moved nearly four hundred miles south-west. Kate told her that Woody, a Californian, had come to study criminology at Oxford, and then worked for the Metropolitan Police in London. Sonia was easy to chat to, and Kate found herself talking about her ill-fated first marriage, and about her two sons.

'Tom,' she said, 'has been living and working up in Edinburgh for some years, happily married and supplying me with grandchildren on a regular basis, which is wonderful. Jack, on the other hand, is still single. He came back from Australia recently, went up to Scotland to see his brother and decided to stay there. He's now found a job up in the Highlands somewhere, as a project manager on some construction site.'

'I've got three; two daughters and a son,' Sonia told her, 'from my first marriage, and I've now acquired three stepchildren with the current husband. Bloody chaos at Christmastime! I was damned glad to get this location job and get away for a bit.'

'Just unfortunate about Crispin Wyngarde,' Kate added casually.

Sonia sniffed. 'He had it coming to him. I'm only amazed someone didn't take a potshot at him long before this.'

'So he wasn't too popular then?'

'No, he was not! But I expect they'll point the finger at me,' Sonia said, 'because I hated his guts and said so. But so did lots of people, including Paul the armourer – and Lucy of course.'

'Lucy?'

'Yes, Lucy Moore, who plays the part of Gwendolyn Tregennys, Mark Pengorran's new love in the film.'

Kate had only seen blonde, pretty Lucy in the distance, and had been struck by her upright posture and riding skills.

'So what did he do to Lucy, or need I ask?'

'It wasn't so much what he did to Lucy as what he did to her father,' Sonia replied. 'Do you remember Byron Bellamy?'

Kate thought for a moment. 'The name's familiar.'

'He was a sought-after actor back in the nineties. Then he did an action film with Crispin.' Sonia shook her head sadly. 'He was required to do a stunt, leaping from a third-storey window, and Crispin had reassured him that all the safety precautions were in place – which they weren't – and poor Byron fell and broke his neck. Spent the rest of his life in a wheelchair and died just a couple of years back.'

Kate was appalled. 'Did he sue?'

'It was the usual story,' Sonia said sadly. 'Byron did get some compensation, but Crispin had a good lawyer and got off without being proved negligent. But he *was*. And, understandably, Lucy detests him.'

'I can't understand why on earth Lucy would want to work for the man who destroyed her father's life and career.'

Sonia sipped her drink and nodded slowly. 'That's exactly what I thought, but Lucy told me she'd had enough of theatre and desperately wanted to get into films. She said she was having panic attacks every time she went out on stage, but she didn't want to give up acting.'

'Maybe she just wanted to get close enough to Crispin Wyngarde to kill him?' Kate wondered if she was pushing her luck, but Sonia seemed blithely unsurprised.

'That thought had crossed my mind,' Sonia admitted. 'Lucy may look fragile, but she's as tough as old boots. She didn't tell Crispin she was Byron's daughter, which is interesting. But *I* know because I've worked with Lucy before and I remember Byron well. Lucy was only a tiny child at the time of the case, and later changed her name, so Crispin never knew who she was.' She glanced at Kate's glass. 'Another gin?'

Kate didn't want this flow of conversation to end. 'That's so kind, Sonia, but I have to drive home.'

'Call that gorgeous husband to come and get you,' Sonia said as she headed to the bar and ordered two more drinks.

Kate took out her phone and called Woody, hoping that he wasn't up to his elbows in carrots at the allotment or something.

Fortunately, Woody wasn't at the allotment.

'Woody, please could you fetch me from The Tinners'? I'm with Sonia, and rapidly getting tipsy, but, honestly, it's all in a good cause!'

'What the hell are you up to now?'

'Give me another fifteen minutes or so, and then I'll have lots to tell you later!'

Sonia returned with two further gins. 'Is he coming? Good. I got a lift here with one of the runners, who's having her hair done, and she's picking me up about half past five.'

It was now five past five, and Kate wondered how many more interesting facts she could extract from Sonia before Woody arrived.

'You know we have suspects here in Tinworthy too?' she asked Sonia, who'd flatly refused her offer to pay. 'Including my sister.'

Sonia looked astonished. 'Your *sister*?'

'Yes, Angie, the one wrestling the gun from Crispin.'

'She's your *sister*?' Sonia studied her for a moment. 'I can see a resemblance now you mention it. But how did your sister get herself that little part with Crispin? Nobody could understand it.'

'They go back a long way,' Kate said drily. 'Angie was once an actress, and she was considered to be quite good, but she's had a love affair with gin for as long as I can remember, which scuppered her chances on more than one occasion. She met Crispin years ago.'

'I can guess the rest.' She looked at Kate knowingly.

'They're trying to make out that Angie had something to do with that blunderbuss being loaded with shot and that, in the so-called tussle, she deliberately aimed the gun at Crispin's heart.'

'How on earth would she know how to load a blunderbuss?' Sonia looked amazed. 'She wasn't some sort of weapons expert, was she?'

'Of course not.'

'It's all down to Paul Bacon, the armourer, of course. He's supposed to be in charge and keep an eye on that bloody gun at all times. He's an alcoholic but reckoned to be excellent at his job, which is why Crispin was keen to have him here. He was sober for a while, but I hear he's gone back to drinking in the evenings lately, down at The Pheasant.' Sonia took a large slurp of gin and leaned forward. 'He got on well with Crispin to begin with, but lately there was a helluva lot of shouting and swearing going on between the two of them, so God only knows what the problem was.'

'Hmm,' said Kate, 'so no love lost between those two either?'

'Not lately,' Sonia confirmed. Then her face brightened up. 'Isn't that your lovely husband I see?'

'Well, well,' said the lovely husband, looking from one to the other, 'are we celebrating or commiserating, ladies?'

TEN

On Tuesday evening when Kate got home, she discovered Woody was still up at his allotment. She made herself a cup of tea, got out a notebook and pen, and decided it was time to make The List.

For every one of her recent investigations, Kate had compiled a list of suspects. Woody had scoffed at first, although he was well aware that it was normal police procedure. Kate, who watched crime dramas avidly on TV, would like to have had a board mounted on the wall so she could pin a photo of the victim in the centre, surrounded by pictures of all the likely suspects. But since she had no board or photos, she had to improvise with a list.

This list wasn't going to be easy to assemble. Just for a start, her own sister would have to be on it. But top of the list had to be Sonia Somerfield, though Kate had a gut feeling that Sonia was innocent and, so far, her gut feelings had been spot on. Still, she had to stay neutral.

So, Sonia Somerfield was placed at the top of The List. The director must obviously have felt deeply for Crispin Wyngarde at one time, before discovering his equal passion for her husband. That certainly wouldn't endear Crispin to Sonia, but it was a long time ago. According to Jilly, 'way back in the nineties'. Had Sonia been biding her time?

Then there was Lucy. Her father's accident would have taken place around the same time as Crispin was romancing husband and wife. She'd been a tiny girl at the time, but according to Sonia she'd been nursing a hatred for Crispin throughout her life. Maybe she'd actually waited until after her father's death to get her revenge?

Kate sipped her tea and sighed. She *had* to add Angie to The List. But *why*, for goodness' sake, when she and Crispin had kept their relationship going and they'd had these trysts over the years? Why would Angie want to kill him when she was plainly still fond of him and he was giving her a cameo in the film? Could there possibly have been any motive? Kate really didn't think so. She knew her sister after all – or thought she did.

Then, Fergal. Why was *he* considered a suspect? Why would he be so jealous of an old lover? After all, Angie had had a considerable number of lovers in her time, not to mention a husband. And doubtless Fergal hadn't had a monk-like existence either. Had he found out that Angie and Crispin were still lovers occasionally?

That only left Guy, and Paul Bacon, the armourer. Guy, too, had been dumped for someone else, but, again, that must have been nearly thirty years ago. Perhaps it was more likely that Guy felt aggrieved about having his name blackened to such a degree that he was never able to work in films again? Guy was, without doubt, an excellent hairdresser with a thriving business, but perhaps what he'd really wanted was fame and fortune in the entertainment industry? In fact, with his looks, he could easily have been 'spotted' and become a star himself!

Paul Bacon had apparently returned to drinking after

being teetotal for years. Bacon was, by all accounts, sober when he was on duty, and so he certainly should have had his beady eye on that blunderbuss at all times, or else had it safely stored under lock and key. If he'd been negligent, that could certainly have riled Crispin and caused rows, but would Bacon have hated Crispin sufficiently to kill him? Or had he left the gun around unattended, so that anyone could have loaded it? That seemed unlikely as he was well respected as an armourer.

She had six suspects on her list. She could think of no one else.

Kate finished her tea. Woody still wasn't home, so Kate decided she'd give Barney a quick walk and grab a coffee at Angie's on the way back to see how she was.

'I'm fed up hearing that Sonia Somerfield thinks you've got such a lovely bloody husband,' snapped Angie as she served Kate a cappuccino. '*This* is the woman who dropped me like a hot potato and who now *dares* to suggest that I might have deliberately killed Crispin by putting lethal stuff in that blunderbuss!'

'She hasn't dared to suggest anything,' Kate said, taking a sip of her coffee and absently stroking Barney's head. He was, as always, living in hope of a cheese-and-onion crisp, a treat normally provided by Fergal. 'The only person who suggested anything of the sort is Charlotte Martin, who, as the detective inspector in charge, has to suspect *everybody*. Even you must know that, Angie!'

Fergal appeared. 'Don't expect any logic from this one, Kate!' he said, placing his hand on Angie's shoulder. 'She's mad as hell to have lost that stupid part and so now we all have to suffer!' He produced a bag of cheese-and-onion crisps and handed them to Kate. The dog, recognising the packet, went crazy.

'It was *not* a stupid part,' Angie shouted, 'and it might well have led to greater things!'

'You're feckin' sixty-four years old!' Fergal roared back. 'And the only reason you got that part was because you dropped your knickers for that old lech! And you were conveniently in the area where he was going to be filming, so he could leave it to you to round up a load of extras!'

Just as Angie opened her mouth to yell back, a young couple walked through the door, and she quickly rearranged her face into as much of a welcoming smile as she could muster. When she'd served them both, and Fergal had taken himself outside, Angie said to Kate, 'Isn't it pathetic how jealous he is!'

'Look, Angie,' Kate said, in an attempt to soothe her sister's bruised ego, while feeding Barney a couple of crisps, 'you'd have felt awful doing that scene again with some other actor and thinking about what happened before. You probably wouldn't have been able to wrench the gun away from him for fear of it going off again. I'm sure Sonia was only trying to help you get over the shock of it all.'

Angie sniffed. 'It was damned unlikely that gun would have fired shot again with police in attendance.'

'That's true,' Kate agreed, 'but I think it might well have affected your performance. Why don't you consider being an extra? You'd probably still appear, however briefly, on screen.'

'*Somebody* has to hold down the fort round here!' Angie looked around, waving her arms expansively. There was only the one young couple, at the table by the window; him with a shandy, her with a Diet Coke.

'You were perfectly happy to leave Emma in charge before,' Kate pointed out.

'But I'm a *suspect* now! I don't want everyone on that set pointing their fingers at me!'

Kate was struggling to maintain her patience. 'Half of the film crew are suspects, Angie! Including Sonia Somerfield herself. Including the leading lady, believe it or not. Including the armourer, who was supposed to be guarding that weapon day and night. And goodness only knows who else there might be who had a reason to blast Crispin to kingdom come! For goodness' sake, Angie!'

'I'll think about it,' Angie said ungraciously. 'And what's that Lucy got to do with it?'

'Apparently her father was an actor too, and thanks to your friend Crispin not taking adequate precautions, the poor man did a dangerous stunt and ended up wheelchair-bound.'

'I never said he was a *saint*,' Angie conceded grudgingly.

Kate had had enough. She finished her coffee, rounded up Barney and headed home, not for the first time wondering why she always had to take on the role of older, wiser sister, when Angie was, in fact, two years her senior. It had been the same all their lives, so she should be used to it by now.

ELEVEN

Kate was looking forward to Wednesday at home. And, perhaps, an omelette for breakfast? When she surveyed the cupboard in the morning, however, she found one lonely egg sitting in the egg box. Kate looked at her watch. Bobby's should be open by now, so she'd nip down there and buy half a dozen eggs while Woody was showering.

Bobby's Best Buys was the one and only grocery store in Lower Tinworthy, where, to put it mildly, he only sold the basics. It was a complete mystery to everyone how he managed to survive on selling so little. Bobby wasn't far off eighty years old, wore a long, grey overall-type coat and boasted, 'If I ain't able to spell it, I ain't able to sell it.' It transpired that there was an awful lot that Bobby could neither spell nor sell, and hygiene wasn't top of his list either. Bottles of milk, eggs and wrapped bread were generally safe bets, but ever since Kate had seen her sister's cat preening himself on Bobby's counter, on the exact spot where Bobby cut his Cheddar into saleable blocks, she'd avoided buying cheese there.

When Kate arrived, Bobby was, as always, puffing at a crafty roll-up cigarette in the storeroom behind the counter, which also lacked daylight and had only one small strip light with which to illuminate the dusty shelves therein. These, as far as Kate could see, held a myriad of tins of tomato soup and processed peas, so she knew better than to ask for consommé or artichoke hearts.

Sighing, Bobby placed his roll-up down carefully on the rose-adorned china plate which he kept for this purpose on a shelf just behind the counter.

'Noisy here last night,' he said by way of a greeting.

'Why was that?' Kate asked.

'Police here *again*.' He gave Kate a knowing look. 'They ain't half interested in that sister of yours.'

'They're interested in everyone connected with the film at Port Petroc,' Kate said dismissively but hoping that Angie wasn't in trouble again. 'Could I have half a dozen eggs please?'

'I've had to put them up ten pence,' he grunted, 'cos every damn thing's goin' up in price and it's a holy wonder I'm in business at all.'

Kate could only silently agree with that. Bobby lived in a tiny flat above the shop, he opened every weekday at nine o'clock and closed on the dot of five, he closed on Saturday afternoons and all of Sunday. Several local businessmen were keen to get their hands on Bobby's dreary habitat, mainly because of its prime position so close to the beach, Angie's café bar, the souvenir shops and the fast-food outlet.

'Why don't you think about retiring then, Bobby?'

'*Retirin'*?' He glared at Kate. 'What would I want to be retirin' for?'

Good question. The shop was his life, where people called in to chat, to give him titbits of gossip and to occasionally buy something.

'Point taken,' Kate conceded. 'OK, could I have my eggs please?'

'Them eggs,' said Bobby, 'are from nice little hens what see the light of day, run in the fields, natural like.'

'Yes, that's why I like your eggs.'

'Cost of feed's gone up, see? Costs money havin' hens runnin' around in a field.'

'Yes, I'm sure.'

'So I've had to put them up by twenty pence.'

Kate scratched her head. 'A moment ago you said you'd put them up by *ten* pence.'

'Them was the small ones,' said Bobby. 'And I know you likes the big brown ones.'

'I don't think the colour makes much difference,' Kate remarked. 'But, anyway, can I have six please?' It was easier to go along with it.

Bobby dug under the counter. 'So what's that sister of yours been up to then?'

Kate shook her head. 'No idea.'

'Polly tells me 'twas your sister what pulled the trigger.'

'It's a *film*, Bobby,' Kate said with a sigh. '*Make-believe.* Doesn't matter who pulls the trigger because the gun wasn't supposed to be loaded with anything other than some stuff to make a noise and a puff of smoke. The police are trying to find out who *loaded* it. My sister wasn't anywhere near when it was loaded.'

Bobby pointed along the road. 'What about *him* then? That fancy man of hers?'

'I really don't think so. Now let me pay you for the eggs because Woody will be out of the shower and looking for breakfast.'

Sniffing loudly, Bobby slid the box of eggs across the counter. 'Never *used* to be like this round here.'

· · ·

'Should we go down to see why the police were back at The Old Locker last night?' Kate asked Woody a little later as they tackled their mushroom omelettes.

Woody shook his head emphatically. 'Why would we do that? It'll only be routine. More coffee?' he asked, wielding the percolator.

Kate nodded. 'Yes please. It's just that Bobby said it was all very noisy.'

'You know how he exaggerates. I do not intend us, on our day off together, to listen to Angie, forever the drama queen, going on and on and on, and then her and Fergal having one of their endless rows. Why don't we go to Boscastle, take Barney for a nice walk along the Valency Valley and then have some lunch in The Cobweb?'

Kate smiled and squeezed his hand across the table. 'Sometimes, Woody, you hit the nail on the head.'

It was when Kate was back in the wardrobe trailer the following morning that Jilly said, 'Funny, isn't it, that Lucy Moore's made an appointment with Guy, your hairdresser, for Saturday?'

Kate shrugged. 'Perhaps she wants her hair done.'

Jilly gave a patient sigh. 'We have a perfectly good hairdresser here on the set.' She pointed to the trailer alongside.

'Maybe she just fancies a change?'

'A change of what? Hannah's never done her hair. All she's been doing is fitting Lucy with a wig each day, because she's got to have this fancy hairdo, all piled up on top, for the story. And Hannah keeps saying how thick Lucy's hair is, and how difficult it is to get it all under the wig. So tell me this: why would Lucy go all the way to Tinworthy to get that Guy to chop off her hair when she could have it all cut off by Hannah right here?'

'I don't know,' Kate confessed. 'Perhaps she fancies him?'

'You're *joking*!' Jilly snorted. 'That's one guy who *ain't* after the gals! Must admit he's dishy though; such a waste!'

'I think he's making someone happy,' Kate said.

'Yeah, that's as maybe, but a lost cause as far as Lucy's concerned. But tell me this: if she's never had her hair cut by either Hannah or Guy, why has she chosen Guy, eh?'

As Kate tied a rope belt round her waist, she said, 'Your guess is as good as mine, Jilly.'

Nevertheless, as she dragged her pail up and down the hillside, Kate did wonder why Lucy had made an appointment with Guy.

Perhaps it was time they had a chat.

TWELVE

On Friday morning when Kate and Woody boarded the bus to take them to location, there was no sign of Fergal. She assumed he wasn't needed for some reason, as the beach scene had been altered slightly. She herself no longer had to carry the pail up and down the hill but had to stir a pot, hanging over a flame, outside the cottage where her character lived.

It wasn't until she was on the way home that Kate began to wonder why Fergal *really* wasn't there, because the group he'd been unloading cargo with were still doing just that. She recalled what Bobby had said about noise and the police being around on Tuesday evening, and wondered if anything was amiss. She should have popped in to Angie's after her visit to the shop, but Woody had been awaiting his omelette. Besides, Bobby had been known to exaggerate.

Nevertheless, when the bus arrived at Lower Tinworthy, Kate decided a visit to The Old Locker was necessary before she climbed up the hill for home.

'I'm just going to pop into The Locker for a minute,' she told Woody, who nodded and carried on walking up the lane.

'I'll start preparing dinner,' he said.

She found an unhappy-looking Angie serving drinks to some early-evening customers. Kate located her favourite bar stool and waited for her sister to finish.

'What's up?' Kate asked as Angie headed in her direction.

Angie groaned. 'I'll get myself a little gin and I'll tell you.' She helped herself to two shots of Bombay Sapphire, then added a miniscule amount of tonic, before slamming the glass down on the counter. 'Sorry,' she muttered, 'should have asked you first what you wanted.'

'I don't want anything,' Kate replied. 'I just want to get home, but I wondered why Fergal wasn't at Port Petroc today? He's not ill, is he?'

'No,' said Angie, 'the bugger's not ill, but he's confined to The Old Locker.' She sniffed, rolled her eyes and took a large gulp of her drink.

'Why?'

'He's "confined to barracks", so to speak, ever since we had a late-night visit from your friend, Charlotte, and half the bloody police force on Tuesday night.'

'They haven't taken him away or anything, have they?'

'I'm beginning to wish they had,' Angie snapped.

'For God's sake, Angie, what's going on?'

Angie took another large slug of her gin. 'What's going on is that Fergal supposedly has a gun licence somewhere, which he can't find and which I didn't know about, and a gun to go with it.'

'So have lots of people surely?'

'And he was a champion shot, in his youth, back in Ireland.'

'So what?'

Angie leaned across the counter and lowered her voice. 'The old bugger was once arrested for threatening to kill some guy in a pub!'

Kate stared at her sister.

'So,' Angie continued, 'they all came barging in here the other night and I honestly thought they were going to arrest him again.'

'But—'

'If he could try to kill someone once, he would be quite fit to do it again, according to your friend Charlotte.'

'She's *not* "my friend Charlotte"!' Kate protested. 'I wish you'd stop calling her that! In fact, she's been a pain in the backside on more than one occasion.' She hesitated. 'So did you *know* about Fergal ever having been arrested?'

Angie shook her head. 'No, I did not! But now that they've investigated his history, they reckon he had the motive and the ability to load the blunderbuss which shot Crispin. But surely the armourer was guarding the gun. And surely Fergal wouldn't have done such a thing when I was the one that had to press the trigger.'

Kate wondered privately if Fergal might perhaps have found it 'poetic' if Angie had pulled the trigger on her one-time lover.

At that moment, an equally gloomy-looking Fergal appeared from upstairs. He nodded morosely in Kate's direction.

'I wondered why you weren't there today,' Kate remarked casually.

'Well I'm sure by now you've heard all the feckin' details from Angie,' he said.

'I still don't see that there's a very valid reason to suspect you,' Kate said diplomatically, keeping her voice down while scanning the customers. Fortunately, no one seemed to be listening. 'I mean, lots of people must be knowledgeable about guns?'

Fergal shrugged while pouring himself a coffee. 'I daresay they are, but they don't all have my history.'

'Like trying to *kill* someone,' Angie added tersely.

'I spent a long time wishing I'd succeeded,' Fergal retorted.
'Michael Barry was a bastard, and he was bloody lucky they got
the gun off me before I blew his feckin' head off!'

Kate was momentarily lost for words.

'Of course if you walk into a bar brandishing a gun,' Angie
said, 'it's probably fair to say that you're not planning on just
ordering a cocktail.'

Kate found her voice. 'But why were you brandishing a gun
in the first place, Fergal?'

'Because I knew Michael Barry was in there and I had every
intention of making sure that he never came out!'

'What had *he* done to upset you?' Kate asked, intrigued.

'It's a long story,' Fergal replied, 'but just for a start, he'd
swindled me out of a large amount of money. A *helluva* lot of
money. He'd also stolen my lovely girlfriend' – here Angie
sniffed loudly – 'and he'd bloody well run over my *dog*!'

'Oh, Fergal!' Kate, being an animal lover, was more
concerned about the dog than the money or the girlfriend.

'So, you see,' Fergal continued calmly, 'I reckoned the world
would be a better place without him. Unfortunately, I was
grabbed from behind before I could press the feckin' trigger.'

'When it comes to digging into Fergal's history,' Angie
added, 'your friend Charlotte's been very thorough.'

'She is *not* my friend!' Kate repeated with a sigh.

Fergal drained his coffee. 'I'm now her new prime suspect.'

'And they've barred you from the set at Port Petroc?'

'Worse than that, they've taken my *gun* away!'

'You had a *gun upstairs in the flat*?' Kate could scarcely
believe what she was hearing.

'Sure,' he said matter-of-factly, 'beneath the bed.'

Kate digested this for a moment. 'But surely guns are meant
to be kept under lock and key, aren't they?'

'True enough, but I just hadn't got around to getting a gun
cabinet. And it's not as if I have a *collection*; I just had the *one*!'

'Either way, he's in trouble,' Angie muttered, heading towards the gin again, 'so is it any wonder that I'm in need of some solace?'

Fergal snorted and shook his head. 'It doesn't take much for Angie to require some liquid solace.' With that, he stomped upstairs.

Kate eased herself off the bar stool. 'It's time I went home.'

'Ah well, you'll have plenty to tell Wonderboy,' said Angie. 'And while you're at it, you can inform him that Fergal has somehow or other found out that I slept with Crispin recently and he's going mad.'

'You can hardly blame him for that, Angie.'

'He's not my bloody husband! I'm a free woman, Kate, and don't you forget it!'

Kate sighed as she closed the door behind her. She'd never understand Angie and Fergal's relationship. But a gun...

'*What!*' Woody almost dropped the grill pan as he turned the steaks over.

Kate poured them both a glass of wine. 'He's certainly a bit of a rogue,' she remarked as she handed him a glass, 'and she's no better. Don't know how Fergal found out about her and Crispin.'

'What a pair!' Woody exclaimed. 'And, frankly, if Fergal was prepared to kill once, it's mighty likely he'd be quite prepared to kill again!'

'But why would he?' Kate asked. 'He thought that Angie's affair with Crispin finished long before he came on the scene, although apparently it didn't. So how did he find out?'

Woody shrugged. 'What really bugs me is that he didn't have his gun securely locked up. He'll be fined heavily for that.'

'I find it hard to believe that Fergal actually *intended* to kill someone once,' Kate said, shaking her head slowly, taking the dish of salad to the table.

Woody was plating up the steaks. 'Everyone's a potential killer, they say, if they're pushed enough. And, let's face it, Fergal's a bit of a mystery really. We don't know a lot about him. Now, enough of all that – let's eat!'

THIRTEEN

Kate was trying to work out the best way to come face to face with the armourer. She had no reason whatsoever to go anywhere near Paul Bacon or the blunderbuss. Having recently become aware of his apparent relapse into drinking off the set, perhaps the best way to find him was by going to the pub. But which one? From what Des and Sonia had said, it seemed Bacon drank in The Pheasant first then carried on at The Greedy Gull.

If he was in The Pheasant, it meant staying on at the end of the day's filming, which meant driving there as opposed to using the bus. Woody would want to know why and would come with her but was unlikely to warm to the idea of visiting The Pheasant after lugging boxes across the beach, or whatever it was extras were required to do. And, if she told him, he would, of course, tell her 'not to interfere', 'leave it to the professionals' and 'not to endanger herself'. He was probably right, but Kate felt she had to meet all the suspects before she consulted The List again – not that she was yet ready to delete anyone's name, much as she wished she could cross off Angie and Fergal.

All this meant that Kate would really need to visit the pub

in Port Petroc quite early on a non-filming day, in the hope that Paul Bacon might show up there. Or did he keep a stack of liquor in his caravan?

She seemed to remember Sonia saying something to the effect that the extras wouldn't be required for much longer, so there was no time to waste. Kate really needed to visit the supermarket, so she could tie that in with a visit to The Pheasant. Woody was extremely unlikely to want to accompany her as he had no great love of shopping, particularly supermarket shopping.

Luck was with her. On Saturday morning at breakfast, Woody said, 'Would you mind if I have a couple of hours up at the allotment later?' He peered out at the grey drizzle. 'They say it's going to brighten up later, so I might wait until closer to lunchtime when it dries up a little.'

'I might go to the supermarket myself,' Kate said casually. 'We could do with stocking up.'

Woody nodded but didn't ask any questions.

The drizzle stopped and the sun emerged about half past eleven and, at noon, Woody was heading to the allotment and Kate was heading to The Pheasant at Port Petroc.

The Pheasant was a typical old Cornish pub, similar to The Tinners' in Middle Tinworthy, except that the ceilings were even lower, with sturdy beams adorned with brass and copper horseshoes, bells and jugs, all designed for the instant concussion of anyone over five feet seven inches. The taller regulars could be distinguished by their permanent stoops as they navigated their way around.

The landlord had few such problems, being only an inch or two over five feet, and not far short of that in girth. He was a jolly little fellow, bald as a coot and known affectionately as 'the monk' by the locals, due to his favoured hooded tops.

Today, the place was plainly swarming with tourists, because there were two large buses in the car park, and Kate had to wait some time to procure a parking space.

As she entered the pub, she could decipher some American accents in the midst of the noisy buzz of conversation. One tall man, looking slightly dazed, was rubbing his head, having made contact with a copper jug, which was still swinging merrily from the beam.

Kate had to push her way through the throng, looking around as she did so in the hope of spotting Paul Bacon – if he hadn't already left for The Greedy Gull. When she finally squeezed her way up to the bar, she could scarcely believe her eyes when she found herself standing right next to the armourer himself, who was sitting on a bar stool, nursing what looked like a large Scotch, staring gloomily into space and paying no attention whatsoever to what was going on around him.

Kate ordered a lime and soda and glanced sideways at him. She hadn't expected it to be this easy and she wasn't quite sure how to approach him.

She cleared her throat a couple of times, but he didn't react at all. Finally, Kate said, 'Excuse me!'

Slowly, Paul Bacon swivelled round to face her, and Kate observed the slightly unfocused eyes and pitted skin of a habitual drinker. She was beginning to feel a little ridiculous, but there was no point in stopping now.

'Er, you're Paul Bacon, aren't you?'

His expression didn't change. 'So what?'

'Oh, it's just that I'm an extra on *Pengorran's Revenge* and I *thought* I recognised you.'

'So?'

Paul wasn't being exactly helpful, but Kate continued anyway. 'Um, my name's Kate Palmer and I'm one of those peasants who's either pumping water from a well or carrying buckets up and down the hillside. It gets a bit monotonous!' She gave a nervous little laugh.

He continued staring at her. 'Your face is familiar; have you worked on films before?'

'No, I haven't and I don't think I will again because it's so boring. Mind you, it certainly livened things up when Crispin Wyngarde got shot though!' she added.

Paul turned back to his drink. 'Horrible bugger, but nothing to do with me.'

'Of course not!' Kate added hastily. She searched her brain frantically for something else to say. After a minute she said, 'I found it particularly scary because my sister, Angie, was playing the part of the mother and trying to wrestle the gun from Crispin's character. I mean, she was the one who actually pulled the trigger, although she had no idea the gun was loaded of course.'

Now she had his attention – he swivelled right round again to face her.

'Angie?'

'Yes, my sister. She'd actually got a tiny part because she knew Crispin and—'

'Angie's your *sister*?' Paul appeared incredulous.

'Yes, she—'

'*Angie Norton*?' he interrupted again.

Kate stared back at him. 'Yes.' How did *he* know Angie? 'Do you know her then?'

'I did once,' Paul replied glumly.

'What? When?' Kate could scarcely believe what she was hearing. Why hadn't Angie said something about this?

'A long time ago,' he said, turning back to the counter and knocking back his drink in one enormous gulp. He then tapped the glass on the bar-top to attract the attention of one of the barmen. 'Want a drink?'

'I've got one thanks.'

There was silence while the armourer waited for the barman to notice him.

'Angie didn't say she knew you,' Kate said, after a minute.

'No, I don't suppose she did.' He'd now got the barman's attention and ordered himself a double Scotch.

'I wonder why she didn't tell me,' Kate said when he picked up his glass.

He shrugged. 'Maybe because she was a bit of a naughty girl.'

'She *was*? In what way?'

Paul turned back to face her again. 'Not for me to say. Why don't you ask *her*?'

'I will.'

Why on earth had Angie never mentioned this? What possible connection could there have been? Kate studied him for a minute. The man had a fine profile and luxuriant greying hair. He looked to be around sixty and must have been rather good-looking once.

She drained her lime soda.

'Before you go,' he said, turning round again, 'let me tell you that I did not like Wyngarde, but it wasn't me who killed the bugger. You can tell Angie Norton that when you get back because' – here he gave her the glimmer of a smile – 'I'll bet you're going straight to her house right now!'

Kate, who intended to do just that, smiled weakly and muttered, 'See you on the set.'

She was about to head back to The Old Locker before remembering she was supposed to be going to the supermarket. Was it any wonder she'd nearly forgotten? Her head was all over the place, and she was now thoroughly overwhelmed by the number of potential suspects she had to contend with and the fact that her sister and the armourer were acquainted.

FOURTEEN

On the way home from the supermarket, Kate wondered if she should impart this piece of unbelievable news to Woody before she tackled Angie on the subject. She decided to play it by ear. If Woody was back home from the allotment, they'd sit down with a cup of coffee and she'd tell him what Paul Bacon had said. Woody, of course, would go completely ballistic and say she had no business hunting down the armourer, and maybe he was right. If, on the other hand, Woody was still up at the allotment, she'd take it as a sign that The Old Locker was where she'd be having her coffee.

Even after she'd unloaded her groceries, there was still no sign of Woody, and Barney was following her around, wagging his tail, which signalled his hope of a walk.

'OK, Barney,' Kate said as she finished stowing everything away, 'let's go!'

She peered out of the window at the beach, where there were still a number of people walking and surfers surfing. She decided there were too many people there to let Barney run free, so she'd take him up Penhallion Cliff instead. It was a bit of a climb, so she'd be ready for her coffee – and Angie – on the way back.

All the way down the lane, across the old bridge and up the path, Kate pondered on what the armourer had said. Angie had undoubtedly been a naughty girl, due probably in no small part to the gin. She'd been considered to have great potential as an actress once, but, frequently, she'd either forgotten to go to rehearsals or forgotten her lines when she got there. How George had put up with her for all those years was beyond Kate's comprehension.

Had Angie known Paul Bacon *before* she married George?

Kate and Barney wandered along the clifftop and surveyed the scene out to sea where a small fishing boat, in the middle distance, was bobbing up and down on the swell. Kate wasn't a good sailor and tried to imagine what it must feel like hauling in nets, or whatever fishermen did, with the world swaying beneath your feet. The very thought of it began to make her feel nauseous.

'Let's go back, Barney,' she called out to the dog after about ten minutes.

As they retraced their steps back down to the village, Kate rehearsed how she might open the conversation with her sister. She rather hoped Fergal wouldn't be around, but, on a busy Saturday afternoon, chances were he would be. It was probably not the ideal time to broach this subject with Angie either. Nevertheless, the sooner she did, the sooner she was likely to find out the truth.

The Old Locker was fairly busy, full of what Angie called 'the newly-wed and nearly dead': those couples who didn't yet have children, and the elderly whose children had long ago got up and gone, meaning they could avoid the school holiday periods.

Fergal was dealing with a queue of customers, along with Emma, the part-time help, and there was no sign of Angie. Kate had never seen the place so busy; standing room only.

Kate waited until most of the queue had dispersed and Emma approached, looking a little frazzled.

'Hi, Kate! You looking for Angie?'

'Yes, I am. Is she upstairs?'

Emma nodded. 'She needed to get off her feet, so she's gone up for a rest. It's been busy here all day.'

This was better than Kate had hoped for: no customers, no noise and no Fergal upstairs. She made her way towards the stairs, giving Fergal a wave as she passed.

Angie was sprawled in an armchair, her feet on the coffee table, reading *Hello!* magazine. 'Oh hi,' she said. 'What brings *you* here?'

'Just been for a walk,' Kate replied casually. 'You look knackered! Shall I make us a cup of tea?'

'Good idea,' said Angie, stroking the dog's head. 'You can dig out a biscuit for Barney while you're at it. I seem to remember he likes custard creams?'

Kate made the tea, gave Barney his biscuit and sat down opposite her sister.

'Some interesting gossip in here,' Angie remarked, laying down the magazine and sipping her tea. 'Amazing what some people get up to.'

'Oh, indeed,' said Kate. 'Talking of good gossip, I met a friend of yours today.'

'Oh yes? And who was that?'

'Paul Bacon.'

Kate noticed Angie's hand wobble and a slop of tea spilling onto *Hello!*, but she quickly regained her composure.

'What are you talking about?'

'You know perfectly well what I'm talking about, Angie.

Paul Bacon said he'd known you a long time ago. I just wondered why you never mentioned that?'

'Why were *you* talking to him?' Angie demanded.

'You haven't answered my question?' Kate said.

'You haven't answered mine either,' Angie snapped.

'OK then. I met him at The Pheasant in Port Petroc.' She had thought of saying that she'd met him on the film set but then decided to stick to the truth.

'What the hell were *you* doing there?'

'I was on my way to the supermarket and needed a pee, so thought I'd stop off and use their loo, and then I thought I'd better buy a drink.' One little lie wouldn't hurt.

'And you just *happened* to bump into him?' Angie looked unconvinced. 'Nothing to do with poking your nose in where it isn't wanted? Got your Miss Marple hat on again, have you?'

Kate shook her head. 'I've answered your question, so now you answer mine. How come you know him? How come he described you as a naughty girl? And how come you never told me?'

'I've had *lots* of little romances that *you* know nothing about,' Angie replied acidly, 'and which were, and are, none of your business.'

'Well what was so "naughty" about this one?' Kate still hoped that her guess that they'd been lovers was wrong.

Angie gulped some tea. 'God knows why he said that. Maybe it was because I was married at the time?'

'What? You were unfaithful to George?'

'Oh, for goodness' sake, don't go getting all high and mighty on me now! You *know* George was away on business half the time and that I sometimes got lonely.'

Kate gave a loud sigh. No sense in censuring her sister now – Angie had always lived life by her own rules. 'How did you meet Paul? When you were acting?'

'No, I met him at our local pub when we lived in Hampshire. He was with a group of friends and was in the army at Aldershot.'

'Was *he* married?'

Angie shrugged. 'Don't think so. He *said* he wasn't. He was an attractive man back then, but he's been in lots of war zones and seen some terrible things. I mean, they get therapy nowadays, but I don't think they did back then. He hit the bottle to dull the memories, very sad. Then he went to Alcoholics Anonymous, or one of those groups, and he gave it up altogether.'

'And where did all those romantic trysts take place?'

'At my place, while George was away. Don't forget I had a young child at the time.'

Kate gave a deep sigh. 'Oh, *Angie*. And you haven't seen him since?'

'Not until we started working on that damned film,' Angie replied, shaking her head.

'But why did you not *tell* me? You must have recognised each other when you were doing the scene with Crispin?'

Angie removed her feet from the coffee table and sat up straight. 'You want to know why? Because I *knew* I'd be quizzed and questioned by you – *that's* why! And I knew then that there was a chance Charlotte Martin might get wind of it, and then *she'd* decide that Paul and I were in league to get rid of Crispin or something.' She sniffed loudly. 'And now I have no doubt whatsoever that you can't wait to leg it home and relay all this delicious gossip to Wonderboy, who, being indoctrinated with police procedures, will immediately pass the information on to Charlotte bloody Martin!'

'Of course he wouldn't, Angie! He doesn't tell tales, and he is *not* in league with Charlotte!'

'Well you *would* say that, wouldn't you? And I expect

you're still making these bloody lists! I bet anything you like that I'll be on there as a suspect before the day is out!'

'Angie, I—'

'Bugger off!' Angie interrupted. 'The dog's getting restless, so time you went home!'

FIFTEEN

'You did *what?*' Woody asked, his mug of tea halfway to his mouth.

'I went into The Pheasant at Port Petroc because I needed to go to the loo.'

'Isn't there a loo in the supermarket?'

'Yes, of course there is, but that was a further ten-minute drive and I didn't think I could wait that long.'

Woody gave her a long hard stare. 'This weak bladder of yours is news to me, Kate.'

'I forgot to go before I left here, that's all,' Kate said, hoping she sounded nonchalant.

'OK, OK, so in you go to The Pheasant, and then...?'

'Well, after I'd been to the loo, I felt a bit guilty, because the loo is supposed to be for customers only.'

'And so you decided to be a customer,' Woody stated, raising an eyebrow, a gesture Kate always found to be extremely sexy. 'OK, you bought a drink, and then *who* should come in but...?'

'He was already sitting at the bar.'

'*He?* Let me guess now: who could possibly be having a

drink in the pub at Port Petroc on a non-filming day? Unlikely to be anyone from Tinworthy, I should think. So who could *he* be, I wonder?'

'No need to be sarcastic, Woody. I didn't know Paul Bacon would be there, did I? But it seemed like fate, you know, me finding myself right next to him when I got to the bar!'

'Quite a coincidence,' Woody agreed, somewhat drily.

'Anyway,' Kate continued, 'we got chatting.'

'Now, I wonder who might have instigated this conversation?'

'That doesn't matter! What does matter was that, when I mentioned something about Angie, and the scene with Crispin and the blunderbuss, he did a double take. "Angie?" he said.'

'Don't tell me he, too, knew Angie a million years ago? She *was* a busy lady!'

'Yes, he *did* know her.'

'*What!*' Woody almost spilled the remainder of his tea. 'But that's ridiculous! She would surely have told you!'

'That thought did cross my mind, which is why I've just been down to The Old Locker.'

'I bet you have! And Angie, of course, denies all knowledge of this guy?'

Kate gulped. 'No, Woody, she admitted to having had an affair with him years ago when George took off on his countless business trips. Paul was in the army at the time and, according to Angie, the memory of his experiences drove him to drink, but then he got help and became teetotal.'

'Well he's certainly not teetotal now, is he? So she had it away with the armourer and she had it away with the producer? Was there anyone on that film set that she didn't have it away with? Should we line up the cameramen, the sound engineers, the editors?'

Kate sighed. 'She always was a *bit* that way inclined.'

'You're telling me! OK, so Angie had her knickers off more

often than she had them on. She told you about Wyngarde, so why didn't she tell you about Bacon?'

'I don't know,' Kate admitted.

'I'll tell you why. Because if the police get to hear about this, they may well deduce that she and Bacon were somehow in league to kill Wyngarde. Let's face it, he was supposedly in charge of the blunderbuss, and she actually pulled the trigger.'

'It *does* look bad,' Kate admitted. 'Will you tell Charlotte?'

Woody shook his head. 'I won't tell her anything, but if she gets wind of it and starts asking questions all round, I will have to tell her what I know. It's for her to find out though.'

'Do you think she will find out?'

'Probably... Who knows?' Woody shrugged. 'Now, I've booked a table for us at The Edge for eight o'clock, so please can we not talk about this all evening? Go have a shower and get your glad rags on!'

The Edge of the Moor, an upmarket restaurant housed in an ancient, one-storey stone building on the edge of Bodmin Moor, was their favourite eating place. It was where Woody had taken her on their very first date – and on many occasions since.

Kate vowed to be good and not permit the names of Paul Bacon or Angie Norton to escape from her lips. They'd have a nice, quiet evening without any drama.

Kate didn't think it was possible to get any more shocks in one day, but, when she and Woody entered The Edge of the Moor, the first person she saw was Guy, the hairdresser, dining with Lucy Moore, the female star of *Pengorran's Revenge*.

'My God!' she exclaimed, tugging at Woody's arm. 'Do you see who I see?'

'Yes, I do. And I am not about to go galloping over there to ask them what on earth they're doing dining together.'

'No, of course not,' Kate agreed as the waiter pulled out the chair for her to sit down. But there was no way she could help studying them over the top of the menu. Why had Lucy come to Tinworthy to get her hair cut by Guy in the first place? The short, pixie style suited her very well indeed and Guy had done a good job, but why were they now dining together?

Guy was his usual suave self, and they were deep in conversation.

'Stop staring and choose what you want to eat,' Woody said. 'Didn't your mom ever tell you that it's rude to stare?'

'She told us a lot of things,' Kate replied, grinning, 'like staying a virgin until we got married and then never looking at another man again!'

'*That* went down well then, didn't it?' Woody murmured, just as the wine waiter approached.

As Woody was ordering the wine, Kate, still studying the unlikely pair, actually caught Guy's eye. He smiled, waved and then continued talking with Lucy. They were plainly still in the middle of their meal so Kate tried to concentrate on her choice of food, with only an occasional glance in their direction.

It was while Kate was about to tackle her lemon posset that Guy and Lucy got up to leave and Guy gave a brief wave as they made their way to the door.

'I rather hoped he'd come over,' Kate said wistfully as she savoured the tangy lemon taste.

'Well, Miss Marple,' Woody said, 'this gives you something else to get your teeth into! Guy and Lucy. Angie and Fergal. Angie and Paul Bacon. Angie all by herself. Fergal all by himself. Paul Bacon all by himself! There's enough there to keep you going for months, my love!' He gave Kate a wicked grin.

'You must admit, though, that these two, Guy and Lucy, are an unlikely pair?'

'Perhaps he likes girls too? Let's face it, she's very pretty. Now can we change the subject *please*?'

· · ·

Kate felt completely relaxed after a wonderful dinner, washed down with a large quantity of very fine wine, greatly superior to their normal supermarket haul. Nevertheless, she couldn't sleep a wink.

After an hour and a half of tossing, turning and trying not to wake Woody up, she crept downstairs to make herself a drink. As she sat down at the kitchen table with a hot chocolate, she could still visualise Guy and Lucy sitting together. Why had Lucy come to Guy to get her hair done? And where was Roly, Guy's partner? *What* was going on?

Then she began to mull over what Woody had said, albeit jokingly, about all the likely twosomes who might have conspired together to get rid of Crispin Wyngarde. For the first time, Kate began to feel a little sorry for Crispin. How sad that this man had, in his time – intentionally or otherwise – alienated so many people who were now all possible suspects for his demise!

Kate got out the hardback notebook where she kept The List. One of her sons had given it to her for Christmas many years ago. It was beautiful, full of floral illustrations with Latin names, and she'd never quite known what to do with it. Now, years later, all her past suspects were written in there, and she was a good halfway through the book. As she located an empty page, she wondered if she should add all the possible partnerships in this particular case.

Guy had seemed an unlikely suspect, but this sudden friendship (just friendship?) with Lucy Moore was weird, to say the least. Her thoughts then turned to Fergal and the gun he'd kept under the bed. Under the bed! Hardly the stuff of James Bond!

Fergal and Angie? Angie and Paul Bacon?

Kate was beginning to get a nagging doubt in her mind

about Angie and Paul. Why hadn't Angie told her that they'd been so close all those years ago? Of course, Kate knew that it wasn't possible Angie was involved in any way in the murder, but she needed to be absolutely certain. Could Paul be using Angie in some way?

There was only one place she could imagine that they could meet up and that would be The Greedy Gull. Perhaps it would be a good idea to go and have a chat with Des.

Kate was glad she had plenty more pages in her notebook. She needed more information.

Had Angie and Bacon met up unbeknown to her? Had Angie and the armourer ever been in The Gull together? Where did Angie go when she had an evening off from The Old Locker? She didn't often visit Kate these days, that was for sure. What had her sister been up to...?

SIXTEEN

It was Wednesday before Kate finally had an opportunity to visit The Greedy Gull.

It was a two-storey, two-hundred-year-old stone building, complete with slate floors, beams and an inglenook fireplace. Des, in one of his more artistic moments, had painted a large gull, with a fish in its mouth, on the white-painted wall on either side of the inglenook. This artistry wasn't just to reflect the name of the pub but also to warn customers that if they chose to sit outside on one of the rustic and rickety benches, there was a good chance of their lunch being snatched away, literally from under their very noses, by a hovering seagull. These gulls hovered over every resort along the north coast and had become expert at snatching anything edible.

Woody had gone to St Austell to get his precious Mercedes serviced, and Kate had declined his invitation to 'come along for the ride'. There was nothing wrong with St Austell, although it could hardly be described as a shopping mecca and, besides, Kate had more important things to do. Like going to The Gull. And that's where she was heading.

It was about quarter to twelve, a few holidaymakers were on

the beach and the lunchtime customers had not yet begun to come in. It would be a good time to catch Des before it got busy. But would he tell her anything, and was there anything to tell?

As Kate pushed open the door, her heart sank. There was no sign of Des behind the bar, only Madge, his other half. Madge rarely emerged from the kitchen, where, single-handed, she cooked or microwaved the daily menu. Madge was a rotund little person, normally dashing about with plates of food, her pink face flushed and her tied-up-on-the-top hair escaping all over the place. So far today her hair was still intact, and she was a paler shade of pink. Kate reckoned that she and Des must be around the same age, mid-sixtyish.

Kate decided she could hardly turn on her heel and go out again because Madge had already spotted her.

'What brings you in here, all by yourself?' Madge asked.

'Oh, just feeling very thirsty. I've been gardening all morning,' Kate lied.

'Thirsty work,' Madge agreed. 'What can I get you?'

'I'll just have half a shandy please, Madge.' Kate could only hope that Des might appear at any minute and Madge would return to the kitchen.

'So where's Des today?' she asked casually as Madge placed her drink on the bar-top.

'He's gone to that new supermarket, the other side of Port Petroc,' Madge replied, 'but he should be back any minute.' She glanced at her watch. 'I need to get back in the kitchen before any customers arrive. I can't be *everywhere*, can I? We need extra help at lunchtime, but Des ain't keen on payin' out. We ain't as busy as we used to be now that your sister's got that place down there, and a licence and all.'

Kate resisted the temptation to apologise on Angie's behalf.

'Talking of Angie, I don't suppose you've seen her here with that Paul Bacon, have you?'

Madge shook her head. 'I wouldn't know, dear, cos I'm

normally in the kitchen. You still on that film down at Port Petroc? How's it goin' after all that murder business?'

'Well it's certainly held everything up considerably.'

'They got any idea who doctored that gun your sister was shootin'?'

'Not yet, Madge. Quite a few suspects though.'

'That Bacon bloke's clutterin' up the car park out there,' Madge said, 'and drinkin' too much in the evenin'. I know he's a good customer and all that, but I wish he'd found somewhere else to park. Does your sister know him well then? Why would they be drinkin' together? Was it her that asked Des to let him plonk his caravan in our car park?'

'I shouldn't think so,' Kate said, beginning to wonder if that was, in fact, the case. 'Des might just feel sorry for him perhaps?'

Madge leaned across the counter. 'I'm going to tell you a thing or two about—' She stopped talking suddenly. 'Ah, he's back.'

'Sorry I been so long,' Des said. 'Supermarket's manic! Had to queue for nearly half an hour at the cashier's.' He nodded at Kate as he carried a box past the bar and into the kitchen.

'You were saying?' Kate asked Madge hopefully.

Madge looked blank. 'Can't for the life of me remember, dear. Couldn't have been very important. I best go help Des unload this lot.'

Kate sat, with The List and a mug of coffee, and waited for Woody to come home. She wondered what on earth Madge had been about to tell her. If only Des hadn't come back at that very moment! Surely it was nothing about Angie and Paul because she'd already denied seeing them, due to being in the kitchen. Kate wondered if her imagination *was* running riot yet again.

'I'm sure Madge was about to say something interesting,'

Kate sighed as she told Woody about her brief visit to The Greedy Gull.

'Were you there in search of Paul Bacon again?' Woody asked.

'No, not entirely. I wanted to find out if Angie had been there with Bacon. I just wish Des hadn't come back the very minute Madge was planning to tell me something. She shut up the moment she saw him coming in the door.'

'Doesn't mean a thing,' Woody said, pouring himself a coffee.

'Do you think she might have suddenly remembered something Des had told her about Angie and Paul Bacon?' Kate added, feeling extremely guilty.

Woody shrugged. 'It's possible, but I'll tell you something, I certainly don't envy Charlotte trying to solve this one, with such a supply of suspects who had good reason to put a shot in Crispin Wyngarde.' Woody stood up and located a packet of his favourite bourbon biscuits from the cupboard. 'Perhaps Charlotte should be told?' he said as he began to open the packet.

'What, do you mean about Angie and Paul Bacon?'

'Who else?'

'No, no!' Kate said, alarmed. 'I'm sure it's purely a coincidence. Don't you go telling her! *Promise* me, Woody?'

'I promise not to tell her. But maybe you should consider having a long, serious chat with your sister, my love, because you just *never* know.'

Kate nodded, too ashamed to tell him that she had indeed considered this but felt too afraid to ask Angie. After all, she *was* her big sister.

SEVENTEEN

'You've got a different outfit today,' Jilly informed Kate when she arrived in the wardrobe trailer the following morning. 'This one's got long sleeves and an over-skirt. They must have known it was going to turn cooler today.'

As Kate struggled into her new, longer robe, she asked, 'Heard any more gossip, Jilly?'

'Nope,' Jilly commented languidly as she bent down with a large pair of scissors to remove some threads sprouting from the hem. 'We're all under suspicion here. I told you already, my money's on Sonia.'

'You really don't like her, do you?'

'Not a lot,' Jilly confirmed. 'Then again, I don't like anyone much on this set. I'll be glad when they've finished shooting the outside scenes and we can get away from this godforsaken place and go back to the studio and civilisation.'

Kate wondered if she dared question her further.

'I know you said you thought that Sonia might have killed Crispin,' she said casually, 'but is there anyone else you suspect? I mean, you know everyone, and you're right here in the middle of it.'

'Except there *were* people I'd never set eyes on before, all swarming over the set, on the day you extras first came on the scene. Any of them could have loaded that blunderbuss thing, if they knew what they were doing.'

'What about the armourer?' Kate asked tentatively. 'Wasn't he supposed to be guarding the gun?'

Jilly straightened up and laid down her scissors. 'Paul Bacon? He should have been, that's for sure, but he's a bit of a nutter. He might not drink on set, but he made up for it in the evening down at The Pheasant. I wouldn't have put it past him to want to kill Wyngarde. Still, my money's on Sonia.'

Kate adjusted her new robe and set off for the hillside.

The next day, they finished filming earlier than usual, and Kate found herself back in Lower Tinworthy at just after half past three. Woody fancied an hour or so at his allotment and Barney was desperate for a walk.

She had a quick cup of tea and a biscuit before setting off with the dog along the beach. Today was cloudy, with a stiff, cool breeze, so there were few people on the beach, only surfers in the sea.

They'd almost got to the far end of the beach when Kate heard a shout behind her and, turning round, saw Angie stumbling along in the sand.

'Kate!'

'What on earth, Angie...?'

'I need to *talk* to you!'

'Why didn't you phone me? I could have called in—'

'No, no!' Angie interrupted. 'I need to talk to you *alone*! Without Fergal around!'

'What's happened now?' Kate hoped Fergal hadn't found out about Angie's relationship with Paul Bacon. 'Is he about to take off again?' Kate asked.

'No, he isn't. Where's that rock you like to sit on?'

Kate pointed to a group of larger rocks at the far end of the beach, one of which she liked to sit on and stare out to sea, listening to the tide either lapping or crashing in, depending on the weather. Many a time she had found solace there. Come to think of it, she'd actually met a wet-suited Woody there!

'I'll race you!' exclaimed Angie, being surprisingly frivolous and reminding Kate of their childhood, when Angie had always wanted to be first everywhere. On this occasion, Kate got to the rocks first, positioning herself on her favourite one and bracing herself to hear Angie's version of their latest altercation.

'I beat you this time,' she told Angie, who was gasping audibly as she selected a rock opposite her sister.

'You didn't used to be faster than me!'

'You're out of condition! You should get yourself a dog!' Kate retorted, stroking Barney's head. 'Well, now that you've had some fresh air, what was it you wanted to talk about?'

Angie sighed and took a deep breath. 'Fergal's asked me to marry him.'

'What? You can't be serious!'

'I'm absolutely serious!'

'Wonders never cease! And have you said you will?'

'Of course not! It just came out of the blue when I was cleaning the toilets!'

'Ever the romantic!' Kate murmured.

'What do *you* think, Kate?'

Kate didn't know what she thought. Angie needed someone to keep her on the straight and narrow, and she was none too sure that Fergal was the man to do that.

'What does it matter what I think? It's your decision,' Kate said, reluctant to give an opinion. She stared out to sea, watching a wet-suited figure crashing through the waves on his bellyboard.

'No, I realise it's not your decision, but I just wondered what you think of the idea?'

'A couple of days ago you said you were having another almighty row. Do you really want to live like that?'

'That was on account of Crispin,' Angie admitted.

'How did Fergal find out you were still having an affair with the wretched man?'

Angie groaned, 'Thanks to bloody Peter Edwards.'

Kate was astonished. 'How on earth did Peter Edwards come into all this?'

Peter Edwards was a local councillor and magistrate, and the long-term lover of Penelope Bowen, who, in turn, was the chairperson of every local committee, the Women's Institute and the Conservative Ladies' Club. Two big fish in a tiny pond.

'Well Crispin had to apply to the local council for permission to take over part of the coastline for his filming, and Peter Edwards was sent to sort it out. And you know Peter! He loved all the hobnobbing with film people, and he got very pally with Crispin.'

'Don't tell me Crispin told him he'd had an affair with you?'

'Yes, he did, the bastard. Edwards wanted to know why Crispin had chosen Port Petroc in the first place, and Crispin told him that was down to me, that we'd been having an affair for years and that I'd suggested the location.'

'So how on earth did Fergal find out?'

'You know Fergal likes a drink in either The Gull or The Tinners' on his evening off?'

Kate nodded, although she could never really understand the attraction of spending precious time off in a similar environment.

'Fergal and Edwards were at the bar together, both a bit pissed. They got talking about the film and then out it all came.'

'Did Fergal believe him?'

'Yes, he did, and he went bloody ballistic! He came home and we had an almighty row!'

Kate shook her head. 'I'm hardly surprised, Angie, with the way you've been behaving.'

'It took a few days, but we made it up.'

'And he's asked you to *marry* him?'

'Yes, because he doesn't want me to be with anyone else, *ever again.*'

Did Fergal honestly think that *that* would call a halt to Angie's colourful sex life? Kate wondered.

'Do you love him?'

Angie sniffed. 'Sometimes.'

'For God's sake, Angie, if you're not sure, *don't!*'

Angie was silent for a moment. Then: 'Do you think he might be trying to marry me for my money?'

'*What* money?'

'Well, you know, The Locker's in my name, and I've a few thousand invested here and there.'

'That hardly places you in the supertax bracket!' Kate knew that her sister had spent most of the money her mother-in-law had left her on doing up The Old Locker.

'No, but Fergal's got *nothing.*'

That much was true. Back in Ireland, Fergal's wife had deserted him for another man, emptied their joint bank account in the process and fled to New York, leaving Fergal penniless. He'd arrived, via London and countless brothers and sisters, in Plymouth, where he'd found a variety of jobs to pay for the rent on his scruffy caravan.

'Didn't he ever train to do anything?' Kate asked.

'No, he went into sales and he worked for his ex-father-in-law until *she* absconded. That's why he's so good with the blarney.'

'So how come he was driving a cab and flogging souvenirs when you met him?'

'Because he couldn't get a decent job in sales at the time.'

Kate didn't know what she was supposed to say, knowing full well that she'd be blamed if she advised Angie *not* to marry him, and Angie was then alone and became lonely. And if she *did* advise Angie to marry him, and it turned out badly or the marriage went on the rocks, Kate would be blamed for that too.

'Angie, I can't tell you what to do. It's your life and your decision.'

'But, seriously, do you think he just wants security?'

Kate shook her head. 'I've no idea.'

'And suppose he's guilty and *did* load up that bloody blunderbuss? What if he ends up in jail?'

Kate stared at her sister for a moment. 'Do you honestly think he is guilty then?'

Angie shook her head wearily. 'No. But I worry a bit because he was so jealous of Crispin. He keeps on about it.'

Kate was becoming increasingly exasperated. 'Who could blame him? For God's sake, I'm not surprised. I'm only surprised that he still wants to marry you. Tell him you need time to think. This isn't a good time for major decisions. I mean, you're *both* suspects! And don't involve me, because whatever I say will be wrong.'

'But do you think—'

'*I* think you should wait until you know your own mind.'

'Why on earth was she asking *you*?' Woody asked as they cooked dinner that evening. 'Can't she make up her own mind?'

'She obviously realises I'm an expert at choosing men,' Kate replied.

Woody grinned. 'There's a certain truth in that! But, for God's sake, why doesn't she just say "yes" or "no" or "give me time to think about it" like any normal human being?'

Kate spread her hands. 'You know Angie!'

'She's older than *you*! How can someone be so immature in their mid-*sixties*?'

'She's always treated me like the older sister. Seriously, though, do you think Fergal might just be looking for some sort of security? Joint ownership?'

'Of course he is. He's put a lot of effort, if not money, into that place, and he's looking to his future. Who could blame him? What I can't get my head round is why, if he believes she's been having it off with Wyngarde, he wants to marry her at all!'

'I hope he loves her,' Kate said anxiously. 'Do you think he does?'

'How do I know? Even at her late age, do you really think Angie's mature enough to settle down with *anyone*?'

Kate shrugged, exasperated.

EIGHTEEN

The following day, Angie phoned mid-morning.

'Just wondered if you and Woody would like to come down for a lunchtime drink, on the house?'

'Are we celebrating something...?' Kate asked.

Angie ignored her question. 'I'm trying out some new, nice little canapés, and I wanted your opinion. See you at half past twelve.' And with that, she clicked off.

'I wonder what she wants?' Woody asked when he came in from the front garden, where he'd been weeding for a couple of hours.

'She told me she wants to try out some canapés or something on us,' Kate said. 'We only need to stay for an hour or so.'

'No longer,' Woody stipulated firmly, placing a teabag into a mug. 'If I start drinking at lunchtime, nothing gets done in the afternoon.'

'An hour only,' Kate agreed.

At half past twelve, when they entered The Old Locker, they found it packed with tourists. Emma, who was behind the bar, waved at them. 'Upstairs!' she said.

Kate and Woody looked at each other and shrugged. *What was going on?*

At the top of the stairs, Kate could hear Sinatra singing 'Strangers in the Night' and the music was coming from the living-room cum kitchen. When Kate pushed the door open, she was astounded to see Angie and Fergal waltzing, close together, round the table. The room wasn't designed for dancing, or for moving more than was absolutely necessary. Angie and Fergal had knocked two very small rooms and a cupboard into what they optimistically called their 'open-plan living area', but it was still a cluttered space, made even tinier by the mini kitchen they'd built into one corner. This left room for only two armchairs, one on either side of the log burner, and a small table, with two chairs pushed underneath, on which to dine. Angie had painted everything white to maximise the feeling of space, but that still didn't leave much room for dancing.

On the table was a magnum of champagne, four glasses and several plates of little nibbles.

'Oh, *here* they are!' Angie disentangled herself from Fergal's embrace and beamed at them.

'What the—?'

'We've just become *engaged*!' Angie exclaimed.

Kate was amazed that Angie had reached a decision so quickly, having thought she'd take weeks to decide, especially in view of the couple's recent ups and downs.

'So you really are planning on getting married?' Woody sounded doubtful – and a little exasperated.

'That's the idea!' Fergal said, looking like he'd had a few celebratory drinks already.

'We wanted you to be the first to know,' added Angie. She looked at Kate. 'You'd better sit down cos you look like you're going to faint or something! I *told* you that Fergal had asked me to marry him, remember?'

'That's wonderful,' Kate said, feeling doubtful. She knew she should be pleased, so she forced a huge smile. 'Well congratulations! When is the big day?'

Angie was pouring out glasses of champagne. 'As soon as possible,' she replied, handing a glass each to Kate and Woody. 'We haven't got a ring yet, but we're going to Plymouth in a few days and we'll get one then.'

Woody sat down on one of the armchairs. 'Well,' he said, 'don't let *us* stop you dancing!'

'Oh, we've finished dancing now,' said Fergal, laughing and holding up his glass.

'Congratulations then!' The four moved closer together and clinked glasses.

'I hope you'll be very happy,' Kate said sincerely.

'We can't decide where to have it. Registry office and then one of the churches for a blessing perhaps?' Angie said. 'Then we either close this to the public for a day and have a small reception here, or we splurge out on a big party in the Ocean Room up at the Atlantic Hotel. We'll get a quote from Marc and Jodi this weekend.'

'You're certainly moving quickly,' Woody remarked.

'And then,' said Fergal, 'we thought we might have a few days in Paris or Rome, sort of a mini-honeymoon, you know?'

'We might need a bit of help with that though,' Angie continued blithely, 'because I'm not sure Emma could manage on her own if it's busy.' She gave an exaggerated smile, first to Kate and then to Woody. 'We might, just *might*, need you to help run this place? Just a day or two perhaps?'

'Unless we go to New York,' Fergal added, 'because then we'd be gone for a week.'

'New York?' Kate asked faintly.

'I have a brother there, you see,' Fergal went on, 'and I

haven't seen him in donkey's years and Angie's never been there and—'

'So you're asking us to run this place for a *week*?' Woody interrupted.

'Thing is,' Angie said, 'we won't get married for another couple of months, by which time all the tourists will have gone home and it'll be nice and quiet here. And Emma would be here too. It would be a *doddle!*'

'No, *not* a week,' Woody said firmly. 'One or two days at the very most, so I should head for Paris or Rome if I were you.'

'But, Woody...' Kate hesitated.

'No, Kate. You're already working at the medical centre two days a week and I'm not having you slaving in here as well. And I'm *not* doing this on my own.'

'But there's Emma,' Angie reminded him.

Fergal was already refilling glasses. 'Have a canapé.'

'I wish you all the luck in the world,' Woody said, sipping his champagne and munching a canapé, 'but I suggest you get a relief couple in to cover for you. I don't know how much they charge, but, for God's sake, how often do you get *married?*'

There was silence for a moment before Kate said, 'Woody's right. You know, what with the medical centre and the film set another two days a week, I am really tired at the weekend, and that's when this place would be at its busiest.'

'Filming should be finished by then,' Fergal said. 'I hear they've only a few more weeks to go.'

'No matter,' said Woody, 'we aren't doing it. A couple of days at the most. The *most!*'

There was a further silence for a moment.

'But it's lovely news,' Kate said brightly, to remove the slight tension in the air, 'and I'm sure you'll be very, very happy.'

'Will you be my bridesmaid, Kate?'

Kate grinned. 'I'd be happy to be your matron of honour,

Angie. You're not planning on a long white dress or anything, are you?'

'Of course not! Ivory coloured, I thought. I mean, I'm hardly a virgin any more!'

'You can say that again,' said Fergal.

'We'll leave you to it,' said Woody, laying down his glass. 'The champers and the canapés were lovely, and thanks for inviting us.'

'We wanted you to be the first to hear the news,' Angie said again, then rolled her eyes heavenwards. 'I must now tell my lovely son in Sweden! I can't imagine *what* Jeremy's going to say!'

'I can't imagine what Jeremy's going to say either,' Kate muttered as they made their way down the stairs and through the bar area. 'He and Ingrid are very pure-living, sporty sort of people, so God only knows what he'll think of Fergal as a suitable husband for his mother.'

'Why do they need to get *married*?' Woody asked as they stepped outside and headed towards the lane. 'Why don't they stay as they are?'

'Like we said last night, it would be security for Fergal. And *we* got married, didn't we?'

'Yes, but you're a woman of taste, Kate! And I *told* you she wanted something! Are we expected to step in every time she wants a holiday?'

'You were right. Thanks for taking a firm stand on that.'

'Well I could see that you were dithering. I know she's your sister, but it's a bit of a cheek to expect us to provide unpaid cover for their jaunt to New York.'

. . .

Kate avoided going anywhere near The Old Locker over the remainder of the weekend. She had no advice to offer Angie, and she still wondered why they were bothering with marriage at their late age. Then she smiled to herself, remembering that it was only a couple of years back that she and Woody had done the very same thing! There was no denying, though, that the advantages of this union would undoubtedly be for Fergal, who was most likely looking for some kind of security and stability. Why else could he possibly consider marrying Angie when she was being so flighty?

And they were forever arguing and falling out, which worried Kate a lot. She knew that's what kept their relationship on its toes, but it was hardly a recipe for a happy marriage. Not only that, Angie certainly couldn't be guaranteed to be faithful, Kate felt sure, after what she'd heard about her sister's relationship with Crispin Wyngarde.

NINETEEN

When Kate arrived at the medical centre on Monday morning, she noticed that Denise had a chic new hairdo.

'Hey, very glamorous!' Kate exclaimed sincerely.

'I've been to your friend, Guy,' Denise replied, moving her head this way and that. 'He's done a good job, hasn't he?'

'He certainly has,' Kate confirmed, 'and he's taken years off you!'

'Oh, do you think so?' Denise appeared delighted. 'If only he was straight, I'd be using all of my feminine charms to get him under my duvet!'

There had been many men beneath Denise's duvet on a regular basis, and she still lived in hope that one of them might hang around long enough to propose matrimony. Although she'd never disclosed her age, Kate knew she had to be in her late fifties, or even early sixties, and that she was aware time was running out. She, and her equally desperate friend, set off on their annual, two-week manhunt every summer, concentrating on the Latins. They'd covered Spain, Italy and Greece quite thoroughly, and amassed a plethora of lovers on the way, but no husbands as yet.

'He was very interesting to talk to,' Denise continued, 'because he knew so many of the people on that film set. He knew the producer – the one that got shot – the make-up woman, and one of the cameramen. Oh, and he knew the man who was supposed to be looking after the gun on the set.'

Kate had been walking away from the reception desk but now stopped in her tracks. 'Do you mean the armourer?'

'Is that what he's called? Can't remember the name.'

'Paul Bacon?'

'That's it!' Denise replied. 'I knew it had *something* to do with breakfast! It seemed ever so funny that the guy who was shot was called Crispin or something, and I kept mixing up the names and coming up with crispy bacon!' She shrieked with laughter.

Kate was so taken aback at the news that Guy knew Paul Bacon that she failed to comment on Denise's inappropriate attitude to a man's death. 'And Guy *definitely* said that he knew Paul Bacon?' she persisted.

'Oh yes, from years ago when Guy was working on a film.' Denise sighed. 'Oh, I *do* wish he was straight. Guy, I mean.'

She turned away as the door opened. 'Ah, good morning, Mrs Bowen!'

Kate's heart sank when she realised that Penelope Bowen was her first patient. As well as being the local bigwig, she was also a terrific snob.

When she got to the treatment room, Penelope came straight to the point. 'I believe your sister is a prime suspect for the murder on the film set at Port Petroc?'

'*Everyone* is a suspect,' Kate repeated wearily, 'not just my sister.'

'Hmm.' Penelope didn't sound convinced. 'Some of the ladies I preside over, and myself as well, rather fancy being extras on this film. I've been told on very good authority that several extras have dropped out on account of that recent *inci-*

dent, and we're quite prepared to fill the breach. It will be so good for the area to have a period film showcasing the beauty of this part of the coast. We're prepared to ignore the nastiness that took place there recently.'

Kate stared at her in disbelief. 'This is the medical centre, Penelope, not the casting department! If you're interested in a part, then I suggest you go and talk to the casting director down at Port Petroc. So what seems to be the trouble, and I mean medically?'

'Oh, I'm feeling rather stressed at the moment,' Penelope replied. 'I think I may have need of some antidepressants or something.'

'Then you must make an appointment with one of the doctors. Perhaps you've got too much on your plate? Delegate some of your duties?'

'Oh no, dear, there really isn't anyone suitable. No one at *all*. What I need is a change of *scenery*, shall we say. I thought that even a *tiny* part in that film might be relaxing – and fun. And it's historical, and I do *adore* history.'

'You'd be better off taking a holiday, Penelope. A nice, relaxing cruise perhaps? A couple of weeks on a Caribbean beach? Swimming with dolphins?'

'Don't be ridiculous, Kate! No, what I need is a new *experience*. Being on a film would probably do the trick.'

'I don't know if they're replacing the extras or not, but I'll ask when I go back.'

Penelope pursed her lips and stood up very straight. 'So you'll see what you can do?'

'I can also make you an appointment with one of the doctors to talk about antidepressants,' Kate said.

'That will not be necessary. I just need a change and a little excitement,' Penelope snapped as she stomped towards the door, slamming it behind her.

Kate sighed.

. . .

When she got home, Kate looked at The List at the kitchen table, thinking about what Denise had said about Guy. Where did he fit into all this? Why did his name keep coming up? How many people had he actually known on that set? He had only told her that he knew Crispin and hadn't even mentioned knowing Lucy Moore, so what was *that* all about? Why would he want to keep that secret, assuming they hadn't just become friendly recently as she'd initially thought? And he'd known Paul Bacon too, but Guy had never mentioned him either. Crispy bacon indeed!

Should she begin adding stars to each name, depending on how likely they were to be the killer? Paul Bacon would merit two stars straight away, and perhaps Guy would too!

One thing was for certain: no one, but no one, must be removed from The List, but she'd have to find some solid information soon so that she could begin to eliminate people.

Kate was thoroughly frustrated that she was no nearer to knowing what had gone on.

It was the Tinworthy extras' final week. On the Thursday, an exhausted-looking Sonia arrived at the wardrobe trailer just as Kate was being kitted out. She barked a few instructions to Jilly, who nodded glumly.

'Have either of you got any paracetamol, or something stronger, for my poor head?' she groaned, collapsing onto a chair. 'I've got the mother and father of all headaches, and we're already two damned days behind schedule, thanks to Crispin. It's just one bloody thing after another!'

'I've got some somewhere,' Kate said, rummaging in her bag then handing Sonia a packet.

As Kate was about to leave the trailer, Sonia stood up and

accompanied her outside. 'I'm told Bacon's been staying in your neck of the woods. He started off at the village pub here, you know. I just hope, for your sakes, he behaves himself because he started getting absolutely bladdered every night at The Pheasant.' She gave a heavy sigh. 'So long as his renewed passion for alcohol doesn't affect his work.'

'When did he start drinking again?' Kate asked.

'So far as I know it was shortly after we came here. I saw him drunk as a skunk in The Pheasant about a week after we arrived, and I know there have been some complaints from the locals. It's a pity he's fallen off the wagon because he was a very reliable armourer. I've worked with him several times.'

'Yes, it's such a shame,' Kate remarked. 'Alcoholism is a terrible disease. Talking of which, how's your asthma doing with that new medication?'

'Absolutely brilliant. I'm so grateful, Kate.'

Sonia had just begun to walk away when Kate remembered Penelope Bowen's request.

'Oh, Sonia, by the way, there are a couple of ladies in Middle Tinworthy who'd love to be extras. Any chance?'

'Bring them along tomorrow,' Sonia replied, 'because that'll be the final day for the extras in this location. We can stick them in somewhere. We need a few more peasants to replace the ones who've left. Do warn them it's only for one day and they'll be wearing rags!'

Kate smiled to herself. She most definitely wouldn't be telling them about the rags.

'I believe there's to be some sort of farewell celebration with the extras,' Sonia said. 'Is it right that it's to be at your local tomorrow night?'

'Yes,' Kate said, 'apparently the extras thought it would be a good idea to have a final get-together. Will you come?'

Sonia shrugged. 'Perhaps, although I should really be

helping with the editing. 'We've only got a few more weeks until we leave here.'

Kate didn't like to tell her that it had been the editor's idea. 'Are you going to be allowed to leave while this murder remains unsolved?'

'No, unfortunately we won't, but we still have a while to go with the main cast, and I'm hoping it'll all be sorted out by then. But for now, I'm off to film your lovely husband,' Sonia said and headed towards the beach.

Everyone was feeling sad on the Friday morning bus.

'It's been a bit of fun,' someone said.

'And the money's been welcome,' someone else added.

'Interesting to see how they make these things.'

'*I'll* be bloody glad not to be staggering around all day with those damn boxes,' Woody muttered under his breath.

Penelope and her two friends had opted to drive down in her car; she was not someone who relished mixing with the hoi polloi. Kate wondered how they'd react when they saw the rags they'd be wearing.

She herself had mixed feelings. She'd enjoyed the experience, apart from Crispin's murder of course, and the money had indeed been very welcome. She'd become quite fond of most of the crew, including Sonia and Jilly, and had found the filming process fascinating. The only person she hadn't got to know was Lucy Moore, and she wasn't over-optimistic about righting that on the very last day.

'We'll miss you,' Jilly admitted as she helped Kate into her robe for the final time. 'You've all been so nice and friendly.'

Kate wondered why extras wouldn't be nice and friendly when they were required to do very little, fed well and paid for the privilege. 'It's been fun,' she said, 'apart from Crispin's killing.'

'And they're no nearer knowing whodunnit, are they?' Jilly asked as she produced another pair of sturdy shoes for Kate, 'but *I* know! Just you wait and see!'

'So you're still convinced it's Sonia, are you?' Kate asked.

'Yes, I am. Who else could it be?'

'I don't know, but I was wondering about Lucy Moore. She's the only person I haven't really met,' Kate said, 'and I'd very much like to talk to her.'

'Don't you go to the canteen at lunchtimes?'

Kate nodded. 'But we normally take a plateful outside with us, to avoid the crush. And sometimes we nip over to The Pheasant.'

'Well,' said Jilly, 'if you go into the canteen at half past twelve on the dot, you'll see Madame Moore sitting there, pushing her veggie lunch round the plate. Or is it vegan? Can't remember, but she doesn't eat much of it anyway.'

'Interesting,' said Kate, planning to do just that.

Noon signalled the end of Kate's peasantry duties and the end of her celluloid career. She knew she'd have to hang around until four o'clock for Woody to finish his box-carrying and for the bus back to Tinworthy. She saw Woody briefly as they set off for the beach and said she rather fancied a canteen lunch today.

'Would you mind if I didn't join you?' Woody asked. 'A couple of the cameramen have asked me if I'd like to join them for a drink at The Pheasant. You'd be welcome to come.'

'No, I'm OK with a meal in the canteen,' Kate said casually. 'I've been meaning to have a lunch there and this is my last chance.'

'You wouldn't be up to anything, would you?' Woody asked, eyeing her suspiciously.

'Of course not.'

. . .

The mobile canteen looked to be about fifty feet long and at least ten wide, and you certainly wouldn't want to come across it on a narrow Cornish lane. It could only accommodate about fifteen people at any one time, so meals were staggered and eating time normally limited to half an hour.

Kate hung about outside, reading and rereading the notices on the board stuck on the side, until she saw Lucy going in.

She waited for a moment, then went in and ordered some soup and made her way to the table where the leading lady was sitting in solitary state.

'Mind if I share your table?'

Lucy shrugged. 'It's a free world,' she said, idly spearing a piece of red pepper from her plate.

Kate took that as an affirmative and sat down opposite. The actress was blonde, porcelain-skinned and slightly built, with a swan-like neck and large blue eyes. She wore a wig for the part, the hair upswept into an elegant chignon and, no matter how hard she looked, Kate couldn't see any joins. She was wearing a full-skirted grey silk dress with a low neckline and tight sleeves, as befitted a lady of the period. As Jilly had predicted, she was gazing down at her plate of vegetables as if wondering what on earth they were.

'This is our last day,' Kate said as a conversation opener.

'Oh?' Lucy was now dealing with what looked like a sun-dried tomato.

'We've all really enjoyed being on the set,' Kate continued, 'and *Pengorran's Revenge* looks like being a fascinating story.'

Lucy chewed daintily for some time, then finally swallowed. 'Not half as fascinating as the *making* of the damn thing,' she said at last, examining a piece of celery on the end of her fork.

'That was unfortunate,' Kate agreed.

'It wasn't at all unfortunate,' Lucy snapped, 'because Crispin Wyngarde had it coming to him!'

Kate cleared her throat. 'I gather he was none too popular?'

'He was an out-and-out bastard,' said Lucy. 'Bedding women – and men – and making money, that was all he was interested in.'

'I guess someone decided to get shot of him?'

'Literally,' Lucy agreed.

'I think you know my friend, Guy, the hairdresser?' Kate asked.

'Oh, lovely Guy! Yes, he gave me a great cut.'

'Didn't I see you with him at The Edge of the Moor a week or two back?'

Lucy was examining a sugar snap pea now. 'Yeah, great veggie food at The Edge. Were you there?'

'Yes,' said Kate, 'I was there with my husband. So you'd met Guy before?'

'Lots of times.' Lucy inserted the sugar snap into her mouth and chomped it carefully with her expensively whitened teeth.

'You've known him a long time then?'

'He was a friend of my dad's, from school. Dad said all the girls fancied him even then, Guy I mean. Shame he's gay.' She was now concentrating on a large black olive. 'I wish they'd serve these pitted. I'm terrified of breaking a tooth.'

Kate decided to go in for the kill. 'So who do *you* think loaded the blunderbuss?'

Lucy gave Kate her full attention for the first time and appeared to be studying her. 'I've no idea,' she said eventually, 'probably Bacon, but I wish it had been me.'

She then picked up a small, unidentifiable white object from her plate. 'Does that look like chicken to you? Or would you say it might be fish?' she asked anxiously, pointing it towards Kate.

'I really don't know,' Kate replied, startled.

'Neither do I. I can eat fish but not chicken. This is supposed to be veggie, and I'm not eating it if there's chicken in it.' She put it back on the plate. 'I've got some organic fruit with me, so I'm going outside to eat that.' She stood up. 'Nice meeting you.'

After she'd gone, Kate was left reeling at the fact that Lucy's father had been in school with Guy. Surely it couldn't be a coincidence that Guy had chosen to work as an extra on a film produced by the man who had ruined the life of his long-time friend?

TWENTY

'I rationed myself to just one pint,' Woody informed Kate as they sat down on the bus for the last time, 'because I'm saving myself for tonight.'

'Tonight? I hope you're not planning to get plastered?'

'No, but I'm planning to enjoy myself. The extras have asked all the crew up for a farewell drink, remember? You haven't changed your mind about coming, have you?'

'No,' Kate replied, 'I haven't changed my mind. I'm looking forward to it. It should be fun.'

'Yes, it should. It'll be interesting to see who, if anyone, turns up. So what have you been up to with this sudden interest in the canteen?'

'Not a lot. Had a bowl of soup and sat opposite Lucy Moore.'

'Oh, *did* you now? And how much information did you manage to drag from her?'

'Quite a bit. Not only is she a very fussy eater, but Guy was a friend of her father's from their schooldays, which explains why she knows him and why they were at The Edge the other night.'

'Are you satisfied that there's nothing underhand going on there?' Woody asked.

'I've been thinking about that. Now we know that Guy was a long-time friend of Lucy's family, perhaps Guy had an extra reason for killing Crispin? Perhaps Lucy was a willing accessory? Perhaps she knew how to load a blunderbuss?'

'I'm amazed you didn't ask her!'

'I only thought about it afterwards,' Kate admitted.

'And I was only joking!' Woody said.

As Kate examined herself in the bedroom mirror, she wondered if the outfit she'd chosen was flattering enough considering she'd be hobnobbing with film and television types, always assuming any of them turned up. She definitely needed the shapewear and the white top that skimmed over her tummy. She knew no one would probably give a damn, but *she* did.

'Are Angie and Fergal likely to be there tonight?' Woody asked as he stood alongside her, looking in the mirror to knot his tie.

'Someone will have to stay at The Locker if Emma's working for Des,' Kate remarked. Because they were doing a buffet for the party this evening, Des had sought the services of Emma, she who frequently worked for Angie and Fergal, to help out at the bar while Madge was slaving in the kitchen.

Kate was wondering if perhaps the green top might look better because it was definitely a night to look her best, the film crew only having ever seen her without make-up and dressed in shapeless rags with 'mud' daubed on her face. Yes, the green was less clingy, so she'd definitely wear that.

'Holy moly!' Woody exclaimed.

For a fleeting moment, Kate thought they must be in the wrong pub, because there was barely a square inch of space in the whole bar, and the noise was deafening. Every single Tinworthy extra had apparently shown up, along with every single member of the film crew.

It took several minutes to edge their way through to the bar, where a perspiring Des was working flat out, and a beaming Emma was being chatted up by a sound engineer. And, swaying gently alongside the bar – and alongside what appeared to be a treble Scotch – was none other than Paul Bacon.

'We must stop meeting like this,' Kate quipped, wondering if he had any recollection of their conversation in The Pheasant.

He appeared to be having difficulty focusing on her. Then he said, 'Angie?'

'No, Paul, I'm Kate, Angie's sister.'

'Well bugger that,' he said and turned back to his drink.

'Ever the charmer,' Woody remarked as they reached the bar to find a hot and stressed Des.

'Never *had* so many people in here,' said Des, wiping his brow.

They ordered their drinks and, when Des came back with them, he pointed at Paul Bacon. 'See he's three sheets to the wind already! He's bought half the bar a drink!'

'That,' said Woody, 'was very generous of him.'

Des leaned across the bar. 'I've told him I want his caravan out of the car park before the weekend's out.'

'Why, what's the problem?' Woody asked.

'He's in here every night and getting so drunk, he's bothering the other customers.'

'So where's he going to go?' Kate asked.

'He's booked in up at the Sunshine Caravan Park. He wants us to call him at nine o'clock in the mornin' to go up there, but he ain't goin' to be capable of towing a caravan that early.' Des

gave a sigh of frustration. 'The way he's drinkin' now, he ain't
going to be capable of that for a few days, by the looks of him.'

'So don't sell him any more,' Kate advised.

'I know I shouldn't, but it keeps him quiet. If needs be, I'll
move that bloody caravan myself. Ruddy great four-by-four he's
got, and a caravan what must be twenty feet long, takin' up two
or three bleedin' spaces in my car park! People are havin' to park
out on the *road*. I'll be glad to see the back of him.' He shook his
head and moved on to another customer.

'Des'll be happy as long as he's making money,' Woody said,
'so he must be ecstatic tonight, although he sure doesn't look it.'

While they'd been talking, Kate had noticed Sonia pushing
her way through to the bar, accompanied by Lucy Moore, who,
with her short pixie haircut and tight jeans, was unrecognisable
as the haughty Gwendolyn of *Pengorran's Revenge*. Kate could
also see Guy and his partner, Roly, near the door, and right next
to the inglenook, young Jilly was being chatted up by one of the
cameramen. There were several other familiar faces from the
film set, and just about every single one of the thirty or so extras
Angie had rounded up.

'I thought this was supposed to be a nice, quiet seaside pub,'
Sonia grumbled as she reached the bar and nodded to them
both.

'It usually is,' Kate said.

After Sonia had ordered gin and tonics for herself and Lucy,
she said, 'Those three last-minute extras you sent me were no
damned good. They turned on their heels and headed for home
after about five minutes!'

Kate had forgotten all about Penelope Bowen and her
'ladies'. 'Why was that then?'

'They thought they were going to swan around in front of
the cameras in silks and satins or something. When they discovered they had to wear scruffy woollen shifts, chop wood and be
a hundred yards from the camera, they couldn't get away fast

enough! Didn't you tell them what they were likely to be wearing, Kate?'

'So sorry, I must have forgotten,' Kate said, feeling only slightly guilty.

'Penelope is our local snob,' Woody explained. 'She's got delusions of grandeur. And a husband in jail, but that's another story!'

'We managed quite well without them,' Sonia said. 'What's the food like here?'

'The usual pub grub as a rule,' Woody replied. 'I've never sampled one of their buffets before.'

'The buffet will do me,' said Sonia. Then, turning to Lucy: 'What about you?'

Lucy pouted. 'Do they do veggie?'

'Not usually,' Kate said, thinking of Madge's meaty curries and lasagne.

'I thought by law they had to provide vegetarian and vegan alternatives,' Lucy said haughtily.

'Des hasn't caught up with the law yet,' Woody said, grinning.

'Doesn't matter,' replied Lucy with a resigned sigh, 'because I had lunch.'

Kate wondered how long the actress could survive on her tiny plate of vegetables. That, of course, was why Lucy was verging on the skinny, while she herself was encased in Lycra.

'We'd better circulate,' said Woody, turning to chat with one of the runners. 'Give me a wave if you find a seat before I do.'

Kate hesitated for a while because she was becoming increasingly worried about Paul Bacon. The armourer was paying no attention to any of them whatsoever, completely focused on emptying his glass.

'Paul,' she said hesitantly, 'don't you think it's time you eased up on the drinks?'

Swaying slightly on his stool, he looked at Kate through unfocused eyes. 'Leave me alone, Angie!'

'I'm not Angie,' she protested.

'In that case, whoever you are, you can piss off!'

Kate decided it was probably wisest to move away from the bar.

TWENTY-ONE

By ten o'clock, Kate had found a table and was joined by Woody. A few people had drifted away and those who remained had quietened down, with the exception of Paul Bacon. He was now perched precariously on a bar stool and talking loudly, presumably to himself since everyone else was giving him a wide berth.

'If Des wants that caravan moved, he's definitely going to have to do it himself,' Woody said. 'With the amount Bacon's been putting away, he won't be safe on the road until at least Monday.'

Just then, there was a rumpus at the bar, with Paul threatening to kill a young man who was standing next to him.

'I was in the army, you know,' Paul was yelling, 'and I've had to kill better people than you!'

'I only asked you to be quiet,' the young man said.

At this, Paul let out a string of expletives, some of which were new even to Kate, and looked as if he was about to attack the hapless youth. The bar went silent.

Woody, his police training kicking in, stood up. 'We can't have a fight in here,' he said, heading towards the bar.

Kate, worried, followed him.

'Don't spoil the evening, Paul,' Woody said quietly as he approached. 'I think you've had quite enough for tonight.'

Des looked relieved. 'See if you can persuade him to go to his caravan, Woody.'

'I'm not spoiling *anyone's* bloody evening,' Paul slurred, swivelling round with his fist outstretched, before slowly slumping towards the floor.

'Come on,' Woody encouraged, hoisting him up and taking his right arm. 'Time for bed!'

Kate took his other arm and, together, they half dragged him out of the door and into the car park.

'What's the betting this thing's locked?' Kate muttered as they got to the caravan.

'Not bloody locked,' mumbled Paul, who'd revived a little in the cool evening air.

Fortunately, he was right because Kate didn't fancy having to search through his pockets. They hauled him in through the doorway into a surprisingly neat, well-designed space. There was a bed at one end, a kitchenette in the middle, complete with sink and cooker, and a chemical toilet at the other end. There was a large glass in the sink and a half-full bottle of Grouse Scotch on the top, so plainly the armourer had imbibed a fair amount before visiting the bar.

As Woody dumped him on the bed, Kate looked around. There didn't appear to be much in the way of food, so presumably Paul dined solely in pubs. The cooker was pristine, as was the sink, but Kate found a plastic bowl, which, along with a glass of water, she placed on the floor beside the bed.

'Just in case he's sick,' she said to Woody.

'Let's leave him to it then,' Woody said, 'because he's almost asleep.'

'I'll wait for a while to make sure he's OK,' Kate said, worried he might be sick while he was lying flat on his back.

They'd tried to roll him onto his side, but he'd rolled right back again. 'He won't be any trouble now, and I'll join you in a few minutes.'

'If you're sure...?'

'I'm quite sure. Go back and tell Des this guy won't be giving anyone any further trouble tonight.'

After Woody left, Kate looked sadly at the supine character draped on the bed. His eyes were still open, but he showed no inclination to sit up. She dug the duvet out from underneath his legs and covered him with it.

'Angie,' he said, looking at her.

'I'm not Angie. I'm Kate, Angie's sister. We met briefly in The Pheasant, remember? I was an extra.'

He screwed up his face. 'You're not Angie?'

'No, Paul, I'm not Angie, and you need to sleep now.'

Kate, aware of the rather stuffy atmosphere, moved towards the kitchen area and opened the window behind the little sink, and another one on the opposite side. She realised Paul was muttering something and turned back to the bed.

He was staring up at the ceiling. 'Shouldn't have taken that money,' he said sadly.

'What money?' Kate asked.

'For loading the gun,' he said, in little more than a whisper. 'Don't tell anyone I took the money, Angie.'

Kate's heart was pounding. Perhaps he'd say more if he continued to believe she was Angie.

'*Who* gave you the money to load the gun, Paul?'

'I'm telling that detective woman tomorrow,' he said quite clearly.

'Who? Detective Inspector Martin? What are you going to tell her?'

'That I took the money.'

'Who paid you, Paul?' Kate asked, hardly daring to breathe.

'I'll tell that sexy detective,' he said, with a faint smile. His eyes were closing now.

'Tell me, Paul, and I'll tell the detective,' Kate said desperately. But even as she spoke, she could see that Paul Bacon had fallen fast asleep.

She sighed and headed towards the door, closing it gently behind her. She stood for a moment outside, trying to digest this information. So he *had* loaded the gun but had been paid by someone else to do so. *Who?*

Back in the bar, Kate confirmed to an anxious Des that Paul was asleep. 'No problem – he went out like a light!'

'I was a bit worried when Woody came back without you, so I had a quick peep just in case you were in trouble, but it seemed quiet out there,' Des said.

'That was good of you, Des.'

Woody had arrived at her side. 'All OK?' Before she could reply, he said, 'Look who's just arrived!'

Kate turned round to see Angie making her way towards the bar. She was in full glamour mode, with eye make-up carefully applied, backcombed and lacquered hair, and a sparkly top.

'Couldn't get away any earlier,' she sighed, 'because it's been manic in The Locker, thanks to this place having a private function. And we didn't have Emma of course.' She waved at Emma, who was working flat out at the far end of the bar. 'Fergal insisted I come up for an hour or so.'

'The party's nearly over,' Kate told her, 'and you've just missed your old boyfriend, because Woody and I had to drag Paul round to his caravan, and he's now passed out.'

'Oh.'

There was no doubt about it – Angie looked momentarily crestfallen but recovered quickly. Was all this glamour for *him*?

'He was drunk then?'

Kate nodded. 'Very.' She wondered if she should tell her sister about Bacon thinking she was Angie but decided this was neither the time nor the place.

'A double gin for my sister-in-law,' Woody shouted to Des.

'Thanks, Woody.' Angie looked around. 'Where's Sonia Somerfield? Did she not show up?'

'She left a little while ago. Why, did you want to see her?'

Angie shrugged. 'I haven't set eyes on her since that awful day when Crispin got shot. Thought I might renew our acquaintance.'

Kate translated that to mean that Angie was still hoping for some sort of part.

'Oh well,' Angie sighed, plainly resigned, 'I'll have my drink and then head back down the lane.'

Kate hadn't had an opportunity to elaborate on the conversation with Paul Bacon until they got home at around eleven o'clock, when she told Woody exactly what the armourer had said.

'You're kidding!' Woody looked aghast. 'He actually admitted that he'd accepted money for loading that blunderbuss?'

'Yes, that seemed to be what he was insinuating, but he wouldn't say from whom,' Kate confirmed, 'only that he was going to call on the sexy detective tomorrow.'

'To confess all?'

'Presumably.' Kate sighed. 'I did try to get him to tell me, but he was determined to save it for Charlotte. The funny thing was, he seemed to think I was Angie!'

Woody studied her face. 'He did? You don't look *very* much alike.'

'Perhaps, in an alcoholic haze, we do?'

'Well we can do nothing tonight, Kate, except crash into

bed. We can only wait to see if he *does* call in to see Charlotte at Launceston tomorrow.'

'But will Charlotte tell us, I wonder?'

'If he accepted money for loading the gun and he tells Charlotte who paid him, then she'll doubtless be arresting the person concerned, hopefully, and we'll all find out soon enough. Then we can forget all this. Come on now – it's time for bed!'

The next morning, when Kate was about to take Barney out for a walk, her phone rang.

It was Des, but she could barely make out what he was saying because he seemed so distressed.

'Slow down, Des!' she said. 'Now, what are you saying?'

'I'm just waitin' for the police to arrive,' he replied, 'but I'm telling you – he's *dead*! Paul Bacon is *dead*!'

TWENTY-TWO

'Paul Bacon is *dead*?' Kate asked slowly, trying to digest what Des had just said.

'I tried to ring Woody, but he ain't answerin'.'

'He's in the shower, Des. What on earth has happened?'

'I went out there to wake him up at nine, like he asked, because I wanted him and his caravan moved before my lunchtime customers come lookin' for parkin' spaces. No answer, see, so I gets worried, like. The door's locked, but it's a bit flimsy, so I gave it a good pull and it crashed open, so in I go and he's lyin' there, *dead as a dodo!*'

Kate gulped and sat down. 'Have you any idea *how* he might have died?'

'Well no, I don't know, but I'm wonderin' if the drink killed him? One thing's for sure, he must have been cold because the heater was on, and the cooker rings, and the grill were all going full blast and the windows were all shut.'

Kate, still in a state of shock, began to remember. 'That's ridiculous!' she exclaimed. 'I opened two windows before I left him last night, and the heater and cooker definitely weren't on, I can assure you. And there's no way he was in a fit state to have got up and put them on. And I definitely *didn't* lock the door.'

'You and Woody had better come down quick, cos the police are on the way and they're going to want to know who saw him last.'

Kate finished the call and put her head down on the kitchen table. She knew she'd opened those windows, there had been no fumes in there, and she had not locked the door.

It was very obvious that she had *not* been the last person to see the armourer alive.

Had the killer struck again?

All the way down the lane, Woody kept asking, 'You're quite sure you opened those windows, Kate? Could they have blown shut?'

'There wasn't a breath of wind last night. And the hinges were quite stiff, so I had to use a fair bit of strength to get them open. It would have taken a force-ten gale to move them.'

Charlotte had already arrived and there were police everywhere, particularly in the car park when they arrived at The Greedy Gull. The entire area around Bacon's large Range Rover and his equally large caravan had been taped off. Kate glimpsed a couple of white-clad forensic officers through the window of the van, and an ambulance standing by.

The detective inspector gave a dramatic sigh as Kate and Woody approached and signalled them to go inside the pub. In the deserted bar, Des and Madge sat wanly on either side of the inglenook, each with a glass of something strong in their noticeably shaking hands.

Kate and Woody sat down at the nearest table, while Charlotte held court in front of the fireplace.

'I'm told you two were the last people to see this Bacon guy alive,' she said, raising her eyes to heaven.

'He was alive when we left him, but obviously someone was there after us,' Woody said.

Charlotte emitted a long, exaggerated sigh. 'But, Woody, didn't you leave Kate in there alone with him?' she asked.

Woody nodded.

'OK, Kate, can you come over here to the snug,' Charlotte asked, 'as I need to talk to you on your own?'

The snug was little more than a small room, at the far end of the bar, in which there were a couple of tables and chairs. Kate reckoned it might have been a storeroom of some sort years ago and had then been knocked into the main part of the bar.

'So,' Charlotte said, sitting down opposite Kate, 'as far as we know, you were the last person to see Paul Bacon alive?'

'Well I obviously wasn't,' Kate said, 'because there was no way he was capable of getting off that bed. He was almost dead drunk.' She then gave Charlotte a detailed account of her final minutes with the armourer. 'He told me that he was going to call on you today. He said he'd accepted money from someone for loading the blunderbuss and he wanted to tell you who it was.'

'Accepted money? Are you trying to tell me that he was being bribed or something?'

'I'm not trying to tell you anything. That's what he said. I tried to persuade him to tell me more, but he wouldn't.'

Charlotte shook her head. 'We now have to presume that someone did not want him to see me today then?'

'That would be my guess. And he seemed to think I was Angie,' she added.

Charlotte regarded her with undisguised astonishment. 'How did he know Angie?'

Kate could have bitten her tongue. Why had she said that? She certainly hadn't intended to involve Angie, but she had to give some sort of a reply now.

'They had some sort of affair many years ago.'

'How very interesting.'

Kate wasn't sure if she could detect sarcasm in Charlotte's voice.

'I assume your sister is unaware of this tragedy?'

'I haven't told her yet. We've only just heard ourselves.'

Charlotte was checking her phone, which was presumably recording this conversation. 'We'll be interviewing her shortly.' She turned back to Kate. 'Why did you stay behind with Bacon when Woody went back to the bar?'

'Because I thought he might be sick, which isn't a good idea if you're lying flat on your back. He didn't appear to be going to throw up, but I left a bowl and a glass of water beside the bed anyway, just in case he woke up feeling dodgy later.'

Charlotte nodded. 'And then?'

'And then I covered him up, opened the two little windows and left him to it.'

'You *opened* the windows?'

'Yes, I did. It was a bit stuffy in there and it was a mild evening.'

'So can you explain why the windows were shut this morning?'

'No, I can't. I swear to you that I opened them.'

'And then you locked him in?'

'What? No, I did *not* lock him in! The caravan was unlocked when we took him back there, and we had no idea where the key was.'

'It was locked this morning. *And* the windows were closed. *And* the air vents had been blocked. *And* the hob, the oven and the grill were all on, according to Des.'

'So are you saying he died of carbon monoxide poisoning?' Kate asked.

'That's what it looks like at the moment, particularly as his face was so red, but we can't be sure until we get it confirmed.'

Charlotte stood up and ushered Kate out into the main bar. 'Woody!' she called.

Woody stood up. 'I hope you're not suggesting that Kate had anything to do with this?' he said as he followed Charlotte into the snug. 'You know that Kate is a nurse, and she was simply concerned about the bloke.'

'Let's hear your side of it then,' Charlotte said.

After about five minutes, Woody emerged.

'I want a complete list of everyone who was in this bar last night,' Charlotte ordered.

Des groaned. 'There must have been a hundred people in here last night,' he said, rubbing his head wearily.

'So was everyone from the film site at Port Petroc here?'

Woody looked at Kate. 'Not sure, but I'd guess most of them were.'

Charlotte whipped out another phone and spoke into it rapidly. 'OK, send a couple of officers over to Port Petroc. I want everyone who was here in The Greedy Gull last night questioned.' She turned to Kate and Woody and asked, 'Did Angie come along too?'

Kate nodded – Angie was at the forefront yet again.

'We shall definitely be visiting *her* later,' said Charlotte before turning her attention to Des and Madge and making them repeat what they'd presumably already told her.

Finally, Charlotte said, 'Well, assuming all four of you are as pure as the driven snow, we have to assume that Mr Bacon had a late-night visitor who was not necessarily in the bar last night.' She turned back to Kate. 'When you entered or left Bacon's caravan, were you aware of *anyone* around who could have been watching you?'

Kate shook her head. 'No, I wasn't, but surely someone could have gone there after everyone had gone home?'

'That would appear to be what happened.' Charlotte switched off her phone. 'There is always the possibility that he committed suicide of course, but, given what you've told me about how drunk he was, that doesn't seem likely. OK, that's all for now. I'll be in touch if I need to ask anything else.'

'I must ring Angie and warn her she's about to be grilled,' Kate said to Woody as they walked back up the lane.

'Interesting that two of her old boyfriends have now hit the dust,' Woody said thoughtfully.

'Very interesting indeed,' agreed Kate, feeling slightly sick.

TWENTY-THREE

'Angie? I've got some awful news. Paul Bacon was found dead in his caravan this morning.'

There was silence at the other end of the phone.

Kate continued, giving her all the details.

'Who'd want to kill Paul?' Angie asked, her voice wobbling.

'That's what the police are trying to find out. I think you can expect a call from Charlotte Martin before long.'

'How did he die, Kate?'

'He was very drunk. The police suspect it might be carbon monoxide poisoning. He seemed to think I was you because he kept calling me Angie.'

'He must have been *very* bloody drunk then.'

Kate wasn't sure how to interpret that so decided to ignore it. 'Charlotte said she wants to talk to you about last night.'

'Poor Paul.' Angie still sounded wobbly.

'Des found him with the windows shut, the air vents blocked and the gas cooker on.'

'So he committed *suicide*.'

'I don't think so. It looks like someone wanted to stop him giving Charlotte some information. I wonder who knew?' It suddenly occurred to Kate that someone might have been eaves-dropping while she was tending to Paul. She had shivers down her spine at the very thought that a murderer might have been lurking outside the caravan. Unless Paul had told someone else?

'Why do I always choose dodgy men?' Angie groaned. 'As if all this wasn't enough, now they're going to charge Fergal with illegally owning a gun and not keeping it in a safe place.'

'That does seem irresponsible,' Kate said, sipping her coffee.

'He did have a firearms certificate at one time,' Angie went on, 'but he can't find it. Probably still in Ireland.'

'Surely you must have noticed the gun in the flat, Angie? So why didn't you check with him if he had a licence or not?'

'I never noticed it, Kate. Honestly! It was under the bed.'

Kate was becoming exasperated. 'You didn't notice it under the bed?'

'It was attached, with tape, to the underside of the bloody bed! How am I supposed to see that?'

'When you were dusting perhaps?'

Angie snorted. 'How often do you dust underneath *your bed*, for God's sake? Tell me that!'

'Not often,' Kate admitted.

'Well then.'

'So, Angie, if it was under the bed, how on earth did the police find out about it?'

'Apparently they had a tip-off, but we don't know from whom?'

Kate could hear Angie blowing her nose. 'I'm sorry to be the bearer of bad tidings,' she said. 'Have *you* any idea who might have wanted to kill Paul?'

'No, I damn well haven't. That's such a stupid question! I haven't even been on the set since that very first awful day!'

'I know. Anyway, be prepared for Charlotte visiting you before too long.'

'Bloody woman!' Angie retorted and ended the call.

. . .

On Monday morning, Kate sat down in her treatment room at the medical centre and waited for the inevitable. That didn't take long.

First through the door was Penelope Bowen, literally bristling. Kate braced herself.

'I want a word with you, Kate Palmer,' she said without preamble as she plonked herself down on the chair. 'First of all, who is this person who, I'm told, was murdered as he slept in the car park of The Greedy Gull?' She paused momentarily for breath.

'Penelope, the person who died was in a caravan at The Gull and the police will doubtless be able to give you all the details. I *can* tell you that it was no one from Tinworthy.'

'I see, but that's not my only complaint. What were you *thinking* of when you sent us down to that *dreadful* film place in Port Petroc, where we were expected to wear the most *awful* outfits, and then spend the day miles away from the cameras doing the most *ridiculous* tasks!'

'If you remember, you *asked* if you could be extras,' Kate reminded her. 'You didn't specify your special requirements such as what you'd condescend to wear or how near the camera you had to be. Now, is there a *medical* problem because that's the only reason why you're supposed to be here? I'm paid by the practice to look after patients not to supply gossip. So, *was* there anything else?'

Penelope stood up and narrowed her eyes. 'It seems to me that there's been one drama after another ever since you, and that sister of yours, came to live here.'

'We haven't caused any of them, Penelope, and it grieves me to point out that one of those dramas took place on your very own doorstep, with your very own husband. Now, I'm really busy this morning, so if there's no medical problem, would you please leave?'

As she headed towards the door, Penelope turned round.

'Peter had some *very* interesting things to tell me,' she said icily.

Peter Edwards was plainly still having an affair with Penelope, which had been an open secret in the area for years.

'Oh, yes?' Kate wondered if this woman was ever going to leave.

'Oh yes, indeed. Of course, Peter got to know Mr Wyngarde rather well when he applied to the council for permission to film at Port Petroc. Said he was a charming man.'

'Well I'm glad *somebody* liked him,' Kate commented.

'I gather that Mr Wyngarde was *particularly* keen on Port Petroc because it was close to where your sister lived, and they'd known each other for a very long time.'

Kate wondered what was coming.

'And then, by coincidence, Peter was in The Tinners' one night recently when your sister's partner was drinking in there. Apparently, he likes to visit other people's pubs on his night off, which seems strange to me.'

Kate certainly wasn't going to admit to Penelope that she had often thought it odd too.

'Your sister's partner was, according to Peter, "three sheets to the wind" and had plainly been drinking for some time. They got round to discussing this Wyngarde, and Peter said how *well* he'd got to know the producer and had wondered what had brought him to this part of Cornwall in the first place. Wyngarde then told him that he'd resumed his old affair with your sister. He chose Port Petroc on *her* recommendation, so they could be close enough to continue their relationship. I understand that your sister's partner was less than delighted with the news.'

Kate said nothing.

'And it might interest you to know that your sister's partner confessed to Peter that he had a gun and knew a thing or two about them. So it is quite apparent to both dear Peter and myself that either your sister or her partner, or perhaps even both of them together, were most likely responsible for the death of Mr Wyngarde.' She smiled sweetly at Kate. 'I now intend to do my duty and inform the lady detective of our findings.'

With that, she swanned triumphantly out of the door.

Kate sat down and took a sip of water to compose herself.

TWENTY-FOUR

It was mid-morning when Sonia Somerfield came in.

'I hope you don't mind,' she said, 'but I am in *such* a state!'

You're not the only one, Kate thought. 'What's the problem, Sonia?'

'Stress!' she wailed. 'I'm supposed to avoid *stress!*' She wheezed. 'I'm probably going to have another attack any bloody minute! Do you *know* how much it costs to lose so many days of filming? A bloody fortune, that's what! Crispin being shot was bad enough, but now the damned armourer's been done in! You couldn't make it up!'

'Very frustrating for you,' Kate agreed, studying the woman Jilly was convinced was the killer. 'You have been taking your medication, haven't you?'

'Oh, I have, and I'm much the better for it, thanks to you. But this damned production is *doomed.*'

Kate thought it best not to discuss what she knew with this woman. 'I can give you some mild sedatives, but otherwise you really need to make an appointment with one of our doctors.'

'I should be beginning to wrap up *all* the location filming by now,' Sonia went on, 'but it looks like we're here for*ever*! It's an ongoing nightmare!'

'We can only hope they find the killer, or killers, soon,' Kate said as she wrote out a prescription. 'It's stressful for everyone, Sonia.'

'Who'd want to kill the bloody armourer, for God's sake? He wasn't exactly a charmer, but he was good at his job and nobody seemed to *hate* him or anything, not like Wyngarde.' Sonia rolled her eyes. 'I've asked for another armourer and, in the meantime, I've got one of the policemen keeping an eye on the weaponry. Have you *any* idea what's going on?'

'I'm afraid not,' Kate replied. It wouldn't be a good idea to tell Sonia about Paul's confession and intention to speak to Charlotte.

And, in truth, Kate really had no idea what was going on.

It was on the afternoon of her Tuesday shift that a distraught Des arrived at the surgery.

'I never go nowhere near no doctors,' he said to Kate by way of greeting, cos I don't reckon on any of them, but I'm feelin' that down at the moment, and I can't sleep or nothin'. This Bacon business has done my head in!' He rubbed his forehead and closed his eyes.

'Sit down, Des,' Kate said, 'and let's give you a quick check.' She took his temperature and placed a blood pressure cuff round his upper arm. His blood pressure was a little high but not seriously so, and his temperature was normal.

'Nothin' wrong with me but stress,' Des protested, 'cos they've taped off half me car park and them police keep comin' in and out, and it's puttin' off me customers. It's a bloody nightmare!'

'Look, Des, I'll just check with Dr Ross to see if it's OK to prescribe you some sedatives, just something for the short term until all this blows over.' She popped in to see the doctor and returned a couple of minutes later. 'Here we are. We'll want to see you again in another couple of weeks and cut down the dosage. You'll probably be fine by then.'

'Don't think I'm ever goin' to be fine again,' Des muttered. 'Forty years I been in the hospitality trade and I've *never* known anythin' like this.'

'It'll get better,' Kate tried to assure him, although not altogether convinced that it would any time soon. 'They'll take Bacon's car and caravan to the police compound and examine everything there, so at least you'll get your car park back.' She handed him the prescription. 'Now, be sure to follow the dosage instructions because these are quite strong. But you need to get your sleep.'

'Thanks, I'll do that,' Des said as he went towards the door.

This film and its crew has turned the whole place upside down, Kate thought. The sooner they found the killer, the better it would be for everyone in Tinworthy.

TWENTY-FIVE

On her way home, Kate decided to call in at The Old Locker and met with a frantic Fergal, who told her that Angie had been taken to the police station for questioning.

'She *has*?' Kate could scarcely believe that Penelope's venom could have spread so quickly.

'Yes, at three o'clock this afternoon.' Fergal looked round at the half-dozen people still in the bar area. 'As soon as they go, I'm closing up. I can't do this evening without Angie.' He looked close to tears.

'Now, come on, Fergal, you can't go to pieces; they've only taken her in for questioning. What exactly did they say?'

'That policewoman detective came in here reading the riot act. Said they had it on good authority that Bacon and Wyngarde had both been her lovers...'

'Well that's hardly proof of anything! What else did Charlotte say?' Kate decided this wasn't the time to tell Fergal about Peter and Penelope's part in all this – or the fact she'd been the one to reveal Angie's relationship with Paul Bacon.

'She said Wyngarde must have threatened to tell me, and that's why Angie paid Bacon to load the blunderbuss.'

'So what did she think Angie's reason was for killing Paul Bacon?' Kate asked.

'She thinks you must have told her what Bacon said to you when you were in the caravan with him, and that he was going to the police.'

'But that's complete nonsense, Fergal!' Kate exclaimed. 'She had no idea he was going to the police. I certainly didn't tell her until after he'd been found dead.'

'Thing is,' Fergal went on sadly, 'I know she's been a bit of a girl, but I do love her. And we were planning on going to Plymouth on Thursday to buy the *ring*!'

'Look, Fergal, I'll go home and get Woody to look into this. They won't be able to keep Angie in for long without charging her, and unless they come up with some sort of new evidence, they've got nothing that will stick.'

She squeezed his arm and headed for home.

When Kate got home to Lavender Cottage, Woody was out. Where *was* he when she needed to talk to him? It was nearly six, so she poured herself a large glass of wine and began to prepare a meal which she was unlikely to be able to eat. Should she phone the police station or wait for Woody?

With great relief, she heard Woody's car in the driveway, and then him whistling as he came in.

He took one look at Kate's face. 'What's happened now?'

'They've taken Angie in for questioning.'

Woody sat down and grimaced. 'Can't say I'm altogether surprised.'

'*What*?' Kate stared at him in astonishment.

'I'm looking at this from a police point of view, Kate. Let's face it, Angie had affairs with both victims and, given that she was planning to get engaged, Charlotte is probably thinking that she didn't want any of her history to be revealed to Fergal. She pulled the trigger on Wyngarde. She came alone to the party on Friday night, and she left alone. She'd be top of my list.'

Kate took a large gulp of wine. 'What are you saying? Do you think my sister is a murderer?'

'I don't think that at all, Kate,' Woody said consolingly, 'but I'm just telling you how the police will look at it.'

Kate refilled her glass while she tried to control her temper. 'So what happens now?'

'I reckon they'll check her bank account to see if she withdrew a large amount of money in the last few weeks to pay someone for something. That could be further evidence.'

Kate sat down opposite him and groaned. 'Oh lord, what do we do now?'

'Let's wait to see if Charlotte contacts us, although I doubt she will. Angie will be allowed a phone call or two, so she may well get in touch. How's Fergal taking it?'

'He's terribly upset and wants to close the bar this evening,' Kate replied.

'He shouldn't do that; he should get hold of Emma, because they may well keep Angie in for twenty-four hours.'

Kate shuddered at what Angie must be going through all alone in a cell and with no access to gin. 'Do you suppose Fergal had anything to do with all this, Woody?'

'More to the point, do *you* think he had anything to do with it? After all, you saw him today. Did he seem genuinely upset?'

'Yes, he did, he really did. I've never seen him in such a state.' And for that reason, she wondered if she should cross Fergal off her list?

'You have to get me out of here *pronto*!' Angie wailed down the phone half an hour later.

'We can't do that, Angie, but they'll have to release you tomorrow unless they get some more evidence,' Kate said, hoping she sounded calm and reasonable. 'Woody said they'll probably check your bank account to see if you withdrew any large sums recently. And after that's been cleared, I'm sure they'll let you come home.'

There followed great, gasping sobs.

'*What*?' Kate asked, beginning to get concerned.

'But I withdrew a thousand pounds a few days ago!'

'God, Angie! Why the hell did you do *that*? *Tell* me it wasn't to pay Paul Bacon!' Kate asked without thinking, her stomach plunging.

'Of course it wasn't to pay Paul Bacon! Why the hell would I want to do *that*?' She sobbed noisily again. 'It was to buy my *engagement ring*!'

Kate sat down heavily in the chair. '*Why* are you buying your own engagement ring, Angie?'

'It's from our joint account, so Fergal's *earned* a lot of that money! We were going to Plymouth on Thursday to this nice jeweller that Fergal met when he was working there, and this guy only takes cash, you see...'

'Have you told Charlotte all this, Angie?'

'Yes, of course I have! I'm not stupid!'

Kate refrained from commenting on that. 'Look, Woody will have a chat with Charlotte, and I'm sure you'll be back in The Locker later tonight, or tomorrow.' She thought for a moment. 'So what have you done with the money you took out?'

'I've hidden it, Kate. Just in case of burglary, or Fergal might go dipping into it for something or other, particularly when he's had a few too many.'

Why was her sister marrying a man who she didn't trust with money?

'But perhaps I should tell you where it is, just in case...'

'OK, Angie.'

'You know the stainless-steel pedal waste bin in the kitchen? It's got a white liner inside, and I've put it underneath that.'

'Won't Fergal lift out the liner to empty it?'

'No, cos I've lined the *liner* with a plastic bag. We just lift out the plastic bag.'

'Oh, Angie.'

'No thief is going to look in there. And neither will Fergal.'

'That's probably true.'

'I'm in a cell now, like a *criminal*! And I shall never sleep on that hard bed, and I shan't eat *anything*, and I shall become quite ill.'

'You'll be OK, Angie. At worst it'll be only for one night.'

I hope, Kate thought as she ended the call.

TWENTY-SIX

Angie was released the following morning, as Woody had foretold.

Kate found her back behind the bar in The Old Locker, scratching her shoulder.

'There were fleas in that place, Kate,' she groaned, 'I'm damned sure of it. How often do those blankets get washed? What filthy person might have been sleeping there before me?'

'You're out now, so try to forget it.'

'You wait, she'll be questioning you next. After all, you were the last person to see him. So take a flea spray with you when you go to the police station.'

'I wasn't planning on going to the police station,' Kate said. 'I think I've told her everything there was to tell.'

'I bet you haven't! That woman is bloody persistent.'

'Did Fergal stay open and cope on his own here last night?' Kate asked, eager to change the subject.

'Yes, he did. It was very quiet, thank goodness. He told people it was my night off, but he didn't elaborate on where I'd gone.'

'So your reputation is still intact, Angie?' Not, Kate thought, that Angie's reputation was exactly the best in the village.

'It's important that no one knows where I was. Promise me that you won't tell *anyone*?'

'Of course I won't. And I trust your cash is still safe in the bin?'

'Yes, I checked as soon as I got back. And you know we were going to go to Plymouth tomorrow to get my ring? Well we're not allowed to go now. We *must* stay in Tinworthy – which means she still suspects us, doesn't it?'

'Very probably,' Kate admitted.

'I'll bet she'll restrict you and Woody as well. Mark my words!'

'Oh, I will, Angie.' Kate was feeling sorry for her sister. 'You'll get your ring eventually. And try not to worry.'

'But I *do* worry! I can't help it.'

'I'm going to do my damnedest to find out who did this,' Kate said with feeling, 'so we can all stop worrying.'

But it was hard *not* to worry about Angie, particularly as she was connected intimately with both victims.

When Kate got home, she brought out The List again. Now that it was known that money was involved, she needed to try to figure out which of the suspects could have paid Paul Bacon to kill Crispin Wyngarde. She decided to cross Fergal off because, no matter how little Bacon would have asked, Fergal wouldn't have had the money. Come to think of it, what sort of money did you have to pay to get someone murdered? Were the police checking *everyone's* bank accounts?

Then she considered her sister again. One thousand pounds hidden in the kitchen waste bin! Kate thought about Fergal. Everyone liked him, including herself and Woody, but she wasn't at all sure he was right for Angie. The very fact of having to hide the money from him… And this friend of his in Plymouth who only took cash…!

With the exception of her long-suffering husband, Angie had a long-time track record of choosing the wrong men, because she rarely went for conventional types, and she was *never* likely to fall for the local vicar.

Kate sighed and went back to her list. She could remove no one from it, apart from Paul Bacon of course, and now Fergal. Unfortunately, she couldn't access any bank accounts. In short, she was no further on with her investigations than she had been six weeks ago.

After lunch, Kate took a look at herself in the bedroom mirror and decided she could now get away with paying a visit to Guy to get her hair done.

'He's off sick, Kate,' Nikki, his second in command, informed her when Kate phoned for an appointment. 'Been off all week.'

'I'm sorry to hear that,' Kate said. 'Any idea what's wrong?'

'Not sure. Something to do with depression, I think.'

Depression? Guy? Surely not!

As Kate ended the call, she wondered if it would be a good idea to go and visit him. He and Roly lived in a flat above the salon, which had a separate entrance, a couple of doors along from Guys 'n' Dolls. She had Guy's mobile number and wondered if she should call ahead, or should she just arrive on the doorstep with some flowers or, perhaps, a bottle of something fizzy?

After some consideration, she decided on the something fizzy because, if he was out or didn't want to see her, she and Woody could put it to good use, since they already had a garden full of flowers.

And so, at three o'clock in the afternoon, Prosecco in hand, Kate rang Guy and Roly's doorbell. At first, she thought there was no one in, but, after a minute, when she was just about to ring again, she heard a shuffling sound that indicated someone was making their way down the stairs.

A scruffy, unshaven Guy opened the door. 'Kate!'

Kate was aghast at Guy's appearance. He, who was normally so well-groomed and dapper!

'I heard you weren't well,' she said, 'when I tried to make an appointment at the salon.' She handed him the bottle of Prosecco. 'Thought you might need some medicine!'

'Come in!' he said, leading the way up the stairs and into a large, sunny, tastefully decorated sitting room. 'Excuse my untidy appearance,' he added, 'but I haven't been bothering much since Roly left.'

'Roly's left?' Theirs had always seemed such a happy, settled relationship that Kate couldn't believe it.

'Yup. Left. Had enough. Gone back to Brighton from whence he came.'

'Oh, Guy, I'm *so* sorry!'

'So am I, but there we are. Now, what will you have? Coffee, tea, Prosecco?'

'Tea's fine,' Kate replied.

As Guy headed towards the kitchen, Kate took a good look around the room. The old building had been lovingly restored with all its original features intact: cornicing, fireplace and a central rose, from which hung a sparkling chandelier. She remembered that chandelier; it had been displayed in an upmarket catalogue, and Guy had asked her opinion on it during one of her highlighting sessions. The walls had been painted a very pale dove grey, the woodwork blindingly white, the rugs pale and long-piled on top of the golden floorboards. The chairs and sofas were all upholstered in pale blue and pink velvets, and it was obvious that no child had ever set foot in this showpiece. There were bowls of roses here and there on the highly polished mahogany furniture.

Guy came back into the room carrying a tray laden with a china teapot and matching sugar bowl, milk jug and mugs, along with a plate of dainty biscuits.

'Roly would kill me for serving you tea in a mug,' Guy said apologetically, 'but I always think cups and saucers are so fiddly, don't you think?'

Kate laughed. 'Can't remember the last time anyone served me tea in a cup and saucer!' She looked around. 'This is such a beautiful room, Guy!'

Guy nodded. 'We had similar taste, thank goodness, and Roly was a trained designer of course.'

'And he's gone for good, do you think?'

'Yes.' He shrugged. 'Which is why I couldn't face the public this week; I was feeling so bloody low. Don't even want to get out of bed in the mornings.'

'You must come to the surgery because we can point you towards some expert help. Is this *all* down to Roly leaving?'

'Yes. It was my own fault for telling him stuff that I thought he'd understand.' He studied Kate for a minute. 'Sugar?'

Kate shook her head and accepted the mug of tea. She kept silent, hoping he might elaborate.

After a few minutes, he said, 'We were OK until that bloody film crew came here.'

Kate sipped her tea, declining a biscuit. 'I think that film crew upset quite a few people, one way or the other.'

'Hardly surprising after two killings,' Guy retorted. 'We'll all be glad to see the back of them.' He looked sadly at Kate. 'I'm still finding it hard to believe that Wyngarde was murdered, and now I hear Paul's been killed too.'

'Did you know Paul Bacon then?'

'Yes, I met him on that one and only film I did. He was the armourer on that as well.'

'You knew him well?'

'Quite well at the time. I hadn't set eyes on him again until

Port Petroc. Why the hell would anyone want to kill him? Or was it suicide?'

'I don't know, Guy. I think they suspect murder, but they haven't had the forensic report yet.' Kate cleared her throat. 'I'm sorry it didn't work out with Roly.'

'He didn't understand, Kate.'

She noticed his eyes were full of tears. 'What didn't he understand, Guy? Would it help if you told me?'

He shook his head for a second then said, 'He didn't like me taking Lucy out. That was my only connection; all I had left of Byron.'

'Byron?'

'Yes, Byron Bellamy, Lucy's father.' There were tears coursing down his cheeks now. 'I loved that man.'

Kate wasn't sure what kind of love he was referring to so said nothing, hoping Guy would expand.

'I'd have done anything for Byron, *anything*! But I couldn't make him walk again. Crispin almost killed him, you know, with that stunt. I'd already hated Crispin after my own brief film initiation, but then I had more reason than ever to want to kill the bastard.'

'I'm not surprised. I could fully understand you wanting to kill him. But that doesn't mean you did?' she asked hopefully.

'No, I didn't.' He drained his mug.

Kate shook her head. 'Why don't we open the Prosecco?'

Guy gave the semblance of a smile. 'Not a bad idea. I'll get glasses.'

He went back to the kitchen where Kate heard him blowing his nose lustily before he returned with two champagne flutes. He opened the bottle and poured two generous measures.

'When I knew Crispin was here and looking for extras for his film,' Guy continued, 'I decided to go for it. And for one reason only: to cause as much chaos as I could to bugger up his damned film. If you remember, they weren't too fussy about us roaming around the set, so I was able to mess up one of the cameras, cut a few wires, nick a couple of scripts, that sort of thing. Childish really, I suppose, but I was determined to hold up filming any way I could, so Crispin would think the place was jinxed. Then, of course, Crispin was killed.' He took a gulp of his drink.

'Is that why you didn't come back after the first day?'

Guy nodded. 'Didn't seem much point. I'd done some damage, and the man was dead. I was ashamed then at what I'd done because I'd meant to annoy Wyngarde, not the rest of the crew.'

'But you got in touch with Lucy?'

'That was the one advantage of being an extra – I met up with Lucy again. We only had time for a brief chat, but I gave her my card' – and here he gave his familiar grin – 'and I told her she needed to get her hair done.'

'Had you not kept in touch with her?'

'I had, until her father died. After that, it was too painful, and Lucy's mother preferred to keep me at a distance.'

'Oh.'

'Byron loved me, you see. Yes, he got married, but, back then, you had to appear heterosexual to the public, and he was a big star. People were very narrow-minded. And women used to fantasise about him being their lover so they didn't want to know that he was bisexual. He really was very beautiful. Tania, the woman he married, knew about us of course.'

'And Roly resented you seeing Lucy?'

'It wasn't so much that he resented me seeing Lucy, it was just that seeing Lucy brought it all back. She looks *so* like her father, and I came home that evening after our dinner at The Edge and poured my heart out to Roly.' Guy blew his nose.

'And Roly didn't like it?'

Guy gulped his Prosecco again. 'I told him Byron had been

the love of my life, that Lucy had brought back all the memories I'd tried to put aside.'

'Was Roly a jealous type then? Surely he didn't resent you being in love so many years ago?' Kate asked, draining her glass.

Guy shrugged. 'It was horrible. Roly said he'd always felt he was second best to someone and he couldn't take it any more.' He waved the bottle of Prosecco in Kate's direction, looking decidedly tipsy.

He'd only had one glass, Kate thought, so she could only assume that he'd had a few before she arrived.

'No thanks, Guy, as I have to drive home.' She paused. 'I didn't really know Roly very well, but I would have thought he was more understanding than that. And Byron's dead... but sometimes grief never goes away.'

'No, sometimes it doesn't.'

'I'm sorry things have turned out like this, Guy. If you continue feeling low, then come to the surgery and we'll get you some help. And I do think that you should get back to the salon.' Kate lifted up some strands of her hair. 'Don't you think it needs a bit of shaping? Come on – your community needs you!'

Guy grinned sheepishly. 'OK, OK, I'll go back on Saturday! Make an appointment with Nikki!'

As she got up to go, Kate turned to him and asked, 'Who do *you* think murdered Crispin Wyngarde, Guy?'

Without hesitation, he said, 'Sonia Somerfield!'

She stopped in her tracks, surprised he even remembered the director's name. After all, he'd only been on the set for one day. 'Why do you think it's her?'

'Because of the way Wyngarde treated her years ago. Did you know that Wyngarde had an affair with both her and her husband at the same time? I think she *definitely* would hold a grudge.'

'How come you know so much about Sonia Somerfield and Crispin Wyngarde?' Kate asked as she reached the door.

'Lucy told me all the scandalous details.'

'Then are you thinking Sonia killed Paul Bacon as well?'

'Obviously. Probably he wanted too much money.'

'Perhaps he did,' Kate said without thinking.

She gave Guy a hug and made her exit.

It was only as she was driving home that she suddenly thought how on earth could Guy know about Paul Bacon and the money?

TWENTY-SEVEN

In view of what Angie had said about the possibility of being confined to Tinworthy, Kate thought it might be a good idea to pay a quick visit to Port Petroc before Charlotte had a chance to speak to her. She was keen to see Sonia, Lucy and even Jilly again, if only to test their reactions to Paul's demise.

It was Thursday, the day Angie was supposed to be parting with a thousand pounds in Plymouth for her ring. Kate wondered briefly if Angie would remove George's wedding ring, which she still wore, before adding Fergal's. What did you do, if you were a widow? She herself had had no such problems because the moment Alex Palmer had exited for the final time, Kate had removed all of her rings and sold them to the local jeweller. She'd have liked a symbolic discarding of them into the nearest bin, but she'd needed every penny to bring up two boys on her own.

Well Angie might not be going to Plymouth, but Kate *was* going to Port Petroc.

'I thought I'd go to the supermarket,' she said casually.

'No need for you to be calling in at The Pheasant this time!'

Woody said cheerfully. 'Why don't you go to the toilet right now before you leave?'

Kate did.

They were filming on the beach with the main characters, including Lucy, and the site seemed almost deserted without the extras. Kate had decided that her excuse for the visit, should anyone ask, would be that she wanted to check on Sonia's health.

There was a policeman, who she hadn't seen before, at the entrance. 'You got a pass?' he asked gruffly.

Kate had had the presence of mind to retain her pass, although it had now expired, and she prayed that he wouldn't check the dates.

He gave it a cursory glance and waved her through. 'Don't go beyond the barrier,' he said, 'cos they're filming.'

Kate decided that the best plan was to head towards the trailers, hoping that Jilly would still be in the wardrobe unit. She was, ironing what appeared to be a silk bodice of some sort.

'What brings *you* here?' she asked, stretching across for a puff of her cigarette, which was positioned perilously on a saucer on the shelf at the side.

Kate decided to be honest. 'I'm being nosy,' she said with a grin. 'I wondered how everyone was reacting to Paul Bacon's death and the police being here again. I had a feeling you might know what was going on!'

Jilly smiled. 'Funny you should say that!' She took another deep drag of her cigarette then placed it carefully back in the saucer. She coughed. 'I'm supposed to be quitting smoking, but what the hell! Not a good time, with all the goings-on around here. I'll start vaping when, and if, we ever get back to London. For the moment, we're all stuck here until they find whoever it was. I'm telling you: if I *ever* have to eat another bloody pasty, or listen to another damned seagull, it'll be too soon!'

'I didn't think you'd be any too thrilled,' Kate admitted. 'I imagine all the crew are feeling much the same?'

Jilly held up the bodice she'd been ironing and folded it on the ironing board. 'Did you hear about Lucy Moore?'

'No, what's *she* done?'

'She tried to *escape!*' Jilly rolled her eyes heavenwards. 'She's been living in a great big Airstream trailer on site, and she was missing her boyfriend who'd been down here for the first week but then had to go back to London. So she apparently organised it that he'd be waiting up on the main road, in the middle of the night, in his car, and she'd creep up there. Everyone who's living on site was asleep, and nobody heard her make her escape, complete with a pull-along suitcase, because the silly cow wouldn't be going anywhere without all her gear, particularly her make-up and that.'

Kate was agog. 'So she got away?'

'Well,' said Jilly, 'yes, she got away from here. Off she goes with the boyfriend and then they go racing through Launceston and onto the A30 doing 110 miles an hour, when they get stopped by the *police!*' She guffawed, took one last drag then snuffed out her cigarette. 'Stopped for speeding and, guess what, when she got to the police station, one of the cops recognised her! Where you going? he asks her, and she comes up with some long-winded story or other, and the boyfriend gets all argumentative and abusive, and so they both spend the night in Launceston Police station! Can you *imagine!*'

'Good heavens!' Kate was flabbergasted. 'Is she back here now?'

'Yes, but Sonia went ballistic! Lucy still had all these scenes to do, and Sonia had to spend the next day trying to get her released, and God only knows what she had to say to get the silly bitch back on site. Can you believe it?'

'Never a dull moment round here,' Kate remarked, wondering if Sonia's already high stress levels had now reached boiling point. 'There must be a lot of bad feeling?'

'Bad feeling! You could cut the air with a *knife*!'

'You know about Paul Bacon?'

'Rumour has it he was killed in his caravan.'

'Yes, he was,' Kate said, 'and it's been discovered that someone paid him to load that blunderbuss with shot, or whatever it is they use to kill people.'

Jilly rolled her eyes. 'I always knew he was a bad lot.'

'Perhaps he was, but so is whoever who paid him. You've no idea who that might have been, Jilly?'

'I used to think it was Sonia. Then I remembered something...' Her voice tailed off.

'What did you remember, Jilly?'

'No, forget it, not important. But now that Lucy Moore tried to get the hell out of here, maybe it was *her*. It's obvious, isn't it?'

'No, it's not obvious. Anyone could have paid him to load the thing. It wasn't *you*, was it?'

'*I* didn't pay him to load the bloody thing!' Jilly shouted. 'Why the hell would I?'

'You tell me.'

Kate was somewhat alarmed to see Jilly's eyes were brimming with tears, and she'd given up all pretence of ironing.

'But do you know who *did*?'

'No, I don't, but I *do* know he loaded the gun.' Tears were now running down her cheeks. 'Oh God, why did I *tell* you that?'

'You *knew* he loaded the gun with lethal shot?'

'I saw him do it.'

Kate considered this for a moment. 'Why did you not tell the police? You could be arrested for withholding information, Jilly.'

Jilly dissolved into tears again. 'They'll arrest me anyway because...' She faltered.

'Because of what?'

'Because I owed him money.'

Kate took a deep breath. 'I think you should tell me this from the beginning, Jilly.'

The girl blew her nose again. 'I've worked with Bacon several times over the last few years. The last time was six months ago in Dorset, and my car – which was on its last legs anyway – finally gave up the ghost.' She sniffed loudly. 'You need a car on location work cos nine times out of ten you're miles away from civilisation or a railway station. Like here. And I've got gear to transport around.'

'Surely the film company looks after you?'

'Yeah, they get you somewhere to stay and all that, and they give you a mileage allowance. Except I didn't have a car, so it would have meant I couldn't move off the site when we had a couple of days off, and I like to go home and see everyone.'

Kate waited.

'When the car broke down, they said it wasn't worth repairing,' Jilly continued, her eyes brimming again. 'And I didn't have any money for a new car.'

'So you needed to borrow some?'

Jilly nodded. 'One of the sound guys was selling a nice Ford Focus, good condition, not too old, and he wanted £6,000 for it. I didn't have £6,000, so he lowered it to £5,500. I didn't have that either, and then Paul heard all this and offered to lend me the money, so long as I paid him back within a year.'

'He didn't give you much time to pay it back, did he?' Kate remarked.

'No, he didn't, but at the time I was desperate to get this car, you see. He wanted £550 a month, which was really more than I could afford, but I very stupidly agreed.' Jilly sat down. 'I saw him load the blunderbuss, Kate.'

'With lethal shot?'

'Yes. And I told him I was going to the police. I'd even taken a video of him doing it on my phone, which he didn't know about. He got a bit nasty then, and he made me an offer. He said if I *didn't* go to the police, he'd reduce the monthly payments for the car.'

'So you agreed?' Kate asked, taken aback.

'No, I said I wasn't going to pay him *any* of it! He went ballistic of course! But I stuck to my guns – forgive the pun!' She gave Kate a watery smile.

'So you didn't go to the police because, in fact, he was paying you £5,500 not to?'

Jilly wiped her eyes. 'When you say it like that it makes me look and feel bloody awful!'

'But he's dead now, Jilly. We already know that somebody paid him to load the gun, but we don't know who.' Kate hesitated for a moment. 'You must tell the police about Bacon loading the blunderbuss immediately, Jilly. Have you kept the video?'

Jilly nodded mutely.

'That's the proof then. It's entirely up to you if you tell them about withholding the money he lent you, because that really doesn't concern this case, and doesn't reflect too well on either of you.'

'Will I be in trouble? Could I lose my job?'

'I sincerely hope not.' Kate made a mental note to talk to Sonia. 'The fact that you've come forward voluntarily with the information should weigh heavily in your favour.'

Aware that Jilly was sobbing again, Kate put her arms round the girl's shuddering body.

'It'll be all right, I'm sure, but it's always best to be honest. Promise me you'll tell the police?'

Jilly nodded. 'Thanks for being so understanding. I really needed to tell somebody.'

TWENTY-EIGHT

This was probably not the ideal day to ask Sonia about her health, but nevertheless Kate decided she'd hover around to see when they were likely to stop this filming session.

It was half an hour before the crew began to leave the site. Sonia was still on the beach and appeared to be arguing with her assistant about something. Kate took a deep breath and moved cautiously down to where Sonia was sitting, stepping over wires and cables as she went.

She cleared her throat. 'Sonia.'

Sonia turned round, the irritation on her face slowly dissipating. 'Oh, Kate, what brings *you* here?'

'Just thought I'd pop in to see how you were, and if the medication was still proving effective.'

'That's kind of you.' She waved her assistant away. 'It must be very effective, because I cannot begin to *tell* you the amount of stress I've been suffering! It's been one damned thing after another!'

'I'm sorry to hear that, Sonia.'

'This set is jinxed! It's been jinxed since day one, and there's no sign of any bloody improvement! The female lead tried to escape, and I had to spend half a day trying to get her released from the police station, and now your detective woman isn't happy with the security here, or the lack of it anyway, so Lucy's being moved from her trailer to the Atlantic Hotel in Tinworthy, from where, they must think, there's less chance of her escaping.'

'Why would she want to escape?'

Sonia gave an exaggerated shrug. 'You tell me! Is it because she can't bear to be without her fancy man – and I can tell you *he's* married with two kids' – here she tapped her nose – 'or is it because she's a *killer*?'

Factoring in what Guy had said to her, it looked more and more likely that it had been Lucy who'd paid Paul Bacon. How else could Guy know about the money? Nevertheless, she wasn't yet ready to exclude Sonia from her list and, if Kate did become confined to Tinworthy, it would be very difficult to speak to her and find out any more.

'Where are you staying at the moment, Sonia? Do you have a luxury trailer on the site here too?'

'No, I damn well don't! I'm in Port Petroc's one and only guesthouse and I'm not particularly impressed.' She shook her head sadly. 'I think they like their guests to be more conventional, and not coming and going at all hours, as I do. And they're not licensed for alcohol! So if I need to unwind – and boy, do *I* need to unwind! – I either have to get a bottle of wine and take it to my room or join the crew in The Pheasant. Believe me, when you've been with them all day, you can do without seeing them in the evening as well!'

Kate's mind was racing ahead. 'Why don't *you* move to the Atlantic Hotel too?'

Sonia shrugged again. 'I hadn't thought of it.'

'You could keep an eye on Lucy, they have a well-stocked bar, and I'm sure they couldn't care less what times you went in and out.' Kate paused. 'Just an idea.'

'Not a bad one,' Sonia admitted, 'providing the police would allow me to drive to and from here each day.'

'Lucy's going to have to make the journey each day too,' Kate pointed out, 'so perhaps you could come to some arrangement?'

'I like the way you try to come up with answers to my problems,' Sonia said with the glimmer of a smile. 'I rather liked what I saw of Tinworthy, so I'll certainly give it some thought.' She glanced at her watch. 'In the meantime, we have to resume filming in ten minutes, so will you excuse me if I grab a quick coffee and pay a visit to the loo?'

'Of course.'

As Kate turned to go, she added, 'Don't forget that, with the exception of Lucy, none of the rest of your crew will be in Tinworthy, and you liked The Tinners, didn't you?'

'I did,' agreed Sonia, 'because it was a real, genuine spit-and-sawdust establishment. You are a very persuasive lady!'

I hope I am, thought Kate.

She grinned at Sonia, gave her a brief wave and took her leave.

Kate decided it might be a good idea to pop into the Atlantic Hotel on her way home.

Marc Le Grand, who owned the place and had transformed it into a boutique hotel, had adopted his French mother's surname but hadn't quite managed to adopt the language successfully, probably due to the fact that he'd been reared by his English father in Essex. However, that didn't stop Marc throwing in as many French words and clichés as he could muster, resulting in frequent Franglais faux pas. Kate knew him well and decided it might be a good idea to forewarn him of a possible further guest. She only hoped he wasn't fully booked.

The Danish receptionist regarded Kate with steely blue

eyes. 'Ah, Mrs Palmer,' she said, 'if you are looking for Mr Le Grand, you will find him in the Ocean Room, where he is having some new lighting fitted.' She was brisk, efficient and immaculately groomed as always.

Kate found Marc barking instructions at an exasperated-looking electrician, whilst doing a great deal of Gallic shrugging and hand-wringing.

'*Mon Dieu!* Why is everything always so *difficile?*'

The electrician ignored Marc, who suddenly espied Kate.

'You would not *believe* how complicated fitting a new light can be! You take out one light, you put in another light, what is so *difficile* about that, eh?'

'Marc, come and have a drink and leave him to it,' Kate said, earning a grateful look from the hapless electrician. 'I'm sure he knows what he's doing, and I have some quite interesting news.'

With much sighing and eye-rolling, he followed her out into the hallway and across to the bar.

'It's always good to see you,' he said, 'and to what do I owe the *honneur* of your visit? And I insist on treating you,' he added, as Kate brought out her purse.

'Just a coffee please, Marc, because I'm driving.'

'*Très bien. Deux cafés, s'il vous plait,* Frederick! And, *pour moi,* a little cognac, I think.'

The barman, who'd been half-asleep behind the bar, jumped to attention. The room was mostly occupied with elderly people who'd commandeered all the comfortable chairs and knew a thing or two about making a drink last as long as possible.

'I understand you've reserved a room for Lucy Moore?' Kate asked once they'd settled themselves at a table near the window and Frederick had delivered the drinks.

'*Oui!*' said Marc, knocking back half of his brandy. He lowered his voice. 'She is *so* beautiful, this Lucy! *Très belle!* I saw her in *The Fledglings*; did you see it?'

Kate shook her head.

'She was *magnifique*! I am so honoured that she has chosen to stay here!'

Kate decided not to mention the fact that it certainly wasn't Lucy's choice.

'Good. Well, Marc, I might just have another guest for you, if you have a room available. The director: Sonia Somerfield.'

'She is beautiful too, yes?' Marc nudged her playfully.

'Not exactly. But she is a very powerful lady.'

'*Fantastique*! I will be very honoured to have her to stay here, and I think the Toulouse suite is free at the moment. It has the most wonderful views of the sea!'

'I'll let her know.'

They chatted for a few more minutes before Kate drained her coffee, thanked him profusely and headed out the door.

TWENTY-NINE

'Would you believe Lucy Moore tried to escape and ended up spending the night with her dodgy boyfriend in the police station,' Kate announced as she walked into the kitchen of Lavender Cottage. 'She's now being moved to the Atlantic Hotel so that, presumably, the police can keep an eye on her more easily.'

Woody looked up from his newspaper. 'Really?'

'I've suggested to Sonia that it might be a good idea if she did the same – moved to the Atlantic, I mean – particularly as she doesn't much like where she's staying at the moment,' Kate added.

Her husband laid down his newspaper and stared at her long and hard. 'You've been to Port Petroc?'

'I told you I was going to the supermarket.'

'The supermarket, Kate, is a mile further on from Port Petroc.'

'Yes, I know, but I thought I'd like to see what was going on.'

Woody stood up and walked towards her. 'Kate, it's not that I disapprove of you trying to sort this out, but I constantly worry about your safety. You *know* that.' He placed his hands on her shoulders. 'Someone on that site is almost certainly the killer of two people, and will not take kindly to you going there and asking questions.'

'I know, but at least this way we'd have the two main suspects in the Atlantic Hotel.'

He gave an exaggerated sigh. 'Actually, Charlotte rang me while you were out and told me about the Lucy incident. Apparently she and the boyfriend were careering along the A30 in the middle of the night, doing 110 miles an hour in a red Ferrari.'

Kate thought it best not to mention that she'd already heard this information and was interested in the further details.

'Doesn't say much for their intelligence that they thought they wouldn't be noticed,' said Woody. 'So I know Lucy is being moved to the Atlantic, but I don't think Charlotte is going to be best pleased at you making arrangements for Sonia Somerfield.'

'I only *suggested* to Sonia that she might like to move to the Atlantic! She didn't say she would, but plenty of people seem to think that she's the chief suspect at the moment.'

'Who thinks that?' Woody asked.

'Well Jilly certainly did at one time, and she thought that was the general opinion on the site.'

'Just Jilly?'

'No, Guy thinks so as well,' Kate said.

'Guy is also a suspect,' Woody said, 'so of course he's going to be pointing the finger at someone else! He's not likely to tell *you* that he suspects Angie or Fergal, is he?'

'I suppose not...' Kate said. 'I found out something interesting today: Guy let slip that he knew somebody had paid Paul Bacon.'

'He did? Well I hope he tells the police that. Look, I know Guy is a friend, but we really can't eliminate him. And what about Lucy Moore? She seems a more likely suspect to me considering what you told me about Lucy's father and Guy's relationship with him.'

He headed towards the cupboard and pulled out a bottle of wine. 'So Guy has more than one reason to kill Wyngarde. Perhaps Lucy Moore and Guy are in this together. We saw them avidly chatting that night at The Edge, so perhaps it was a joint effort? Perhaps they were scheming how to get rid of Paul Bacon?' He held up the bottle. 'Drink?'

'That's exactly what I was thinking. Yes please – I could do with a drink.'

Woody shook his head sadly. 'In spite of that, I don't believe anything or anybody until I have some sort of proof. That's my police training for you!'

Kate knew this made sense. 'So do you think I'm right that we should be checking up on Sonia Somerfield then?' she suggested as she accepted the glass of wine.

'I do,' Woody said with conviction.

'I've already checked her out on IMDb.'

'What's that?'

'It's a film-industry database. She's had an illustrious career as a film director, she's been married twice, with the first marriage ending in a blaze of publicity, as well you know. She has three children. Work, though, appears to have dried up since 2017, which is probably why she decided to do this film, even if it meant working with Wyngarde again.' Jilly had also told her that.

'Or maybe because it would give her the opportunity to get her revenge?' Woody suggested. Jilly had said that too.

Kate sighed. 'Nothing can be ruled out yet, can it?'

'Paul Bacon can. He may well have loaded the blunderbuss so, strictly speaking, he's guilty of the killing, but at someone else's behest.'

Kate had kept the best for last. 'Jilly, the wardrobe girl, can verify that Paul Bacon loaded the blunderbuss with intent to kill,' she said, 'which verifies what Bacon told me and what I then told Charlotte, although I'm never really sure she believes me. Jilly even has a video!'

'Well that sure is something,' Woody agreed, 'but unfortunately we're still no nearer to knowing who might have paid him.'

'At one time Jilly was quite certain it was Sonia, but, since Lucy tried to escape, she's now considering Lucy as well.'

'In other words, Kate, she's got no idea.'

Kate nodded. 'I fear you're right.'

'I hope you persuaded her to give this belated information to Charlotte?' Woody took a swig of his wine and looked thoughtful as he swilled it round his mouth.

'Of course. And I think she will.'

Kate went on to tell Woody about the loan for the car, the amount Bacon was asking for each month, and Jilly refusing to pay or she'd tell the police what she'd seen.

'Nobody comes out of this smelling of roses,' Woody said sadly, 'and we're still left with the same old suspects.'

'I wonder how much Bacon was paid? Or wanted to be paid?'

'I don't know what the going rate is these days for killing someone,' Woody replied, 'but it'll be a helluva lot.'

'Therefore it *has* to be someone with a great deal of money, hasn't it?'

'Not necessarily. It could be someone who hasn't yet paid,' Woody corrected, 'and has no intention of parting with a penny of it.'

'Would *you* kill someone if you hadn't been paid in full?' Kate asked.

'Not a decision I'm ever likely to have to make, or would agree to in the first place. But no, I probably wouldn't. Perhaps we need to find out how desperate Bacon was for money? Would he accept a deposit before he set up the blunderbuss, on the promise that the rest would be paid as soon as Wyngarde had been officially confirmed dead?'

'How much would a deposit be, do you suppose?' Kate was thinking about Angie's cash in the bottom of the kitchen bin. She really didn't want to believe that her sister could be involved. Besides, surely a thousand pounds wasn't enough.

'There's always the chance that Charlotte knows a great deal more than we do,' Woody said thoughtfully, gazing at Kate. 'Angie and Fergal are still suspects, you know.'

'You're right.' Kate knew that she was devoting more time to the other suspects than she was to her sister and Fergal. It was natural that she'd want to distance Angie from all this. But she'd gone over the circumstances again and again in her mind and could come up with no good reason why Angie would want to kill a man she was plainly fond of, and who'd given her the tiny, treasured part in the film.

Fergal, of course, was a different matter altogether. He'd been infuriated by Peter Edwards' revelations about Angie, yet he'd recovered sufficiently to want to marry her, and he'd been so upset about her being arrested Kate had been inclined to strike him off The List. But Fergal had a fiery temper, he knew a thing or two about guns, and he'd once been arrested for attempted murder. He would certainly have been one of Kate's prime suspects if he hadn't been Angie's partner.

Woody's comment had got her thinking. She'd have to try to have a chat with Fergal on his own.

THIRTY

Kate went back to The List, refilled her mug with tea and gazed out of the window at the sea, hoping for inspiration or, even better, a sudden breakthrough!

She wondered if she should move Fergal to the top of The List but decided that was hardly fair until she'd had a chat with him.

Then there was Guy. She hoped she'd left him in a slightly more cheerful frame of mind than when she'd first arrived at his flat. At least he'd been persuaded to go back to work.

She pondered over what he'd told her: his great love for Byron Bellamy; his fondness for the daughter who so reminded him of Byron; Roly's apparent jealousy.

Kate could see why Guy might well have wanted to kill Wyngarde, but Paul? What reason would he have to hate Paul that much? She supposed that, if it *was* Guy who'd paid to bring about Wyngarde's murder, then *he* would have had to pay Paul Bacon to load the gun, and perhaps Paul wanted more money? Or maybe he hadn't been paid at all? All possible.

Guy and Roly had been together on the night of the party and presumably went home together. But did Guy come back later in the night? Why, for that matter, had Guy, without hesitation, named Sonia Somerfield as the likely killer? Could it be because he wanted to draw attention away from himself and Lucy?

Kate sighed loudly. She couldn't help wanting to exclude the people who mattered to her most. If it wasn't Angie, and it wasn't Fergal, and it wasn't Guy, then who the hell had killed Paul Bacon? And who had been responsible for the death of Crispin Wyngarde?

Perhaps Jilly was right; perhaps Sonia Somerfield *had* finally got her revenge. Perhaps *she'd* paid Paul to load the blunderbuss? Perhaps, perhaps, perhaps...

Kate was only too aware of how complicated this case had become. She needed to know more about Paul Bacon, but, other than googling, how to find out? She got out her laptop.

There were several Paul Bacons listed on Google, but only one appeared to be sixty-one years old and an armourer, which could hardly be classed as a common occupation. He'd served thirteen years in the British army and had seen action in Northern Ireland and Bosnia. Married, divorced, no children. Began his career as an armourer on film and TV productions in 1994. It then went on to list the films he'd worked on, but aside from the production Jilly had mentioned him working on six months ago, there were no other credits in the last three years. Had he been out of work then? If that was the case, perhaps Paul Bacon would have been grateful to spike the gun for a few extra thousand pounds?

Kate's mind kept returning to Byron and Lucy, and so she googled Byron Bellamy first. Byron, born in Canterbury, Kent, had gone to RADA, and had appeared in several productions at the National Theatre and the West End, before being snapped up by the film industry and becoming a Hollywood heart-throb. An accident on set had ended his career when he was only thirty-eight.

Then Kate turned her attention to Lucy, who was listed as being the daughter of the famous actor, Byron Bellamy. She had inherited his outstanding talent and she, too, had gone to RADA, then won several lead roles in West End shows before making her screen debut in *The Fledglings*, in 2018. There was no indication of any follow-up to this film, so it looked like what Lucy had told Sonia about wanting to get into films again after a long spell in the theatre could be true, even if Crispin Wyngarde was the producer. Presumably Wyngarde hadn't been doing his research, or surely he'd have known that Lucy Moore was Byron Bellamy's daughter, and might well have thought twice about offering her a contract?

Kate's googling was interrupted by a phone call from Marc Le Grand.

'I just wanted to say *merci!*' he gushed excitedly. 'A Madame Somerfield has just booked with us, and she will be *very* happy to occupy the Toulouse suite!'

I daresay she will be, Kate thought, *after a joyless stay at the Port Petroc guesthouse.* Nevertheless, she was delighted that Sonia had heeded her recommendation.

'Thank you for sending her to me,' Marc continued, 'I am so grateful. Like Miss Moore, she is unable to say how long she will be staying, but it will be for at least a week.'

Kate reckoned it was likely to be a lot longer than that.

'She has asked me for your phone number so that she can thank you herself,' Marc continued, 'but I wanted to check that out with you first.'

'That's OK, Marc. Do, please, give her my number.'

Kate sat back and smiled to herself. At least, hopefully, all her eggs were now in one basket.

On Saturday morning, Sonia phoned.

'Thank you, Kate, for recommending this place. I have a

very nice couple of rooms with sea views, and Lucy is just along the corridor so I can keep an eye on her. I'm in the bar right now and wondered if you, and your lovely husband, would care to join me for a drink?'

'I'd love to, Sonia, but Woody's gone to do some repairs on the house that he lets out.'

'Shame, but *you* must come! Please!'

Kate glanced across at the vacuum cleaner she'd just plugged in. That could definitely wait. 'I'd love to,' she replied.

THIRTY-ONE

When she arrived at the Atlantic, Kate found Sonia and Lucy sitting in armchairs by the window of the bar. Sonia got to her feet and greeted Kate warmly with a hug, then pulled another armchair over from a nearby table. Lucy remained seated.

'You've met Lucy, haven't you?'

'Yes, we shared a table in the canteen once,' Kate replied, and Lucy gave a brief nod of acknowledgement.

Sonia, her hair tied up messily as usual, was in peasant mode today: multicoloured long skirt of Indian fabric, with some red and blue wooden beads to match, dangling over her red T-shirt, along with her spectacles. Lucy was in tight white jeans and a tight white halter top, all of which highlighted her slim figure and perfect golden tan, real or otherwise. They were both drinking what appeared to be Martinis, complete with olives.

'A drink?' Sonia asked, turning towards the bar. 'These Martinis are pretty good.'

'I'll just have a Diet Coke please, as I'm driving,' Kate replied.

'Can't you persuade the gorgeous husband to collect you again?' Sonia asked with a twinkle in her eye.

Kate laughed. 'Not on this occasion. He's on the roof of his old cottage replacing a couple of slates, so he wouldn't thank me for asking him!' She sat down and glanced at Lucy, who seemed to have become obsessed with examining her perfect, oval, unvarnished fingernails.

'Lucy's been learning her lines,' Sonia said as she returned and deposited a Diet Coke in front of Kate, 'so I've rewarded her with something to moisten her tonsils.'

'Do you have many lines to learn?' Kate asked Lucy.

'Too damn many,' Lucy replied, scowling at Sonia, 'and I'm supposed to have the weekend off.'

'You're *supposed* to be the female lead in this production,' Sonia reminded her, 'and that involves knowing your lines so we don't have to keep doing retakes. Honestly, this bloody film will be the death of me!' She sighed and took a large gulp of her Martini, just as the receptionist came in, phone receiver in hand.

'Miss Somerfield? Important call!'

'Oh bugger,' said Sonia, standing up and almost tripping over the hem of her skirt. She spoke into the phone for a moment, then turned to the two of them. 'I've got to take this call elsewhere,' she said, 'so please excuse me, ladies.' She then headed towards the door.

This was an opportunity Kate had been hoping for: to have a private word with Lucy, who hadn't been exactly forthcoming on their previous encounter.

'I think I mentioned that we have a mutual friend in Guy?' Kate remarked casually.

Lucy looked up from her fingernails. 'Yes, you said he did your hair.'

'Yes, he does my hair and, like I told you, he's become a good friend,' Kate replied.

'He was a great friend of my father,' Lucy said.

'Ah,' Kate exclaimed, 'the wonderful Byron Bellamy!'

Lucy appeared startled for a brief moment. 'You remember him?'

'Of course I remember him! How could I not! He was such a fine actor, and so handsome!' Kate hoped she wasn't overdoing it.

'You've seen some of his films?'

No, she hadn't, but fortunately Kate had memorised the name of one of them. 'Oh yes, in particular *The Man from the East*!' Hoping not to be questioned, she continued hurriedly, 'I was so sad to hear about his awful accident.'

'It was horrendous,' Lucy said. 'He left home one morning big and strong, and ready for action, and he came home six months later, paralysed from the neck down.' She sighed. 'They did everything they could for him at Stoke Mandeville, but they couldn't repair his broken neck.'

'Guy did tell me that Crispin Wyngarde didn't take the necessary safety measures,' Kate said.

'Bloody right!'

Kate cleared her throat. 'I did wonder why you'd ever want to work with the wretched man who'd wrecked your father's life?'

Lucy leaned forward and looked her straight in the eye. 'I intended to get my revenge,' she said. 'I knew that the arrogant bastard wouldn't have done much research, and I was right. He hadn't the slightest idea who I was.'

Kate knew she had to be careful with what she said next. 'So...?'

'So I had a look at the script and could see a couple of places where he might be killed. And I also knew the armourer might be short of money because he hadn't had much work recently.'

'Was he?' Kate felt a rising sense of excitement. Had her guess had been right?

'Yes, and not only that, he'd made some bad investments. He told me on the first night here, when we were all having a drink in The Pheasant, before he got plastered.'

Kate had to ask. 'So he could have been bribed?'

Lucy gave Kate that slightly unnerving, steady stare again. 'Oh yes, he could be bribed all right. But do you know what? Someone else had the same idea and got there before I did.'

Kate, astounded, digested Lucy's remarks for a moment. Was the woman being truthful, or was her disarming honesty designed to divert attention away from herself? She was an actress after all, so could this all be an act?

'Then who do you think it was that got there before you did?' she asked at last.

'No idea,' said Lucy, with a shrug, 'but it saved me a job.'

Kate was astonished at how matter-of-fact she sounded. There was little she could say in reply.

'There must have been some other people on the crew who disliked Wyngarde then?' she asked hopefully after a minute.

'Nobody liked him,' Lucy replied, 'but I don't really know who else could have hated him as much as I did.'

'You don't suppose Guy might have done it on your behalf?' Kate asked hesitantly.

Lucy appeared horrified. '*Guy*? Are you *serious*?'

'Only because he might have guessed what you were planning and wanted to protect you – being the gentleman he is,' Kate added hastily.

'No,' Lucy said firmly, 'not Guy. Definitely not Guy! I thought you were his *friend* – how could you suggest something like that?'

Before Kate could reply, Sonia returned, looking very pleased with herself and full of apologies. 'So sorry to dash away like that! But thank God I'd already given my agent this phone number, because my mobile's up in the bedroom on charge.

Apparently I've got an offer of some work in New York after I wrap up this production. I think that calls for a bottle of champagne, don't you?'

Judging by the scowl on Lucy's face, champagne seemed to have been the last thing on *her* mind.

THIRTY-TWO

Kate had been persuaded to have a glass of champagne before making her exit, and arrived home to find herself face to face with the vacuum cleaner again. Not only that, Barney in his enthusiastic welcome had managed to knock over a pot plant, scattering soil and gravel across the carpet. She wondered how long it would take her to become bored with residing in a nice hotel and drinking Martinis on a Saturday morning. Sighing, she switched the Dyson on.

While vacuuming, Kate's thoughts returned to her conversation with Lucy. Had she spoken the truth? And if she had been pre-empted, then who had pipped her to the post? There were so many people on the crew, and it could have been any of them.

And why was Jilly so convinced that the killer was Sonia?

It was shortly after Kate and Woody had finished lunch that Charlotte Martin arrived at the door. Briefcase under her arm, she sat down at the kitchen table, where she'd parked herself several times in the past and, without preamble, asked, 'Was there some reason, Kate, why you decided to join two other suspects at the Atlantic Hotel this morning?'

Kate was rendered speechless for a moment before asking, 'Is there some reason why I *shouldn't* visit acquaintances in the Atlantic Hotel?'

Charlotte rubbed her chin thoughtfully. 'No, but it struck me that you might be playing detective again.'

Woody got to his feet. 'For God's sake, Charlotte,' he said angrily, 'why can't Kate visit anyone she likes?'

'Calm down, I'm not saying that she shouldn't, but I just wonder why she did,' Charlotte remarked calmly, brushing an imaginary hair off her pink, cashmere-covered shoulder.

Kate, who'd been filling the kettle, sat down at the table opposite. 'I was invited for a drink by Sonia Somerfield,' she said.

'Are you close friends then?'

Kate couldn't believe she was being questioned about anything quite so mundane. 'We are not *close* friends,' she snapped, 'but we became quite friendly after I came to her aid when she was suffering an acute asthma attack on the set. I also suggested to her that it might be a good idea for her to move to the Atlantic, since she wasn't particularly happy with the guesthouse at Port Petroc.'

'And so she took your advice?'

'Yes, she did.'

'And were you aware that we had already moved Miss Moore to the hotel?' Charlotte asked.

Kate nodded. 'Yes, I did know. And I'd heard about her recent attempt to escape.'

'In view of that, we're keeping a close eye on Miss Moore, and would have preferred that she'd remained isolated from the rest of the crew.'

Kate shrugged. 'I don't quite know where this conversation is leading, Charlotte. I was invited for a drink. I went. End of.'

'Hmm.' Charlotte was gazing out of the window at where Barney was enthusiastically chewing a bone on the grass. 'What I really came to tell you was that you are both now confined to Tinworthy – Higher, Middle and Lower – for the time being, until this case is solved.'

'Why, Charlotte? Why us?' Kate asked.

Woody stared at Charlotte. 'Presumably because we're still suspects?'

'Precisely. This applies to all the suspects who live here, including your sister and her partner,' Charlotte replied.

'What about Sonia Somerfield and Lucy Moore?' Woody asked.

'They will be escorted to Port Petroc and back by police each day they need to be on set,' Charlotte replied.

'Let's hope then that you and your team find the killer very soon,' Kate said, giving her the sweetest smile she could muster. She stood up again. 'Would you like a cup of tea?'

'No thank you,' Charlotte said, standing up and smoothing her immaculate navy-blue pencil skirt. 'I must be going.' With a wave, she made her way towards the door.

'What was *that* all about?' Kate asked, watching through the window as Charlotte got into her car.

'Search me,' replied Woody.

'*Now* do you see why I went to Port Petroc the other day?' Kate asked. 'I had a feeling this might be coming, and at least we've now got the two main suspects from the film set in Tinworthy.'

'I'm not quite sure what the advantage of that is,' Woody remarked, frowning.

'It means that I can keep in touch easily with both Sonia and Lucy,' Kate said, 'and they might just provide a few clues. They've both got nice suites so it'll cost a bit.'

'No doubt Limelight Films are having to foot Lucy Moore's

hotel bill,' Woody said, 'although she's probably got quite enough money to pay for it herself.'

'She had a luxury Airstream caravan out at the site,' Kate said.

'I wonder then why they didn't bring that here and park it somewhere?'

'Maybe she preferred to be in a hotel.'

'Could be,' Woody agreed. 'Perhaps she wanted a nice, flushing toilet.'

THIRTY-THREE

When Kate was leaving work on Monday, she popped along to the shops to buy a newspaper and almost collided with Roly, Guy's partner, who was loading boxes into the open boot of his silver Audi. He was a tall, dark, good-looking man, albeit with a receding hairline.

He turned to Kate as he slammed the boot shut. 'I guess Guy told you I was leaving?' He looked close to tears.

Kate nodded. ' And I was so sorry to hear it,'

'Yeah, well. That's the final load. Oh God, Kate, I don't want to be leaving.' He sniffed loudly.

'You won't be coming back then, Roly?'

'I shouldn't think so. I'm back in my old place in Brighton now, and just came back today to collect the remainder of my stuff. It's so damn sad to be leaving, but I don't want to be living with such a likely suspect.'

Kate, horrified, asked, 'Why do you say that?'

'I have reason to.' He glanced at his watch. 'I suppose I'd better get on the road because it's a long way. Oh, this is so *awful*! I love him so much, you know.'

'Roly, come and have a drink with me in The Tinners' *please*. I hate to see you leave here looking so sad.'

Roly considered. 'Guess I could have a pint of shandy before I hit the road. Thanks, Kate – why not?'

She was thinking quickly and wondering what on earth he'd meant by the remark about Guy being such a likely suspect. 'I guess you'll be back from time to time though, to see your mother?'

Roly's mother, Jodi, had married Marc at the Atlantic Hotel quite recently.

He nodded. 'Occasionally.'

In The Tinners', they both opted for lemonade shandies, as Roly had a five-hour drive ahead of him, as opposed to Kate's five-minute cruise down the hill.

As they raised and clinked their glasses, Kate asked, 'Why did you refer to Guy as a likely suspect?'

Roly wiped his mouth with the back of his hand. 'It grieves me to say this, but I think Guy killed Wyngarde.'

'Why do you think that?' Kate asked, shocked at Roly's candour.

'He'd been badly treated by him when he was working in the film industry back in the eighties. He was very young, but he never forgot that. Then, just a short time ago, I discovered another reason why he hated him so much.' He wiped his eyes and blew his nose.

Kate remained silent, having a good idea as to what he was about to tell her.

'He was madly in love with Byron Bellamy years ago. It was the "love of his life", he told me, And, as I'm sure you know, Wyngarde wrecked Bellamy's life, so that gives Guy a further motive, doesn't it? As if all that wasn't hurtful enough, it turns out that Lucy Moore is Bellamy's daughter! She's the female lead in the film, you know?'

Kate nodded.

'I overheard Guy and Lucy talking together. They'd both wanted Wyngarde dead, wanted revenge,' Roly continued.

'But, Roly, they weren't the *only* ones who had reason to hate Wyngarde.'

'I'm sure you're right. But tell me this: why did he take thousands out of our joint account? And refuse to tell me why?'

Kate was truly dumbstruck for a moment. 'Are you *serious*? *Thousands*?'

'Yeah, thousands.' He didn't specify how many thousands, and Kate didn't like to ask. 'You got any idea what the current assassination rates are, Kate?'

She gulped. 'Oh God, Roly.'

'And I expect Miss Moore was withdrawing thousands from her account too. Depends how much the armourer wanted, I suppose.' He wiped his eyes again.

'So are you saying that Guy and Lucy Moore, between them, paid Bacon a large amount to load the blunderbuss?' Kate asked.

'That would seem to be the only explanation,' Roly said, 'but *I'm* not about to shop him. Let the police do their job. I just don't want to be around to see him being arrested. I still love him so much, Kate.'

'But, Roly, in that case, you must think that Guy killed Paul Bacon as well? Weren't you with him all that evening at The Gull?'

'Not *all* evening, Kate. I popped in to see Mum and Marc for an hour or so on the way back, but Guy said he was exhausted and wanted to go to bed.'

Roly drained his drink. 'Anyway, that's enough of all that. I'll be off, cos I've got a long drive ahead of me. And I have to get away from here, because it's breaking my heart.'

Kate reached out and touched his hand. 'I'm so very sorry. I honestly don't know *what* to think any more. I just cannot imagine that Guy is guilty of such heinous crimes though, I really can't!'

Roly sniffed and shook his head sadly.

'Roly, I happen to know that Guy loves you very much.'

'Maybe, but I reckon I'm a poor second to this Bellamy bloke.'

'No, you're not! Byron Bellamy was a long time ago, a tragedy that happened in the past. Surely we've all loved and lost people at some time? And, just occasionally, you get a sharp reminder, as Guy did with Lucy, which brings it all back for a while. But it doesn't mean that he loves you any less.'

Roly said nothing for a moment, just stared sadly into his glass. 'I don't mean to be jealous,' he said, 'but I can't help it.'

Kate placed a hand on his. 'You mustn't be jealous of a ghost. Guy has moved on. He may have loved Byron at one time, but he loves you now. Surely you wouldn't expect him not to have loved before?'

Roly remained silent, and finally Kate said, 'Promise me you'll think about it?'

He nodded slowly.

'The film crew will disappear, hopefully, before long, and Guy will be lonely and sad. He's going to need you.'

Roly drained his drink, stood up and put an arm round her. 'I guess you're right, Kate, and perhaps I did overreact, but I do need to get away now to sort myself out.'

'When you've done that, come back. I'm sure Guy will be waiting.'

He smiled. 'It was sweet of you to listen to me bleating on. Best be on my way.'

Outside The Tinners', they hugged briefly.

'I'm sure you'll be back before too long, Roly,' Kate said as he got into his car.

He shrugged, smiled and started up the engine. She could see tears in his eyes. And she wondered what it meant.

THIRTY-FOUR

Kate had become increasingly confused by the Wyngarde case, to the point where she was having problems sleeping. It didn't help that she was so desperate to exonerate Angie. She couldn't get it out of her head that there was still a possibility Angie had been involved, in any way at all, with Crispin's murder. Then she worried that she could even *contemplate* suspecting her own sister.

It was something she didn't want to talk to Woody about because, although Woody was fond of Angie, Kate knew he did consider her to be something of a loose cannon. And there was no denying that he was right. Not only that, Woody was well trained in detection skills, and he doubtless considered Angie as likely a suspect as anyone else. And it wasn't *his* sister.

Deep down, Kate didn't think for one moment that Angie *was* capable of pointing a gun at Wyngarde's heart, knowing it would kill him. She knew her sister better than anyone and, although Angie might act irresponsibly at times, she wasn't a bad person and certainly not a killer. And that killing had, without doubt, been premeditated and well set up beforehand. Good actress though Angie undoubtedly was, her reaction to the killing was obviously so spontaneous that it couldn't possibly have been put on. This, as far as Kate was concerned, eliminated Angie, who was incapable of that sort of forward planning. So why was she still worrying?

She was also concerned about Angie's proposed marriage. At their ages, she could see no good reason for Angie and Fergal to marry, other than for legal or financial security. Then she laughed out loud; who was *she* to talk? Still, it didn't change the fact that Fergal would benefit from the marriage far more than Angie.

Fergal: happy-go-lucky and full of charm. Kate didn't think Fergal was a killer either but felt it was high time she had a chat with her prospective brother-in-law.

The opportunity to chat with Fergal came unexpectedly when Kate popped into The Old Locker on her way home the following evening and found him there on his own.

'Oh hi!' he said, when he finished serving a couple of teenagers with cappuccinos. 'You've just missed Angie, because she's had to go to the minimarket. We're just about to run out of tinned tuna and Bobby, needless to say, has none in stock. I don't know how that feckin' shop stays open.' He shook his head. 'She's gone to that little grocery in Tinworthy, near the church, because she's not allowed to leave the village. As you *know*.'

Kate nodded. 'I actually wanted to have a talk with you, Fergal.'

'Well that's nice. Shall I get you a coffee? An Irish one?' He raised an eyebrow.

'A cappuccino is fine for me thanks.'

When he placed the coffee in front of her, he asked, 'Now, what did you want to talk to me about? That you're secretly *madly* in love with me?'

Kate grinned. 'That goes without saying, Fergal! It's just that I'm really worried about Angie.'

'Now why would you be worrying? She's fit as a fiddle.'

'I can't help worrying about her being a suspect.'

'For Jaysus' sake, Kate! Don't tell me you suspect your own *sister*?'

'No. I just wish she wasn't mixed up in this whole horrible business.'

'Don't we all wish that? Surely they'll find that killer before much longer so we can all relax?'

Kate sighed deeply.

Fergal was studying her, frowning. 'You don't think *I* had anything to do with this whole feckin' business, do you?'

'No, Fergal, I don't. But I had a visit from Penelope Bowen the other day, and she seems to think you *are* a prime suspect because of your recent meeting with Peter Edwards.'

'Peter Edwards?'

'Yes, you know who he is; he's been having it off with Penelope for years, and you met in The Tinners' recently. And if what she said is true, then it seems that both you and Edwards had some sort of drunken chat that night, and he told you about Angie and Wyngarde.' Kate was keeping an eye on the door, because she knew Angie would be back before long.

Fergal groaned.

'I'm understandably concerned not just about Angie but about you too,' Kate said, 'because it now looks as if you might have had even *more* reason to polish off Wyngarde than just being jealous of an old flame.'

'Have you told that woman detective all this?'

Kate shook her head. 'No, I haven't, but I think you'll find that Penelope has.'

'Jaysus! Just a minute...' He moved along to serve a young couple who'd just come up to the counter.

Kate waited while he served them and wondered if it had

been wise to have this conversation. But surely it was best he knew the truth?

When he finished serving, he poured himself a lager and positioned himself in front of Kate again.

'Interfering old cow,' he said morosely.

'I presume you mean Penelope?' Kate asked with a grin.

'Well of course I do! I'd forgotten herself and Edwards were thick as thieves. And, to be honest, Kate, I really had *no* idea until then that Angie had still been seeing Wyngarde. I suppose I must be bloody thick! So, yes, I was angry.' He took a large gulp of his beer.

'You honestly didn't know about this until he told you?'

'Of course not! You're not suggesting I became an extra just so that I could bump off Wyngarde?'

'No, *of course* I'm not suggesting that, Fergal! But the police might think that way. And they already know you once threatened to kill someone.'

'Bloody Edwards! Bloody Penelope! But thanks for telling me.'

He leaned forward and looked into Kate's eyes. 'I've learned some hard lessons over the years, Kate. I was young and irresponsible that time in Ireland when I threatened Martin, but I've had to grow up, believe me. I love Angie very much, and the last thing I'd do is have her in a position to pull a trigger on *anybody*, not even bloody Wyngarde. I love her far too much for that.'

Kate smiled faintly. 'Knowing what she's like, I sometimes wonder why you'd want to marry Angie?'

He looked genuinely amazed. 'Because I love her, that's why. And she's still a single woman, so I have no right to complain about her behaviour, have I? If we get married – properly married, with vows and everything – then surely she'd be faithful?'

'I hope so,' Kate said, trying not to sound too doubtful, and trying to dismiss thoughts of Angie's dalliance with Paul Bacon, while she was married to George.

She finished her coffee, said goodbye to a still worried-looking Fergal and headed up the lane for home.

There was something about Fergal that was almost childlike – an intensity, an innocence. Kate didn't think this was in any way contrived. What you saw with Fergal was what you got. It seemed he'd been taken advantage of, one way or the other, for most of his life, and Angie hadn't helped by resuming her affair with Wyngarde.

Crispin Wyngarde had been the cause of so much anguish; an oversexed, selfish, arrogant man, who left trails of misery in every direction. Could she honestly blame anyone who might have wanted to kill him? What was interesting was that no one had tried to do so before now. Was it purely coincidental that this should have happened in Cornwall, close to several of his victims?

Her chat with Fergal had convinced her, and strengthened her gut feeling, that he was innocent and that he hadn't been lying. He might be penniless, but she was certain that he did love Angie and seemed to be marrying her for all the right reasons.

Kate arrived home, got out The List, and erased Fergal's name. Then she felt guilty at having eliminated him and not Angie. She didn't think Angie was guilty either, but, for some reason, she decided not to remove her from The List just yet.

Now she was going to begin worrying about why she *hadn't* removed her.

Kate poured herself a large glass of wine. This case was getting a bit too close to home for her liking...

THIRTY-FIVE

Des Pardoe had never been exactly cheerful, but he had been known to stretch his rubbery face into a smile occasionally, and he was always pleasant and polite to customers.

On Wednesday evening, when Kate and Woody popped in for a pre-dinner drink, they found Des looking even more morose than he generally did. There was none of his usual remarks, such as 'How's our local film stars then?' or 'I expect you'll soon be off to Hollywood?' or any of his habitual quips, which was as near to joking as Des could generally manage.

'I've never seen Des look so miserable,' Woody remarked as they grabbed a table near the window. 'He's got a face like a fortnight of frost.'

Kate could only agree. 'He's not been the same since the night of Paul Bacon's murder,' she said, wondering if he'd taken the sedatives she'd given him, and if they were helping him to sleep. If he was still suffering from sleepless nights, that would account for his look of exhaustion.

'They've taken the car and caravan away now,' Woody pointed out, 'so it's not as if they're still cluttering up the car park.'

A little later, Kate decided she needed a word with Des. 'Fancy another one?' she asked, tapping Woody's empty glass.

'Can't say no to an offer like that, ma'am,' he replied, exaggerating his American accent.

Kate picked up the glasses and made her way to the bar, where Des was serving a couple of hikers. She overheard one of them ask, 'Do you do food in here?' followed by Des's curt reply, 'That board on the wall behind you ain't no ornament.' He was referring to the blackboard upon which Madge wrote out the menu available each day in her best handwriting.

Kate saw them exchange glances before one of them said, 'Let's go down to that place on the beach where you're made more welcome.' Then they both walked out.

Des rolled his eyes as he turned to Kate. 'They must've been bloody blind if they couldn't see that bloody great board!'

Kate ordered the drinks and, when Des delivered them, she said, 'You're not yourself at the moment, Des. Have you been taking those sedatives?'

He shrugged. 'When I remember. You know what? Finding that bloke dead in the caravan has done my head in, Kate. I keep reliving going in there and finding him; just can't get it out of my mind.'

'You must try to forget it, Des, because you don't want to lose customers, do you? Perhaps you should make an appointment with one of the doctors and they'll prescribe you something stronger.'

Des grunted. 'There's days when I think I want to pack all this in.' He waved his hand around the bar. 'I fancy goin' off and buyin' one of them motor caravans, so me and Madge can just take off.' He stared longingly out of the window.

'Oh, you *can't* leave The Gull, Des!' Kate said, alarmed. 'What would we do without you?'

'You'd buy your booze from a new landlord, that's what you'd do,' said Des, without a trace of a smile.

Well that's me told, Kate thought, as she carried the drinks back to the table.

Woody made light of it, but Kate continued to worry about Des. She certainly hoped he wouldn't be swanning off in a motor caravan because The Gull definitely would not be the same without him. She liked Des, but she didn't like to see him tetchy like this, and she now had him to worry about, as well as Angie and Guy and Roly – the list went on. None of this helped her insomnia of course, and it was with some relief when Woody told her about the retired police get-together in Truro on Saturday afternoon. He'd obtained special permission from Charlotte to make the trip since it was a police event.

'It's just a load of old guys swapping stories about how brilliant we all were,' he told her with a grin, 'and it'll involve a lot of beer.'

'Which means you should book yourself a hotel room,' Kate said.

'I guess you're right. Would you mind if I stayed away overnight?'

'Of course not,' Kate said truthfully, with immediate visions of being able to toss and turn in bed all night without worrying about waking Woody.

He smiled. 'Well don't sound so damned pleased about it! I'd appreciate a little sighing and sobbing, maybe some beating of the brow!'

Kate obliged with a couple of sighs and a sobbing sound.

'Don't overdo it, honey! Anyway, I guess that means I'm cleared to go!' He regarded her thoughtfully for a moment. 'You're not planning on doing any detective work, I hope?'

Kate smiled sweetly. 'As if!'

THIRTY-SIX

On Saturday, shortly after Woody had left at lunchtime, Kate decided to visit the Atlantic Hotel in the hope of 'bumping into' either Sonia or Lucy. It was a warm, sunny afternoon, and she reckoned that, if neither of them were in the reception area or the bar, there was a chance they might be out by the pool. The pool was another of Marc's innovations since he'd taken over the hotel, along with renovating the entire interior.

There was no sign of either woman in reception or the bar, and there was no sign of Marc either, which was fortunate since he always wanted to engage in conversation. Kate ventured out to the rear of the property which faced south-west and, according to Marc's blurb, 'guaranteed sunshine all day long'. This was a rash statement, even by Marc's standards, considering the vagaries of the Cornish weather. At least it had a view across some fields of grazing sheep towards the sea in the distance.

Most of the turquoise blue sunloungers were empty, apart from an elderly couple near the doorway and one woman in a white bikini at the far end. Kate reckoned this certainly wasn't likely to be Sonia but was almost certainly Lucy. As she drew closer, she recognised Lucy's slim brown body and oversized sunglasses.

'Hi!' Kate said.

Lucy lifted her sunglasses up and opened one eye. 'Oh, hi!'

'I was just passing,' Kate lied, 'and wondered how you and Sonia were doing?'

'We're OK,' Lucy replied, sitting up and positioning the sunglasses on top of her head. 'Just bored. And a bit cold.' She donned a white shirt over her bikini.

'Let me buy you a drink,' Kate said, looking around for a waiter. She signalled to a dark-haired man in a white jacket who was serving drinks to the elderly couple. 'What'll you have?'

'Well thank you. I'll have a dry Martini then.'

As Kate gave her order to the waiter for one dry Martini and one white wine spritzer, Lucy chimed in, 'With lots of olives please.'

The waiter bowed and smiled and, as he turned away, Lucy said, 'He's Carlos, and he's Spanish.'

Kate chuckled. 'Is he from Barcelona then?' She recalled the hapless Manuel from the TV comedy *Fawlty Towers*.

Lucy stared at her in astonishment. 'Yes, he is. How did you know that?'

'Oh, just a guess,' Kate said, realising Lucy was probably too young to have seen *Fawlty Towers*. She cleared her throat. 'I paid a visit to Guy recently, because he was off work with depression.'

'Yeah? That would probably be on account of Roly taking off.'

'You knew about that?' Kate asked.

'Sure. There were lots of contributing factors though. Nothing is ever as straightforward as you might think.'

'That's for certain,' Kate agreed. 'But Guy did say something that puzzled me. He seemed to know that Paul Bacon had been paid by someone to load the gun and kill Wyngarde, and that was confidential police information.'

At this point, Carlos returned and deposited the drinks on the table, while openly ogling Lucy. Kate paid, and Carlos moved away slowly and unwillingly, still admiring Lucy.

Lucy yawned. 'What were we talking about?' she asked idly, taking a sip.

'I was telling you that I wondered how Guy could have known that Bacon had been paid by someone to load the gun which killed Wyngarde?'

'Because I told him,' Lucy replied.

'You did? So you knew too?'

'Of course I knew.' Lucy took another sip and nibbled an olive. 'I thought I told you that I wanted to kill Wyngarde, but somebody else beat me to it.'

'You didn't actually say you'd approached Paul Bacon.'

'Oh, I approached him all right.' Lucy fished another olive out of her Martini. 'I told you I studied the script and could see this golden opportunity to kill the bastard,' she said matter-of-factly. 'I told that policewoman all this because she obviously had me down as guilty when I tried to escape from that damned place.'

'OK, so how did you know that someone else had the same idea?'

Lucy sighed. 'When I asked Bacon how much he wanted – and I had the cash all ready – he sneered at me. Said he'd had a better offer and had accepted it.' She smiled. 'I'm sure that, if he hadn't been so drunk, he'd just have taken my money as well and said nothing. At least it's saved me a life sentence.'

'It certainly has,' Kate agreed, sipping her drink, amazed at Lucy's candour. 'I don't suppose he told you who'd paid him?'

'Of course he didn't! But whoever it was must have paid him a fair amount, because I'd offered what I thought was a fortune! It meant borrowing some from Guy; he's such a good friend!'

That explained a lot, so far as Kate was concerned, but now she wondered anew if this proposed assassination attempt had been planned as a joint effort. Lucy and Guy? Guy must have known what she wanted the money for. Not that it mattered much now since, fortunately, they hadn't succeeded in bribing the armourer. And if what Lucy said was true, then she could remove both of them from The List. It was looking more and more like Sonia was the killer.

As if on cue, Sonia, resplendent in a purple kaftan and an enormous straw hat, emerged from the building and made her way along by the side of the pool to where they were sitting.

'Oh. Hello!' she said to Kate. 'What brings you here?'

'Just wondered how you both were getting on?' Kate replied casually.

'We're getting on OK,' Sonia replied, glancing across at Lucy, who was ignoring her. 'It's nice to have a decent room, a decent bar and a pool. Great idea of yours, Kate.' She hesitated. 'The meals are very elaborate but bloody expensive. I went to the fish and chip shop the other night – delicious!'

An idea suddenly occurred to Kate. 'I'm on my own this evening,' she said, 'because Woody's at a police reunion in Truro, so why don't you both come to my house for dinner?'

'What a lovely idea!' enthused Sonia, looking at Lucy.

'Makes a change from here,' Lucy said, draining her Martini. She smiled at Kate. 'Thank you.'

Kate produced a card and handed it to Sonia. 'That's my address. Get a cab, and I'll expect you around seven. OK?'

'OK,' they both chorused.

As Kate drove down to Lower Tinworthy, she began to question her own sanity. She had only a few hours to prepare a meal for a famous film director and an equally famous actress, who, no doubt, were accustomed to haute cuisine. Still, Sonia had said something about the fussy meals at the Atlantic, and how she'd enjoyed escaping for some fish and chips, so perhaps the solution was to cook something simple.

She seemed to remember, from her first encounter with Lucy in the canteen, that fish was OK, and chicken wasn't. Kate knew she had a few different types of seafood in the freezer, and decided to defrost these and make one of her acclaimed fish pies. Followed by apple crumble perhaps? There was plenty of wine in the cupboard, and she'd chill a few bottles of white as soon as she got home.

Kate dropped in at the mini-market in Middle Tinworthy on the way home to buy some Cornish clotted cream to accompany the crumble, plus some olives – with Lucy in mind – and, not least, some dry vermouth to accompany the gin, also with Lucy in mind. It was important to get these two ladies – Sonia in particular – into a talkative mood.

Having completed her shopping, Kate beavered away all afternoon putting the meal together, at the same time wondering if she was about to be entertaining a cold-blooded murderer.

Woody rang at four o'clock, having just arrived in Truro.

'What are you doing?' he asked.

'Oh, just pottering about,' Kate replied vaguely.

'I hope you're not up to something?'

'Woody Forrest, you are a very suspicious man!'

'I have good reason to be,' he replied, 'when I consider your penchant for taking matters into your own hands!'

Kate laughed. 'I promise to behave myself!'

But, she thought, *I can only hope that my guests won't.*

THIRTY-SEVEN

At quarter to seven, Kate had tidied the kitchen, set the table nicely and had everything ready to cook, while she ensured she had all the ingredients ready for a cocktail or three as well as the wine, chilling in the fridge.

The taxi pulled up at ten past seven, and the two women disembarked, clutching bottles of wine and bunches of flowers. Kate thanked them profusely and settled them in the sitting room.

Lucy had poured herself into some skinny white jeans, which she'd paired with a deep-pink silk shirt, while Sonia wore another of her kaftans, this one in emerald green with a great many wooden beads stitched into the front, amongst which her spectacles dangled.

'Isn't this nice!' Sonia settled herself on the sofa and spread the folds of emerald cotton around her. 'Such a delightful place, Kate! All this and the gorgeous husband – you don't know how lucky you are!'

'Yes, I'm certainly lucky,' Kate agreed. If only they knew how lucky she really was, in view of the many narrow escapes she'd endured, thanks to her acquired sleuthing skills!

Sonia was a straightforward gin and tonic lady.

Lucy asked, 'Any chance you could put a dry Martini together?'

Kate thanked her lucky stars she'd had the presence of mind to stop at the mini-market and get the vermouth.

'I'll do my best,' she said, before heading into the kitchen where she'd left the likely ingredients laid out on the work surface. She hoped she'd got the ratio of gin and vermouth correct, then added a twist of lemon and a couple of olives for good measure.

She carried the drinks, along with a few canapés she'd prepared earlier, into the sitting room. There was much clinking of glasses and murmurs of approval, and Sonia said enthusiastically, 'This is so generous of you!' She took a large gulp of her gin. 'So much nicer than a Saturday evening in a hotel!'

'The restaurant was fully booked anyway,' added Lucy, 'being Saturday night.'

They spoke about the village, about Kate's family and about her decision to move to Cornwall, meeting Woody and her job at the medical centre. Sonia did not elaborate on her own first marriage but spoke about her children, and referred to her current husband without much enthusiasm.

Lucy enthused about her boyfriend, how wonderful he was, how rich he was, but that they had no plans to get married just yet. At this, Sonia gave a loud snort, no doubt referencing his marital status, and received a poisonous look from Lucy.

The evening was proving to be a great success. The meal was pronounced as delicious, and a great deal of wine was imbibed following a great deal of gin. Sonia had adjourned to the sitting room, where she was making a fuss of Barney, and left Lucy in the kitchen to help Kate load the dishwasher.

The wine seemed to have aided Lucy, in particular, in opening up considerably. As she passed plates to Kate, she remarked, 'I'm so glad I didn't need Guy's loan, and now I've been able to pay it back. But, do you know, I'm not sure he even realised what it was for! He's such a sweetie!'

Kate stiffened. 'Lucy, are you telling me that you've paid Guy back however much it was that he lent you?'

'Yes, I have. But what's it to do with you, if you don't mind my asking?'

'The money isn't important; what's important is that Roly's left because he had no idea why Guy had taken so much money out of their joint account, and he thought that Guy might have used it to bribe Bacon. And Guy, if you aren't already aware, is *devastated*! Theirs was a real love match, you know.'

'Ouch!' Lucy looked genuinely astonished. 'I really didn't know that was why Roly had taken off. But it would explain why Guy has been looking so awful recently. There shouldn't be a problem now that the money's back in the account.'

'I'm not sure about that,' Kate said. 'I think you need to get in touch with Roly and tell him exactly what's been going on, and how Guy wasn't really clued up as to what precisely the money was for. And, most importantly, stress how desolate he is now.'

'Do you really think I should, Kate?'

'Oh, I do,' Kate replied with feeling.

Sonia, at least, seemed extremely happy. 'I'm *so* looking forward to working in New York,' she said, the second they joined her in the sitting room, 'and I've just got to get this bloody film in the can as soon as possible, because I want to be over there by the middle of November.'

'What's happening in New York?' Kate asked.

'It's a documentary about Brits living in the States,' Sonia replied, 'and I really want to do it. They've got to have solved these bloody murders by then surely?'

'Too damn right!' agreed Lucy. 'I'm desperate to get back to

London.' She turned to Kate. 'Your husband's a detective, isn't he? Does he have some idea who killed these two?'

'He's an *ex*-detective,' Kate pointed out, 'and no, he has no idea.'

'Well I'm only delighted somebody managed to kill Wyngarde,' Sonia said, 'because otherwise I wouldn't be going to New York.' She swigged some more wine.

'Really? Why's that?' Kate asked.

'Because Wyngarde was originally the producer of the American programme, and he was doing his best to block me from directing it, even though the studio wanted me,' Sonia said. 'We had a mutual hate-filled relationship, you see. But Karl Endberg's taken over as producer now, and he got in touch immediately.'

This didn't add up, Kate thought as she refilled the wine glasses.

'But, Sonia,' she said, 'how come you were working with Wyngarde here, on *Pengorran's Revenge*?' Would Sonia confirm what Jilly had told her?

Sonia leaned forward across the table, almost toppling her wine glass as she did so. 'Oops!' She retrieved the glass in a practised way, just in time, and took an enormous slurp. 'Because the money was so good! He wrote *Pengorran's Revenge*. Did you know that?'

Kate nodded.

'It was his bloody vanity project! Lousy script, and no one else wanted to direct the damned thing. No one!'

'Really?' Kate said.

'Yes, really. Believe me, he tried just about every damn director on the *planet*! Nobody wanted to know.'

'But you agreed?'

Sonia gave a little hiccup and drained her glass. 'Yes, I agreed to do it. And do you know why?'

Kate certainly did want to know why and hoped Sonia was

about to tell her. 'I'd had a couple of years off, because my daughter had problems. My marriage wasn't great and I wanted to get away for a while. So, a couple of months on the Cornish coast – what wasn't to like? And he was paying over the top because he was determined to get a director, although I daresay the lazy bastard could have directed it himself.' She smiled. 'And there were a few details I wanted to attend to.'

'Were there?'

'Yes.' She nodded. 'That man was a sexual predator, Kate. A bad lot. The first one I knew about was a young actress. She couldn't have been more than sixteen or seventeen, and he abused her.' Sonia sighed deeply. 'She was probably flattered that he fancied her, poor kid. Rumour has it, he got her pregnant then dumped her, and shortly afterwards she took her own life. *That's* the kind of man we're talking about.' Sonia shook her head slowly. 'Let's not talk about the bastard any more, because it's been such a lovely evening, and that meal was delicious, Kate, by far the best since I came down here.'

'Absolutely,' Lucy agreed. She looked like she might fall asleep any minute, but, nevertheless, she groped around for her glass and glugged some more.

Kate had been careful not to drink too much herself, and she was determined to try to extract some more information from Sonia before they left.

'Well it certainly couldn't have been easy working with Wyngarde then?' she tried again.

'You're right, it wasn't. I did my best to try to improve his bloody awful script, but he wasn't having it. I can't pretend to be sorry he's dead.'

'Me neither,' said Lucy.

Sonia glanced at her watch. 'We've had a lovely evening, Kate, but it's time we left. I'm going to call the cab.'

She produced a phone from the pocket of the kaftan. As she

waited for a reply, she said, 'We must reciprocate. You and Woody must join us for a meal one evening at the Atlantic.'

She then ordered the cab, and both women got unsteadily to their feet. Kate watched them leave, still no nearer to discovering the truth behind Wyngarde's demise...

THIRTY-EIGHT

Kate cleared up, sat down and seriously considered abandoning The List. She'd all but eliminated both Lucy and Guy on account of what she'd learned from Lucy, who'd been so honest, and freely admitted she'd planned to kill Wyngarde, if only she'd got there first.

She couldn't, or wouldn't, believe that Angie was in any way involved, and so that left one obvious suspect, particularly after this evening's conversation: Sonia herself.

Like all the suspects, historically Sonia had good reason to hate Wyngarde, but, unlike everyone else, she had an up-to-date motive as well – Sonia badly wanted to work on this documentary in New York, and the only person standing in her way had been Wyngarde. She freely admitted she was glad he was dead. It just had to be her.

Kate sighed, switched off the lights and went to bed.

Woody arrived home just after ten o'clock the following morning. He'd had a great time, having encountered some of his old buddies, including a couple of guys from the Met who'd retired to the West Country. They'd had a four-course dinner and drank a great deal of wine and beer.

'We decided we should do another event with wives,' Woody continued, 'sometime before Christmas.'

'Oh good,' Kate said vaguely.

'I'm real sorry I left you on your own last night, but you ladies would not have appreciated some of the conversation that went on! My God, some of the stories...! Anyway, did you have a nice, early night?'

Kate took a deep breath. 'Not exactly, no. I did some entertaining.'

'And who exactly did you entertain?'

'Well after you left, I popped in to the Atlantic—'

'Now, why would you do that?' Woody looked suspicious.

'Having recommended Sonia to stay there, I thought it only polite to make sure that she was satisfied.'

Woody narrowed his eyes. 'And is she? Satisfied?'

'Oh yes, and so is Lucy Moore. But the food's quite expensive, so I thought I'd invite them both down for some supper. We had fish pie, followed by apple crumble and, if I say so myself, it went down very well.'

'Very nice too,' said Woody.

'Yes, it was.'

'So no doubt you've solved this case then, Miss Marple?'

'Not quite,' Kate said, smiling, 'but I think I may be a little closer to solving it, if my hunch is right. Just for a start, I think we can eliminate Guy and Lucy.'

Woody looked at her with raised eyebrows. 'Really?'

Kate went on to tell him about Lucy approaching Bacon with a fistful of money – some of it borrowed from Guy – to bribe Bacon to load the gun and kill Wyngarde. She had not, Kate said, been the first to approach him and was told that he'd received a better offer from someone else. 'She did say that she was relieved to have avoided life imprisonment,' Kate added.

'I wouldn't count on that,' Woody said drily.

'Why not?'

'Sometimes, my love, you are extremely gullible, that's why.' Woody sat down with a mug of coffee.

'But surely...' Kate began.

'Kate, you only have *her* word for the fact that he'd had a better offer. I'm not saying she was lying, but she could be, to put you off the scent.'

Kate groaned. 'I suppose you're right, but I still think she was telling the truth. And I'm pretty certain that the killer is Sonia Somerfield. Did I tell you she had an offer to work in New York?' Kate proceeded to inform him about how Wyngarde had tried to block Sonia from getting the job. 'She's the only person, Woody, who has an up-to-date reason, as well as a historical one, for getting rid of Wyngarde. Don't you agree?'

'Does Charlotte know about this up-to-date reason of Sonia Summerfield's?'

'I don't know. I don't suppose Sonia would think to tell her.'

'Well, as you think it's such a factor, don't you think you should inform her?'

'I suppose I should... Do you think this makes Sonia a more likely suspect?'

'I agree she's a suspect, but so is everyone else. I'm damn sure Charlotte would have charged someone before now if she had any kind of likely proof.'

'When you say "everyone else", are you including Angie and Fergal?' Kate asked anxiously.

'Kate,' Woody said, in a tone that indicated his patience might be becoming sorely stretched, '*you* are a suspect. *I* am a suspect. *Angie* and *Fergal* are suspects. Possibly half of the film crew are suspects for all I know, as well as Sonia Somerfield, Lucy Moore and Guy of course. I've no doubt Charlotte is working hard to get this thing solved, but she must lack the necessary proof to make any arrest.'

'So we're really no further on in trying to solve this thing?' Kate said.

'We are no further on in trying to solve this thing,' Woody confirmed.

Maybe not, Kate thought, *but I'm not about to give up yet!*

THIRTY-NINE

Since Kate had stopped being an extra, the Tinworthy public, for the moment at least, had stopped coming into the surgery with imaginary complaints in order to badger her for information about the murders. Thus, after an uneventful day at work on Monday, Kate made her customary visit to The Old Locker on her way home. She found both Angie and Fergal looking remarkably cheerful.

As Angie placed a coffee in front of her, Kate remarked, 'You're both looking very chirpy today!'

'Well,' said Angie, 'that's because we've reached a decision. First of all, we've decided to get married on the third of November, at the registry office, followed by a blessing at St Swithin's afterwards, because Fergal is Catholic so we thought that would be nice, and then a reception at The Atlantic. Surely to God, even Charlotte Martin will have solved this damned crime by then.'

'Let's hope so. Great news,' Kate concurred.

Angie glanced across at Fergal, who was on the phone. 'He's been talking to the brewery for ages,' she said. She leaned closer to Kate. 'He found the *money*!'

'He did?' Kate asked.

'What happened was that the plastic bag split and the liner got all messy, so Fergal lifted out the liner to clean it, and there it was!'

'I suppose there was always a danger of that happening,' Kate said.

'Yes, but it's usually me who empties it,' said Angie, 'so it really was a case of Sod's Law. Furthermore, Fergal almost chucked the money out because I'd put the notes in a plastic bag and he thought it was more rubbish! Can you believe it?'

'Yes,' replied Kate, 'I can. But at least you seem very cheerful about it.'

'Well, you see, I told Fergal it was for my ring, but, in the meantime, I'd been doing a bit of thinking.' Angie nodded sagely as if discussing the international monetary fund.

'And?'

'And I thought to myself, do I really need a ring? We've no idea when we're going to be able to get to Plymouth and, anyway, I have several nice rings, including George's, and when do I ever wear them? So we've paid the cash back into the bank, and we're going to put that thousand aside for our honeymoon in New York!'

'Yes, I suppose that's a good idea,' Kate said, her mind in a whirl with visions of herself and Woody spending a week toiling in this place, despite what he'd said.

'But you're not to worry,' Angie added, 'because I *know* what you're thinking! You think you're going to be here running the place, but Emma has a new boyfriend called Carlos, currently working in the Atlantic Hotel, and they want to get some experience of running a little business like ours before they open their own one, in the spring, in Tavistock.'

'That's certainly a relief,' Kate admitted.

'So keep the third of November free,' said Angie, 'and you can be my maid of honour.'

'How could I refuse? You've certainly made all your arrangements!'

'Yes, we have. We're going to have a wonderful week in New York, where we can stay with Fergal's brother, see the sights and the lights, and even do some early Christmas shopping. Another coffee?'

'No thanks,' Kate replied, sliding off the bar stool. 'I'd best be getting home.'

Woody, who'd become quite a chef, was preparing dinner, so Kate was able to sit down with a glass of wine and listen to his experiences with the new tenants of his cottage across the valley.

'Said they didn't realise it would be halfway up a hill and, apparently, the husband's got a dodgy leg.' Woody shook his head. 'The photograph clearly *shows* it's halfway up a bloody hill, and it's mentioned in the blurb! And they've got a car anyway, so what the hell are they going on about?'

Kate nodded in sympathy. 'Some people are *born* awkward! I have some interesting news though.'

'Yeah?'

'Yes, Angie and Fergal are tying the knot on the third of November, followed by a week in New York, *and* they've found someone to run The Locker!' She proceeded to tell him about Emma and the boyfriend.

'Well that's something,' Woody agreed. 'So they've managed to find enough money for a trip to New York?'

'Yes, the money Angie had hidden in the bottom of the kitchen bin to pay for her ring. She's decided she doesn't need a ring after all, so she's paid the money back into the bank.'

'Hmm,' said Woody, busying himself with removing a pot from the oven.

Kate had expected more of a reaction. 'You don't sound wildly thrilled.'

Woody shut the oven door. 'If I was in charge of this case, Kate, I'd be asking myself why Angie withdrew a thousand pounds *before* the death of Paul Bacon and then paid it back in *afterwards*.'

Kate was flabbergasted. 'You're insinuating that Angie withdrew that money to pay Paul Bacon?'

'I'm not insinuating anything, Kate. I'm stating a fact.'

'No one in their right mind would accept a mere thousand pounds to kill someone surely?'

'No, they wouldn't. But it could have been an instalment, a final instalment even, and now it's no longer needed.'

'An instalment? You honestly think Angie had been dishing out thousands?'

Woody shrugged. 'From a police point of view, she could have been.'

Kate gasped. 'But Angie doesn't have that kind of money, Woody!'

'How do you know?'

'Because she's always had to be careful with money, and you were there yourself when she said they could probably only afford a weekend in Paris or Rome.'

'Yes, but that doesn't mean she didn't have the money. It could mean that they wanted the money for other purposes.'

Kate stared in horror at her husband. 'Are you telling me that you think she was emptying her bank account to pay Bacon to kill Wyngarde?'

Woody put his hand on her shoulder. 'Calm down, Kate! I didn't say that at all. I said "for other purposes", and I meant just that. But I'm looking at it from Charlotte's point of view because she'll be naturally suspicious. She may even be able to access Angie's bank account, which, frankly, you can't.'

. . .

Kate refused to believe that Angie was paying the armourer in instalments; the whole idea was utterly bonkers! Why would Angie want to kill anyone with whom she was having an ongoing relationship and who'd given her a part in his film? She just wouldn't! In fact, Angie couldn't kill the proverbial fly! And how ridiculous it was to even contemplate Angie having the kind of money required to hire an assassin! But if Kate thought it impossible, why had she not crossed her sister's name off The List?

Of course, Kate realised, she really had no idea how much was in Angie's bank account, because they'd never shared such details. Her sister had inherited not only from her late husband but had also benefitted from his mother in France, who'd died quite recently. Angie had spent a fair bit of money renovating The Old Locker, but...

Kate hated herself for even *thinking* along these lines. She wasn't feeling particularly well disposed towards Woody either for putting the idea into her mind in the first place. But Woody was, of course, first and foremost a detective, trained to think logically and suspect everyone until he had good reason not to.

Which was precisely what Charlotte Martin would also be thinking.

FORTY

Something was nagging at the back of Kate's mind, and it concerned her last visit to Jilly in the wardrobe trailer. Jilly had begun to say something about Sonia, and then stopped, claiming it wasn't important. Kate should have questioned that, made her say what she'd been going to say, because every thought, every idea and every recollection was crucial at this time.

There was only one problem: Kate wasn't allowed to leave Tinworthy. And she could hardly ask to accompany Sonia and Lucy under police escort! Even if she could, it would mean spending the day there until such time as filming finished and the two women were returned to the hotel. However, Kate did need to be there at some point during filming hours because she wouldn't have a clue where to find Jilly other than in the wardrobe trailer. There was no two ways about it – she'd have to break the rules and, somehow or other, get herself to Port Petroc.

Kate decided she'd tell Woody she was taking Barney for his walk up to the woods behind the church in Middle Tinworthy, and afterwards she'd risk driving on from there. Surely the police weren't checking every single car leaving Tinworthy! Of course they weren't, because the vast majority of Tinworthy residents had had nothing to do with the film and were perfectly free to go wherever they wished. She just had to look like one of them. It was certainly worth the risk if it meant finding out who the killer was and getting Angie off the hook once and for all.

On Wednesday morning, Kate took Barney for a long walk through the woods in the hope that he'd be tired and would sleep in the car while she visited the film site. The leaves were beginning to fall now, and they crunched underfoot as she and Barney walked.

The walk completed, and with Barney on the rear seat, Kate set off in her red Fiat and, for the umpteenth time, rued the day she'd chosen red, which was always more noticeable than the dark colours and the silvers when she was trying to keep a low profile. Her heart lurched every time she saw a parked car alongside the road – could it be the police?

However, the journey was uneventful, and it was with some relief that Kate parked in the makeshift car park in the field overlooking Port Petroc cove. Fortunately, Barney looked happy to sleep in the back of the car, so Kate made her way towards the wardrobe trailer, praying that Jilly was still there.

For a moment, her heart almost stopped when she entered the trailer and found a tall, red-haired girl hanging up some costumes.

'Where's Jilly?' Kate asked.

'She'll be back in a moment,' the girl said. 'She had to go down on set because one of Lucy Moore's costumes has split.'

Kate wondered if her fish pie and apple crumble were guilty of making Lucy's seams part company, given that Lucy had eaten much more than she usually did.

It was ten minutes before Jilly finally came through the door.

'Hey, what are *you* doing here?' she asked.

'I needed to talk to you about something,' Kate replied. Then, indicating the red-haired girl, she added, 'Anywhere we can talk privately?'

'I'm just going,' said the girl and, with a couple of outfits over her arm, she made her way towards the door.

Jilly closed the door behind her. 'So what did you want to talk about?'

'This may sound strange,' Kate said, 'but, when we spoke last time, you said that, at first, you suspected the killer was Sonia. And then you seemed to remember something and stopped in the middle of whatever it was you were going to say.'

'Did I?' She shrugged.

'Yes, you did.' Kate gave her a hard stare. 'Do try to remember, Jilly, because it stuck in my mind that it could be important.'

Jilly hesitated. 'It might have been something Paul Bacon said one of the last times I saw him,' she admitted.

Kate realised she was holding her breath. 'And what was that?'

She sighed. 'Well we'd had a bit of a row, as you can imagine, after me not paying back the loan and everything. It was in The Pheasant that evening, and he was three sheets to the wind as usual.'

Kate nodded.

'And he was ranting on about what a cow I was, what a shitty lot everyone on the set was, and then he said something like, "I wish I'd never set eyes on that bastard who's made me a killer."'

Kate took a deep breath. 'Are you sure?'

'They mightn't have been his exact words, but that's more or less what he said – about wishing he'd never set eyes on the bastard. Now, that to me would mean a man, wouldn't it? I mean, Bacon wasn't sparing with his adjectives, and if it had been a woman, I think he'd have said "that bitch" or "that cow" – see what I mean?'

'Yes, I do see what you mean,' Kate replied, her thoughts in turmoil. 'And he definitely indicated that "the bastard" had made him a killer?'

Jilly nodded. 'So that was when I began to think it couldn't be Sonia – or Lucy.'

'I think you should tell the police about this, Jilly, because it could be very important. If it was a man, then that would halve the list of suspects. You're really sure it could be a man?'

'I think so. You see, when I challenged him about it, he *realised* he'd let it slip and made me promise never to tell anyone. And that was another reason why he agreed to forget the loan.' Jilly bit her lip. 'I think I'm able to break that promise now he's no longer here – what do you think?'

'I think you're right.' In fact, Kate could only think that, if what Jilly said was accurate, that meant the killer was likely to be either Fergal, Guy or, heaven forbid, Woody! She had to keep reminding herself that both she and Woody were still suspects in the eyes of the police. But if the person who *paid* Paul Bacon had *killed* Paul Bacon, Kate knew it couldn't possibly be Woody because he'd been with her the whole time after she'd left Bacon in the caravan.

As she drove home, Kate decided she wouldn't mention this visit to Woody. After all, she'd broken the rules by going to Port Petroc in the first place, and now that she had such a massive clue about the killer being male, she'd try to work it out for herself. Therefore, the first person she must try to eliminate from The List – again – would be Fergal.

FORTY-ONE

The following afternoon, Angie appeared at the door of Lavender Cottage.

'I've given myself a couple of hours off, and I wanted to show you these photos of Fergal's brother's place, where we're going to be staying when we go to New York,' she said, accepting a cup of tea from her sister.

Fergal's brother had plainly done a great deal better for himself than Fergal had, because the apartment that Angie was proudly displaying on her phone appeared to be very luxurious.

'What's his name, and what does he do?' Kate asked.

'He's Barry, and he's something or other in real estate, and this apartment is only a few minutes, on the subway, from the centre of Manhattan. Fergal hasn't seen him in years.'

'Well that sounds wonderful,' Kate said. It suddenly occurred to her that if Fergal really *was* the man who'd paid the armourer, they wouldn't be going to New York or anywhere else. 'Let's just hope that Charlotte Martin finds the killer before then,' Kate added lamely.

Angie sipped her tea. 'She must! But, God knows, it's taking her long enough. I'm only surprised that you haven't come up with a name yet, Miss Marple!'

Give me time, Kate thought as she smiled sweetly.

'So I need you to get a move on, so I can get married!' Angie said before she drained the rest of her tea and headed towards the door.

When Kate was clearing the tea things away, she spotted Angie's phone down the side of the sofa. She either hadn't put it away properly, or it had fallen out of her bag. Kate picked up the phone and stared at it for a moment. She was about to call Angie's landline to tell her, when a thought occurred. If she could access Angie's bank account, she would be able to see if that thousand-pound withdrawal was a one-off, or if it was one of several. Since theirs was now a joint account, and Fergal didn't appear to have any other money, it would be an indication, surely, of his innocence or otherwise.

Feeling extremely guilty, Kate sat down and gazed at the phone for a moment. Should she proceed to check her sister's bank account? It certainly wasn't something she'd normally dream of doing but surely it would be in Angie's interest now?

Having persuaded herself that it was, she then wondered how to access Angie's bank details. She found the banking app and wondered what the password might be. There was a chance it would probably be the same as all her other passwords: Cunningham. Cunningham was their mother's maiden name, and Angie had said she used it all the time because she could never remember anything else. It was worth a try.

Kate clicked on the app and waited. Finally, up came a request for the third letter, the sixth letter and the seventh letter. Counting them off on her fingers, Kate tentatively typed in the letters and waited anxiously. She couldn't believe it when the bank details came up on the screen. She hated herself for looking, and prayed no one would ever know, but this *had* to be in a good cause.

Kate looked rapidly down the list of payments, one eye on the door in case Angie realised she'd left her phone behind and came rushing back. Unsurprisingly, there were more payments out than there were payments in, so she was able to see straight away that the thousand pounds had been paid in very recently. It took much longer to carry on down to see when it had been taken out. Having found that, Kate carried on scrolling, on and on and on. There was no sign whatsoever of any further withdrawals, and Kate had reached three months back before she heard Woody's car in the drive.

Just to make sure, she locked herself in the toilet and checked another couple of months. Only the usual payments in and out. Sighing with relief, Kate switched off the app and the phone, and emerged into the kitchen.

'Had a visit from Angie this afternoon,' she said cheerfully after Woody had pecked her on the cheek, 'and she's left her phone behind. Would you like to see photos of Fergal's brother's apartment?'

Later, while Woody was watching football on TV, Kate went into the kitchen and took out The List from where she'd hidden it at the back of the tea-towel drawer.

Everything depended on Jilly's statement; had Bacon really said 'bastard'? Jilly wasn't the most reliable witness in the world, but she had been pretty definite about that. And Bacon had apparently admitted it to Jilly when she'd tackled him. Why, then, had Jilly not come out with this information before? She'd originally insisted it was Sonia, and then suspected Lucy, and now this... Surely, now that Bacon was dead, her promise not to tell was no longer valid? *After all*, Kate thought, *she's just told me.*

It was the only real clue Kate had. She could eliminate Fergal, and she could certainly eliminate her husband, so who was left if it was a man?

That only left Guy.

There followed another sleepless night. Now that Kate had eliminated Fergal, she was becoming increasingly concerned about Guy. Lucy had indicated that Guy had lent her the money she needed without being fully aware of what it was for, but was that likely? After all, Guy was a businessman, and nobody's fool.

As if he'd known he'd inhabited her dreams, Guy rang up the very next morning.

'Kate,' he said, 'do you fancy a drink at The Tinners' at lunchtime – my treat – today or tomorrow?'

Kate was taken aback by this unusual invitation. 'Well yes, Guy, of course...'

'Today then?'

She thought quickly. 'Yes, today's fine. I'll walk the dog up in the church woods and join you in the pub afterwards.'

'That's great. I take my lunch break between twelve and one, so how about I see you in there at twelve-fifteen?'

'Yes, fine.'

Guy had never invited her for a lunchtime drink before, so what on earth was that all about?

FORTY-TWO

While she and Woody were having breakfast, Woody asked, 'Are you up to something, Kate?'

Kate almost choked on her toast. 'Me? Of course not! Why do you ask?'

'You seem deep in thought a lot of the time, and I have a feeling you didn't sleep too well last night.'

'You're right,' Kate admitted, 'I didn't. Nevertheless, I am not *up to something*.'

'Hmm,' he said, studying her, 'not sure I believe you. Now you know I'm having my dental check-up today? Charlotte was gracious enough to give me special permission. What are your plans?'

'I thought I'd take Barney for a nice long walk and get some fresh air in my lungs so that, hopefully, I'll sleep better tonight.'

He was still regarding her with some suspicion when, an hour later, he got into his car and set off for Exeter.

That was the thing with Woody; he knew her so well, and he missed nothing. Kate made up her mind she'd tell him about Guy, anyway, later in the day. She'd make it sound as if she'd just bumped into him.

. . .

Barney liked pubs, and The Tinners' liked dogs, so, after their walk, Kate took him with her into the pub, where she found Guy already standing at the bar.

'What'll you have?' he asked.

'I'm not driving, so I'll have a gin and tonic please.'

'Shall I make that a large gin? You've not got far to stagger down the hill and, let's face it, pub measures are pretty stingy.'

Kate allowed herself to be persuaded to a large gin and tonic as they settled themselves at a table in one of The Tinners' many nooks and crannies. The tiny multi-paned window, next to where Kate was sitting, might well have had a view of the sea once, before they had built the estate of houses opposite. Kate noted that Guy seemed considerably more cheerful than he had when she saw him last.

'You're looking happier, Guy.' She clinked her glass against his.

'That's because I am.' Guy set his beer glass down on the table and wiped the foam from his lips with the back of his hand. 'First of all, Lucy has paid me back the money I lent her, so my bank balance is considerably happier too. She said she was very glad she hadn't needed my loan.'

'Did she ever tell you why she wanted the money?' Kate asked tentatively.

'She didn't tell me when she asked to borrow the money, but she seemed desperate so I lent it to her. She only told me what it was for when she paid me back,' Guy replied. 'She wanted to pay Bacon to load the gun in order to kill Wyngarde. But she was too late, and thank God for that! It would have broken my heart if she'd done it and been found guilty, although I can understand she wanted retribution for him crippling her father. If she'd told me what it was for, I'd have tried to talk her out of it. I would never have played a hand in allowing Byron's daughter to risk going to prison! That's not what he would have wanted.'

Kate nodded as she sipped her drink.

'But, most of all, I wanted to thank you, Kate. Roly got in touch with me not long after he'd left, and said he'd seen you and that you'd made him think twice about what he was doing. I was able to tell him about the loan, and that I didn't know what it was for when I lent Lucy the money and that it had been paid back into our account. So it's all right. And he's coming back.'

'I'm so glad I managed to persuade Lucy to contact Roly and tell him the truth.'

'So am I! And thank you so much!' He paused. 'Roly's always been impetuous, you know. He was quite convinced I was paying that armourer to kill Wyngarde! Which I suppose I was – indirectly.'

'You do realise that, if she'd succeeded, you'd have been an accessory?'

Guy considered. 'I suppose I would, but I genuinely didn't know when I lent her the money, although I doubt the police would have believed that. I'd have happily wrecked Wyngarde's hair, and taken a few nicks out of his neck, but I could never actually kill someone.'

'No, I don't suppose you could.' Kate was becoming more and more convinced that Guy was innocent, and more and more mystified about who Jilly's 'man' might turn out to be.

'So,' Guy continued, 'when Roly comes back, we'd like to treat you and Woody to a meal at The Greedy Gull, because that way you can have lots of drinks and then walk home afterwards.'

'Guy, that is so generous of you, but—'

'No buts,' insisted Guy.

. . .

Roly, Kate discovered, came back on the Saturday. On Sunday, Guy rang up and asked if he and Roly could treat them to that meal in The Greedy Gull on Monday evening. 'I know you work Mondays,' he said to Kate, 'and so I thought it would be nice if you didn't have to cook in the evening.'

Kate was delighted, Woody less so.

'Do we *have* to go?' he asked.

'Of course we do!' Kate looked at him in amazement. 'It's a lovely gesture and it's because I had that chat with Roly and then Lucy, which apparently saved their relationship.'

Woody grinned. 'Are you setting yourself up as a relationship counsellor then?'

Kate laughed. 'Just another string to my bow! I may take that up when my Miss Marple talents fade.' She sighed. 'I'm beginning to think they're fading fast, because I'm damned if I know who did these killings. Anyway, don't you *want* to go?'

Woody sighed. 'It's just that Chelsea are playing...'

'You can watch it on catch-up when we get home,' Kate said firmly.

When they first arrived at The Greedy Gull, Kate was astonished to see Fergal, of all people, working behind the bar, and there was no sign whatsoever of Des.

'Fergal! What on earth are you doing here?' Kate asked as soon as she spotted him, leaving the others to sort out a table.

Fergal finished serving some drinks to a group of youngsters and made his way to where she was standing.

'It's my night off, believe it or not, so I thought I'd come up for a quiet drink – would you believe?'

Yes, that she could believe. What she couldn't believe was that Des would leave Fergal in charge behind his bar. 'So where's Des?'

'Good question. Very depressed apparently. Doesn't want

to face the public, can't cope any more. Poor old Madge was going crazy when I came in, trying to serve drinks and sort out food. What else could I do?'

'Oh, Fergal, that's so kind of you!' Kate realised she seriously needed to chat with Des to make an appointment to see the doctor, because it was obvious he was in need of antidepressants.

Guy had appeared at her side. 'Don't let her pay for any drinks,' he said to Fergal, 'because this is my treat.'

'Talk later, Fergal,' Kate said, patting his arm, as she went to join the others at their favourite window table.

'What the hell is Fergal doing behind the bar?' Woody asked. 'Don't tell me he and Angie are taking over The Gull as well!'

'Des isn't too well,' Kate replied briefly, 'and Madge was having a problem on her own.'

At this point, Guy returned with a couple of bottles of wine, with which Kate and Woody toasted Guy and Roly's renewed relationship.

Apparently Roly had thought about what Kate said all the way to Brighton.

'I used to love Brighton,' he said, 'but suddenly I realised I didn't want to be there any more. I almost got straight back in the car and came home to Cornwall there and then! However, I was too tired to contemplate doing anything and decided I needed a good night's sleep and then see how I felt in the morning. Then I got a call from Lucy. She told me about your chat regarding Crispin Wyngarde, and how you'd persuaded her to tell me about the loan, and how Guy had no idea what she wanted the money for.'

'I called him in the morning,' Guy said, 'to tell him about the money and everything. But Lucy had already told him. It was all a massive misunderstanding really.'

They gazed fondly at each other before Roly said, 'Well we must order some food. What's the steak like here?'

'Excellent,' Woody confirmed, and Kate nodded.

'I'll never understand,' he said, looking across at Fergal as Guy got up to order four steaks, 'why people who run bars spend their precious evenings off visiting other people's pubs.'

'Just as well he did,' Kate said, watching Fergal hard at work, and much busier than he would be in The Old Locker. She decided she'd pop in after work the next day and try to persuade Des to make an appointment to see the doctor, and to have a chat with Madge, who must be worried sick.

'I've never known Des to be like this before,' Kate remarked to Woody as they walked home.

'He's not been happy since the night of Bacon's killing,' Woody added.

'Don't forget it was Des who had to break into the caravan the next morning and find him dead like that,' Kate said, 'which couldn't have been a pleasant experience, and it's obviously affected him.'

'Hmm, I think you're right. Poor old Des.' Woody said thought-fully. 'Perhaps it's time he did retire, although I'd hate to see him go.'

'I feel sorry for Madge too, because it can't be any fun trying to run a pub single-handed – drinks and food – and worrying about Des as well.'

'I've known Des for a good ten years now and don't think he has a history of depression,' Woody said, 'but I guess it can come on at any time.'

As they arrived back at Lavender Cottage, Kate remem-bered something. 'A few weeks ago, Madge started to tell me something while Des was out, but then he came back and she stopped abruptly. Perhaps she'd been going to tell me he'd had problems in the past.' She wondered if it would be a good idea to have a look through his old notes at the medical centre to see if she could get to the root of his difficulties.

'In that case,' Woody said, 'I suggest you have a word with her, woman to woman, and persuade her to persuade him to get some help. I'm sure your Doctor Ross could prescribe something to get him up and running again, or else refer him to somebody who could.'

'I'll see what I can do,' Kate said.

The following day, when Kate got home from work, she had every intention of having a cup of tea and then wandering down to The Greedy Gull to have a word with either Des or Madge, depending on who was behind the bar. Woody had gone seafishing with a friend who had a new motorboat and didn't expect to be back until around seven o'clock. They were keeping within the Tinworthy fishing limits, so he couldn't be accused of leaving the area.

Kate had just kicked off her shoes, filled the kettle and switched it on, when there was a knock on the door.

'Fergal!' Kate was surprised, to say the least, because Fergal wasn't one for social calls.

He looked agitated. 'Can I have a word, Kate?'

'Of course. Come in! I was just about to make some tea.'

He gave a semblance of a smile. 'You might need something stronger.'

Kate felt some stirrings of panic. 'Why, what's wrong? Is Angie OK?'

'Yes, yes, Angie's fine,' Fergal reassured her. 'She's busy on the internet trying to find an outfit for the big day. Emma's helping out at The Locker, but it's quietened down now anyway.'

Kate placed a mug of tea in front of him on the kitchen table and sat down opposite, looking at him expectantly.

Fergal took a sip. 'I had a long chat with Madge last night when we were clearing up.'

'Poor Madge. She was probably glad to have someone to talk to.'

'I learned some very interesting facts,' Fergal continued.

'About what?'

'About Des. Did you know that this is his second marriage?'

Kate shrugged. 'No, I didn't, but I'm not altogether surprised, since just about everyone I know has been married before.'

'Well Des was married years ago, when he was young. And he had a daughter.'

Kate was amazed now. 'How come he never talks about her?'

'Because she died.'

'Oh, Fergal, that's *awful*! Poor, poor Des! I had no idea!'

'She was only seventeen, and she hanged herself.'

FORTY-THREE

Kate felt her eyes fill with tears. 'Oh my God!'

Fergal drained his tea. 'Seemingly she was mesmerised by some film producer. According to what Des told Madge, once he knew he'd got her pregnant, he completely lost interest in her. She couldn't face life with the fact that, not only was she pregnant, but he'd dropped her, and her hopes of an acting career were over.'

'I can't believe this. That poor girl.' Kate wiped her eyes. 'You're right, I do need something stronger. Shall we have a brandy?' She got up and withdrew the brandy bottle from the cupboard, poured two glasses and handed one to Fergal.

They both sipped silently for a moment.

'You're probably thinking what I'm thinking?' Fergal said.

'Yes.' Kate took another sip. 'Wyngarde. But we've no proof.'

'No,' Fergal agreed, 'we haven't.'

'What does Madge think?'

Fergal shook his head. 'I don't really know, but she did seem very, very worried.'

'I'm not surprised. What can we do?'

'Well I've offered to help out again tonight, so maybe I can find out some more to substantiate our suspicions.'

'Be careful though, Fergal,' Kate advised, 'just in case.'

'Oh I will,' Fergal replied, gulping the remainder of his brandy. 'You know me: I can charm the birds from the trees, so I'll be subtle. Now I'd better get going.'

After he'd gone, Kate sat down and tried to digest what she'd just been told. Surely Des Pardoe had every reason in the world to want to get his revenge on the producer – who must surely be Crispin Wyngarde? Of course there was no proof because Paul Bacon could tell no one now who'd paid him. Had Des gone out to the caravan that night after everyone had left? Had Paul told him he'd be going to the police station the next day? It was all beginning to add up.

Kate felt sick.

Woody returned with two beautiful sea bass, which he then gutted, cleaned and filleted at the sink while Kate told him about Fergal's visit and the tragic tale of Des's daughter.

He stopped and turned round to face Kate, the knife still in his hand. He looked horrified. 'I know what it might look like,' he said after a moment, 'but Des is no killer.'

Kate still hadn't told him about her visit to Jilly and Jilly's insistence that the killer was a man.

'Maybe not,' she agreed, 'but it's one thing to physically kill someone, close up, with a knife or a gun or something, and altogether different, and less personal, to pay someone else to do it. And let's face it, even Paul Bacon didn't get his hands dirty.'

Woody went back to his task and patted the fish fillets dry on some kitchen paper before turning to face Kate. 'Yeah,' he said, 'I get what you're saying, but I'm still convinced Des couldn't do such a thing. And it would mean that he'd killed Bacon as well.'

'Listen, Woody. You have two daughters, right? Try to imagine one of them – Donna, for instance, as she's in the business – being treated like that by Wyngarde. I bet *you'd* feel like murdering the bastard!'

'I probably would,' he agreed, 'but how long ago was that? Why would Des wait for what must be around twenty years to kill the man responsible for his daughter's death? Doesn't make sense.'

'Maybe this was his first opportunity,' Kate suggested. 'Maybe he's been waiting for just the right moment. Maybe he could hardly believe his luck when Wyngarde landed almost on his doorstep?'

Woody sat down. 'What happens now?'

'Fergal's working there again tonight, and he's going to put some feelers out.'

'He should be careful,' Woody said, 'just in case poor old Des really is a killer.'

'Should we be telling Charlotte Martin this?'

'Let's wait until we know a little more.'

It was exactly nine minutes past five on Wednesday morning when Kate was wakened by her phone ringing.

'What the...?' muttered Woody.

Kate rolled over, rubbing sleep from her eyes, and picked up the phone. 'Angie! For God's sake, do you know what *time* it is?'

'I know, I know, but I'm desperately worried!' Angie's voice kept rising. 'Fergal hasn't come *home!*'

'Well he was working late at The Gull, so he's probably asleep there.'

'But he *always* comes home! It's not as if we had a row or anything!'

'Angie, what exactly do you expect me to do about it at this hour of the morning? I expect he'll be asleep in his car! It wouldn't be the first time!'

Woody switched the light on.

'But *why* wouldn't he have come home?' Angie persisted.

'Perhaps Madge asked him to stay because she was worried about Des,' Kate continued, looking at Woody and feeling more and more anxious. They'd both been worried about Fergal last night, and it was beginning to look as if they had good reason to be, but she didn't want to tell her sister that. 'Look, Angie, he'll probably crawl through the door around seven o'clock.'

'Do you really think so?'

'Of course I do. I'll pop round later and make sure everything's OK.' She switched off her phone and stared at Woody.

'I take it Fergal hasn't come home?' Woody asked.

'It wouldn't be the first time,' Kate said.

'No, and he was working at The Gull last night,' Woody said, 'so he probably got pissed and slept in his car. Again.'

'Exactly, but she seems very worried about it,' Kate said, feeling increasingly uneasy. 'I'm wide awake now, so I think I'll go downstairs and make myself a hot drink then take Barney down to The Gull to check if he is sleeping in his car.'

'Good idea,' said Woody, 'and I'm coming with you.'

They both hurriedly got dressed, putting on warm jumpers and stout footwear.

As they were dragging on their coats, Kate said, 'Surely there isn't any need for Angie to worry?' She said it more in hope than expectation.

'Weren't you listening to me last night when I warned you about Fergal needing to be careful?' Woody asked, sounding almost angry. Kate knew it was anxiety.

'But you know what Fergal's like,' she said. 'He's a free spirit and he doubtless imbibed countless free spirits from happy customers in the bar last night. He could have fallen asleep and Madge offered him a bed for the night. Or, more likely, he staggered round to his own car, knew he wasn't fit to drive and fell asleep in the driving seat. That was probably around midnight and he wouldn't have phoned Angie in case she was asleep. There might be no need to worry at all really.'

'I hope you're right, Kate! I hope we are overreacting, but your sister would never forgive us, and we would never forgive ourselves, if we went back to bed and hoped for the best.' He handed her a torch.

'Thanks.' In spite of her fears, Kate was almost amused that it was Woody who was suddenly taking the lead. He wasn't telling her not to get involved now!

Just as they were walking out the door, Angie rang again.

'There's still no sign of him,' she told Kate, her voice wobbling.

'Which just means he's fast asleep somewhere,' Kate said consolingly, hoping she sounded convincing. 'Woody and I are going to take Barney for an early walk and see if there's any sign of him.'

'I want to come with you!' Angie shouted.

'No, don't do that,' Kate soothed. 'You need to be there for when he gets back.'

'OK,' Angie replied, 'but since you're up, would you mind coming down?'

'We'll be with you in half an hour or so, although I'm sure he'll probably be back by then.'

'Well done, Kate,' Woody said as she came off the phone. 'If there is a problem, the last thing we need is Angie in hysterics.'

They made their way slowly down the lane to The Gull.

'There's his car,' Woody said, shining his torch towards the far end of the car park, where it was hidden away in a corner.

The torchlit trees cast eerie shadows and Kate shuddered – and not with cold. Nevertheless, she felt relieved.

'If he'd taken his car for such a short journey, surely that meant it was his intention all along to sleep in the car and not get home in the early hours and wake Angie up.'

'Possibly,' Woody said.

They made their way towards the car, Kate happy in the knowledge that they would find Fergal fast asleep inside.

But the car was empty.

Kate felt a jolt of fear but was determined not to think the worst just yet. 'He must be asleep inside the pub then,' she said bracingly. 'There's no sign of life there yet, so we best go to try to reassure Angie.'

Woody said nothing as they carried on walking.

On arrival at The Old Locker, they found a distraught Angie sitting at one of the tables, her head in her hands, a glass of gin in front of her. 'Have you seen him?'

Kate had to admit that there was no sign of him, including in his car. Despite how early it was in the morning, she decided not to comment on Angie's gin.

'If he was drunk or exhausted, Kate, he'd have gone to sleep in his car. He's always said it's really comfortable.'

'Perhaps he felt ill or something, and Madge persuaded him to sleep it off in the pub,' Woody suggested.

'Or maybe Des was being a bit difficult and Madge wanted him to stay for a bit of support,' Kate added.

Angie held her gaze. 'It's just that I have a bad feeling about this,' she said gloomily. 'I didn't want him to go there last night again. What the hell's wrong with Des anyway?'

'He's been a bit strange ever since he discovered Paul Bacon dead in his caravan,' Kate replied.

'Maybe it's time he saw a doctor then,' said Angie. 'And if they need help at The Gull tonight, then Emma or someone can go, so Fergal can stay at home.' She paused. 'But where is he?'

'We'll call at The Gull on the way home, Angie,' Woody said.

'Would you?' Angie sounded relieved.

'Yes, we will,' Kate said. 'They should be awake by then, and I'll bet he's fast asleep, spreadeagled on Madge's settee.'

Angie's lip trembled. 'What if he's not there?'

'He's got to be there,' Kate said firmly, hoping she sounded more confident than she actually felt. 'If by any chance he isn't, we'll set off to look for him. Try not to worry, Angie.'

Kate and Woody made their way back up the lane. When they got to The Greedy Gull, Kate stopped and peered in through the window to see Madge polishing an array of brass knick-knacks on the bar top. The door was ajar.

'You wait here,' Kate told Woody. 'We don't want to worry Madge too much.'

'OK,' Woody agreed as Kate wandered in.

'Oh, hello,' said Madge. 'What brings you in here so early?'

'Angie rang me to say that Fergal didn't come home last night and I wondered if you'd seen him.'

Madge shook her head, 'No, I haven't seen him, not since last night. But I'm glad you're here: I'm proper worried cos I don't know where Des has got to. It's years since he's been on a binge and I'm wonderin' if that Fergal persuaded him to go on drinkin' somewhere. I don't know what to think, Kate.'

'I don't think they could have gone out on a binge because Fergal's car is still in the car park.'

Madge stopped polishing. 'He'll be asleep in his car then.' Madge looked relieved for a moment. 'I expect Des is in there too?'

Kate was becoming aware of a sinking feeling in her stomach. 'No, I've already looked in the car. Fergal isn't in there and neither is Des. I thought Fergal might be here? Had a few too many and zonked out on your settee?'

Madge shook her head. 'Oh no, m'dear, he ain't here. He was still around when I went to bed around quarter to twelve. He was ever so helpful, Kate, putting everythin' away, tidy like. To be honest, I don't know how I'd have managed without him last night.'

'Then where are he and Des, Madge?'

'Dunno, dear.' Madge's face became tense. 'You're gettin' me a bit more worried now.'

'When did you actually see Des last, Madge?'

'Well he came down ever so late, and he and Fergal were chattin' away. I left them to it, cos I was knackered.'

Kate's sense of foreboding was increasing by the minute. 'Don't worry, Madge. We'll find him.'

FORTY-FOUR

Woody had gone back to the far end of the car park and was inspecting the inside of Fergal's car as Kate walked over to him. 'He left it unlocked,' Woody said, 'as he always does. Any news?'

'Fergal and Des have both disappeared,' Kate announced.

'Disappeared?'

'Yes. Fergal isn't in The Gull. Madge is going frantic because there's no sign of Des either.'

'Well if they're both missing, it's a pretty good bet that, wherever they are, they're together,' Woody said.

Kate nodded. 'Fergal was still at The Gull just before midnight, when Madge went to bed, and he was chatting to Des apparently...' She paused. 'Woody, I'm so worried. If they're not in Fergal's car, and they're not in The Gull, then where the hell are they? You were the one who said Fergal should be careful.'

'Try not to worry,' Woody said. 'We'll find them.' He reached out and clasped Kate's hand. 'Perhaps Fergal started to walk home and fell asleep on the way?'

'It's only a ten-minute walk for goodness' sake! And what

about Des? Are they together somewhere, or what the hell's going on?'

Woody looked thoughtful. 'OK, I can see you're worried. They can't have gone that far, so we should find them in no time. Wait here a moment,' he instructed. 'I'm going to double-check with Madge to make certain there's still no sign of Des.'

Kate waited, feeling more and more tense as she watched the sun rise over Higher Tinworthy.

'Still no sign of Des,' Woody said as he returned. 'Madge told me the same as she told you – that they were together around midnight, and that the two of them were deep in conversation about something.'

'I find that a bit worrying,' said Kate.

'Yes, it is,' Woody agreed, his face grim as they set off down the lane.

There were a couple of cottages further down, one of which was a holiday let and currently empty, and the elderly lady in the other one, still in her dressing-gown, confirmed that she'd seen or heard no one last night.

Kate looked up at the leaden sky and wondered if a storm was brewing. It was so quiet, it was eerie, as if the village was hardly alive.

'I really don't know what to say to Angie,' Kate remarked as they arrived down in the village, with the old grey stone bridge straight ahead. The road, at this point, veered round to the left, alongside the river, past the row of shops – including The Old Locker – towards the sea and the cul-de-sac at the end. To the right of the bridge was a well-worn footpath which followed the river inland for almost a mile. 'They surely wouldn't have gone along there,' Kate said, indicating the footpath.

'Why not? They must have gone *somewhere*. But more likely they went towards the sea or the cliffs. Look, I'll search the beach area and head towards the cliffs.' Woody hesitated.

'Have a quick stroll along the river, just in case. You know where I'll be, and call me if you find them.'

Kate thought that unlikely but, along with Barney, nevertheless set off along the path, soothed temporarily by the sound of the rush of water lapping against the stones in the middle of the river. At this point, the river was fairly shallow, but a little further on were a couple of deep pools, greatly favoured by local anglers.

It was as she approached the second pool that Kate saw the two men, one standing and one lying on the ground, on the bank. She felt as if icy fingers were creeping up her spine, followed by a moment of near paralysis, before the shock subsided and she could take a deep breath. Slowly, she approached Des, who was standing a little unsteadily, an empty whisky bottle on the ground beside him, and tried to pass him to get to Fergal.

'What's going on, Des? What's happened to Fergal? Why are you here? Everyone is worried sick!'

Des didn't move, apart from slowly, very slowly, shaking his head and holding out his arm to bar her way.

'Let me pass.'

Kate pushed past him. He tried to resist but stumbled aside. She bent down to tend to the crumpled form of Fergal. He was completely unconscious and had a nasty cut on the side of his head. Then, as she frantically tried to find a pulse, she became suddenly aware that Des had moved and was now towering over her.

'Leave him *alone!*' he growled.

Kate, aghast, had detected what she thought might just be the slightest indication of a pulse, and she turned Fergal onto his side, as well as she could, into the recovery position. Before she could do anything else, Des had grabbed her by the collar. Furious, she stood up to face him, at the same time digging her phone out of her pocket to call Woody and 999.

'No!' Des snarled.

'We have to get help for Fergal,' Kate said, bringing the phone to her ear. As she did so, his hand shot out against hers, and her phone flew into the depths of the water.

'Des!' Kate was now really afraid. Des wasn't exactly steady on his feet, but he was bigger than she was and he was in a strange, menacing mood. She tried to keep her voice from shaking. 'I have to get help for Fergal,' she repeated.

Barney began to growl then to bark frantically, jumping up against Des.

'No,' he said firmly.

But she could see that he was staggering slightly and she had to get past him somehow and go to find help. With all her strength, she pushed him backward. Des lost his balance completely and collapsed in a heap into the rough grass at the side of the path.

She was afraid to leave in case he recovered sufficiently to get up and – horror of horrors – perhaps tip Fergal into the water, since he seemed so determined that she not get help for him.

Des was now frantically struggling to get up, and she went back to check Fergal's pulse. It was there – faint but there. Kate breathed a quick sigh of relief before she looked down at Des, who'd given up the struggle and was now reclining against a network of brambles, and swearing loudly.

'Des,' Kate said, 'I've got to go and get help.'

'You're going nowhere,' snarled Des and reached inside his jacket. Suddenly there was a gun in his hand, and he was aiming it straight at Kate. His hand was firm considering how unsteady he was.

Kate felt a frisson of shock then utter fear. Surely Des would never shoot her! But he wasn't really the Des she knew. Barney began to bark again.

'Des, where did you get that gun from?'

He shrugged. 'Where do you think? I took it from Bacon's caravan when I was sure he was dead. Thought it might just come in handy.'

Kate decided to get straight to the point. 'You did it for your daughter didn't you, Des? I can understand that, and I might well have done the same in your shoes.'

He let out a strange sound, which Kate suddenly realised was a sob.

'How do you know what I did? Who told you?'

Kate wondered what she should say next. 'Des, I—'

But he obviously wasn't interested in her answer.

'She was my only child,' he interrupted, wiping away tears with the back of his hand. 'She was so beautiful. Don't know how I managed to produce anyone so lovely.'

'I wish I'd known her,' Kate said. 'You must have been very proud of her.' She saw that his hand which held the gun had now relaxed a little. She moved towards him, hoping she could grab the gun somehow.

Des noticed and suddenly the gun was pointing at her again, straight and steady.

'I was. Proud of her.' Des was staring at the river now, tears streaming down his cheeks. 'She was so bloody thrilled to get that part! I can remember her comin' in and tellin' us...' His voice broke again.

After a minute, he regained his composure. 'That bastard Wyngarde couldn't leave her alone! And she was that flattered; thought he was goin' to marry her, for God's sake!'

'He was a horrible man,' Kate said quietly.

'She was havin' his baby,' Des went on, 'and he didn't want to know. He'd found someone else by then.' He paused. 'Have you any idea what it feels like to walk into your shed and find your child hangin' there?'

'I don't even want to imagine it,' Kate replied, her eyes blurring with tears at the very thought of either of her sons becoming that desperate.

'I've dreamed for years of killin' the bastard but didn't know where to find him or – to be honest – how I'd do it. I'm not a violent man, see. And then the film company came to Port Petroc, along with Wyngarde, and I met Paul Bacon when he comes drinkin'. Ten thousand he charges me before he'll agree to do it, and another ten after Wyngarde's pronounced dead. That's all the money I had in the world, Kate. I got nothin' now. Nothin'. Becky's mother died of a broken heart, and Madge ain't goin' to want to know me after this.'

'Nonsense, Des. If she loves you, she'll stand by you. What you did was understandable after all,' Kate said in an effort to soothe and calm him.

He looked at her surprisingly steadily. 'Maybe killin' Wyngarde. But then Bacon's plannin' on goin' to the police, to tell them everythin'. And after all the money I paid him and he'd promised he wouldn't say nothin'. I had to stop him, Kate.'

There was a further silence for a moment before she asked, 'What about Fergal?'

'Fergal says he needs to clear his head and wants to go somewhere quiet where we can talk. Somewhere no one can hear us, he said. So that's why we went for this walk up-river. Nice 'n' quiet. No one around.'

In the distance, Kate thought she could hear the faint sound of footsteps some way off. Barney pricked up his ears and suddenly set off back down the path. 'What did he want to talk to you about, Des?'

'He twigged, see? I reckon Bacon maybe said somethin' to him, and then he tells me Madge has told him all about Becky, and he's put two and two together and all that. He goes on about goin' to the police and clearin' his own name, and I'm thinking to myself: is this bugger wantin' money from me too? I ain't got a penny left in the bank, and that's the truth, Kate.'

'So what did you do?' Surely, Kate thought, Fergal wasn't after money?

'I put some of them pills in his drink, so he was staggerin' around when we got here, and then I knocked him on the head. I can't have him goin' to the police but...' He slumped a little and his head fell to one side as his words tailed off.

Kate waited to see if he would say any more, but he remained silent.

'Is Madge aware of what's been going on?' she coaxed.

He shook his head sadly. 'No, and I don't want her bein' involved in any of this. None of it's her fault.' As he spoke, his head fell forward, but the gun remained steady.

'How much of that whisky have you had, Des? What else have you taken?'

He lifted his head and gave her a lopsided grin. 'I've drunk the whole bloody bottle and taken every one of them pills you gave me. And a few others to boot.' He was still holding the gun.

Kate was aware of the approaching footsteps coming at a run. She stiffened and moved towards Des to try to grab the gun.

FORTY-FIVE

'What the...?' For only a second, Woody stopped, before lunging forward and wresting the gun from Des's now drooping hand. Kate, trembling with a mixture of terror and relief, had never seen Woody move so fast. As he grabbed the gun, Des slumped backward.

Kate bent over him. 'Des, Des! Don't go to sleep...'

'Let him be,' Woody said, helping her up and hugging her tight. 'You didn't answer my calls...'

Kate crouched down by Fergal, who was now moaning quietly, while Woody dug out his phone and dialled the emergency services. 'Two men requiring urgent medical attention,' he said, before describing their exact location. He turned to Kate. 'There was no one around on the beach or the cliffs, so I tried to call you. I panicked when I couldn't get a connection.'

Kate smiled wearily and nodded towards the water. 'It's down there somewhere.'

'Was that Des?'

'That was Des, when I tried to phone for help.' She stood up and leaned against Woody. 'I think there's a possibility Des has taken a lethal dose of pills and alcohol.'

Woody wrapped his arms round her again. 'Why the hell did I let you come along here on your own?'

'Because we needed to cover the area, and I just happened to come across them,' Kate replied. 'I'm really worried about Fergal and his head injury.' Her eyes filled with tears. 'At first I thought he was dead, Woody, and it made me realise how fond I've become of him and what he means to Angie.'

'You've done all you can, my love. The paramedics will be here soon.'

They did arrive very quickly, along with Charlotte Martin, who appeared a little more dishevelled than usual. Perhaps, Kate thought, she'd been having a lie-in with her new doctor boyfriend and had to leave in a hurry.

Charlotte looked from Kate to Woody and back again. 'When did you last see these two?'

Woody explained about their visit to The Greedy Gull the night before last, when Fergal had been working behind the bar because there was no sign of Des, then about Fergal working there again last night, and Madge's reckoning that they must both have left the pub sometime after midnight.

Kate told her about Fergal's visit after that first night, and how Madge had told him all about Becky, Des's beloved daughter. She spoke of Angie's early-morning panic call because Fergal hadn't come home; how they'd walked down the lane, seen Madge in the pub and discovered that Des hadn't come home either; how they'd gone to search for the missing pair.

Once the two men, who were in a stable condition, had been carried along the path to the waiting ambulances, Kate raced to The Old Locker to alert Angie. She found her sister sitting at a table in the deserted bar, drinking what could only be more gin.

'Kate!' Angie stood up a little unsteadily, holding on to the back of the chair for support.

'It's OK, Angie,' Kate said in what she hoped was a soothing tone, 'we've found Fergal and he's on his way to hospital at this very minute. Now, calm down...' She took Angie's arm.

Angie, wild-eyed and wailing, was stumbling towards the door.

'We're going to take you to the hospital right now! No need to panic. He's had a nasty knock on the head, but I'm sure he'll be OK.' As she spoke, Kate was mentally crossing her fingers.

'I've got to see him *now*!' Angie yelled. She turned back to her gin, which she downed in one before sending the glass flying. 'My coat – where's my *coat*?'

Kate found the coat, and her bag and keys, then led her out to where Woody was sitting in his car, engine running.

Fergal, his head heavily bandaged, was drifting in and out of consciousness when they arrived at the hospital.

'Oh, Fergal!' Angie planted some gin-fuelled kisses over his mouth and nose. 'God, Fergal, you scared the hell out of me!'

He lay in solitary splendour in a small, square ward, the walls painted a strange shade of pale green and the floor covered in some high-gloss dark-blue linoleum. Outside the door, a policeman stood guard.

Kate decided to leave them in private and went out to talk to the nurse in charge.

'He seems a big, strong man,' the nurse said cheerfully, 'but we'll be keeping him in for a few days because you can never tell with a head injury.'

'You wouldn't know what happened to the other man, would you?' Kate asked hopefully.

The nurse shook her head. 'No, he was whisked away to Derriford, I think. Do you want me to check?'

'No, no,' Kate said hurriedly, 'because his wife should be with him now.'

The police had gone straight to collect her when the ambulances left. Kate didn't hold out too much hope for Des, and she wondered how poor Madge was coping.

Woody had just arrived outside the door of the ward – he'd dropped them off before going to find a parking space. 'Has he come round yet?'

'I think he's beginning to,' Kate replied, 'but I doubt you'll get much sense out of him for a while yet. I'll go check.'

Inside, she found Angie leaning over Fergal and talking softly. She turned when she heard Kate come in. 'He's prattling on about God knows what.'

Kate saw that he was awake and leaned over to see if she could decipher anything he was saying.

'The fecker tried to kill me,' Fergal said very clearly.

Afterwards, it was one of the worst weeks that Kate could remember. There were visits to the police station, Charlotte Martin giving them both the third degree, there was Angie going backward and forward to the hospital, and there was an utterly confused and distraught Madge, who didn't seem to know which way to turn.

The late-summer visitors were disappearing, and the village was in a state of complete shock. Des had been a popular landlord. Des *was* The Greedy Gull! Madge closed up the pub and went off to stay with friends in Plymouth, so she could visit Des more easily. Angie, with help from Emma, kept The Old Locker open, and everyone called in with cards and gifts for her to take to Fergal.

On the twenty-fifth of October, Des Pardoe passed away in Derriford Hospital, Plymouth, due to organ failure. The private funeral took place in Bristol, where Des hailed from originally, with only Madge and a few police officers in attendance.

'Did Madge *really* not know?' Kate asked for the umpteenth time as she and Woody sat down on either side of the wood burner that evening, a glass of wine in hand.

'I don't suppose we shall ever *really* know,' Woody replied soothingly. 'She was very loyal, so I wouldn't be altogether surprised if she had an inkling of what was going on.'

'Poor Madge.' Kate sipped her wine and found her eyes welling up again. 'And poor Des too. As parents, I suppose we can understand why he did what he did.'

'Unfortunately, it snowballed,' Woody remarked, 'and who knows what might have happened next?'

'What do you mean?'

'Well if Des realised Fergal knew, then he might have thought that Angie knew too, and even us.'

Kate gasped. 'You're not suggesting he'd have gone round killing everyone in sight?'

Woody shook his head. 'You never know what might happen when a man's as desperate as Des was.'

Kate sipped her wine, lost in thought.

FORTY-SIX

It was the day of Angie and Fergal's wedding. The couple had requested that only Kate and Woody be present at the registry office to witness their union, and that everyone else gathered at St Swithin's, at midday, for the blessing. As a tribute to her new husband's nationality, Angie had chosen an emerald-green dress and coat in which to get married.

'You'll give me away at the church, won't you, Kate?' she'd asked.

'But you'll already have been legally married!' Kate had protested.

Angie had insisted. 'Yes, but it'll look nice for all Fergal's family.'

Kate could hardly refuse such an honour, although she could recall many a time over the years when, driven mad by her sister's antics, she'd gladly have given her away to anybody.

St Swithin's Catholic Church was full to overflowing. Half of the village appeared to have shown up, along with a surprising number of Connollys. Angie had spent days trying to locate all of Fergal's far-flung siblings. Her success was such that not only had the brother in London and the sister in

Glasgow shown up, but also a brother from Dublin and one from Galway. Since each sibling came with a partner, that made eight noisy, non-stop chattering Connollys all embracing Angie and Fergal. The brothers living abroad had, unsurprisingly, declined the invitation.

They got to the church gate, Angie tottering on her four-inch emerald heels as they climbed out of the taxi and up the steps. As Kate took her sister's arm to steady her, she had an overwhelming compunction to giggle. She looked at Angie, who obviously felt the same and had already begun to shake with laughter. How crazy was this – two sisters, in their sixties, giggling like teenagers before entering a church for what was a solemn event.

'God, Kate, I've really got the giggles now!'

'Have you been on the gin already?'

'Just the one, honestly!' She met Kate's eye and tried to straighten her face. 'Could this be the daftest thing I've ever done?'

'Probably,' agreed Kate, and they both dissolved into laughter again.

'For heaven's sake, try to think of something sad,' Kate said as they hovered at the door.

With difficulty, they composed their faces and made it up the aisle to where an anxious-looking Fergal stood, alongside Woody, who'd reluctantly agreed to be best man.

'You don't need a best man for a blessing,' Woody had protested, but Angie had insisted that it all be done in as traditional a manner as possible, bearing in mind that Fergal's siblings had come a long way for this event and would expect some semblance of a ceremony.

It was with relief that Kate handed Angie over to her new husband, and she and Woody were able to sit down in the front pew, finally relieved of their duties.

The elderly priest, Father Paddy Reagan, who covered

several parishes including Tinworthy, had come from about two miles away. He was a jovial little soul: short, plump, bald on top with prolific white sideburns and a huge, gappy smile. He was happy, he said, to act as God's representative, and to bless the union of these two mature people. When he'd finished the little ceremony, he wished them long lives and much happiness, at which point the whole church burst into applause.

The Connollys were all on top form, commenting on how lovely Angie was, and how lucky Fergal was to have found himself such a wonderful bride. Not for the first time, Kate wondered privately where they'd all been when a penniless Fergal had arrived from Ireland some years before. He could certainly have done with their support then.

'Sure, our Fergal was always a bit of a divil himself,' said the brother from Dublin to Kate, as they all gathered together outside the church, 'but he had the divil's own luck with that woman he married!' He was referring to the runaway wife.

'She'll be one of our family now,' said the sister from Glasgow, who was clad in what resembled a set of curtains: full length and vividly patterned with purple berries and autumn leaves.

'Looks like our Fergal's done well for himself,' the Galway brother said, looking approvingly at the emerald-clad Angie.

'Oh, indeed,' said Kate.

They'd come from all over Tinworthy to celebrate Angie and Fergal's happy day. There'd never been a party like it in Lower Tinworthy before, everyone said as they spilled outside, clutching their glasses and trying to make themselves heard above the full-volume Irish dance music that Fergal had unearthed from somewhere. Fergal had had no idea – when he posted an invitation in the *Tinworthy Gazette*, inviting all and sundry to the proposed party – that anyone would actually show up. But show up they did, and in force.

Angie, still in her emerald-green dress and heels, gin glass in hand, was reigning supreme. Kate and Woody were circulating with some people they hadn't seen in years. They chatted to Jane and Joanne, who'd recently got married, but not by Jane's father who was the local vicar. He had never approved, but they'd found someone who did. Then they chatted to Guy and Roly, who planned to do exactly the same thing and had got the name of the obliging vicar.

There were Sue and Denise from the medical centre, who were getting quietly pickled in the corner by the window, along with Fergal's curtain-clad sister. No sign of the husband. And Polly Lock! Polly had sold The Old Locker to Angie. She had a colourful love life as well as an insatiable appetite for gossip, and she was deep in conversation with the Galway brother.

'Haven't they done a great job with this old place?' she shouted to Kate, pausing in her chat with the Irishman.

'I agree,' said Kate, looking around at Angie's autumn-themed decorations – garlands of berries, lots of pumpkins and some bright orange-and-green autumn leaves. The curtain-clad sister would melt into the background if she stood in one place for too long.

She found herself next to Marc and Jodi from the Atlantic Hotel. '*Ma chérie*, we have so much more space at ze hotel!' he lamented with a Gallic shrug.

That was as maybe, Kate thought, but Angie and Fergal had insisted on having the party at The Old Locker.

Kate stopped suddenly, spotting a familiar face. Who *was* she? Of course – *Maureen Grey*! Poor Maureen who'd lost her little girl in that hit-and-run accident. Maureen smiled and introduced her new friend as Edward, or was it Edgar? No matter, Maureen looked happier than Kate could ever remember.

Someone touched her elbow. Kate *knew* that face, but *who* was *he*?

'Jordan Jarvis,' he explained, 'but you probably don't remember me?'

Of course she remembered that face! Jordan – the eager young reporter from the *Cornish Courier* who'd badgered her years ago, at the very time that she was helping Maureen.

'Jordan! You were aiming to work for *The Times*!'

'Well guess what? I got there!' He beamed happily. 'Just a few months ago! I'm home for the weekend to see my folks.'

'Congratulations, Jordan! I'm so pleased for you!'

He lowered his voice. 'Who's that gorgeous girl over there?'

As Kate followed his line of vision, her eyes alighted on Melissa Bowen. 'Not sure she'd be the one for you,' she said. 'Melissa has been engaged countless times, but no one has yet succeeded in getting her to the altar.' She noticed that Basil, Melissa's latest conquest, was absent, so perhaps the girl was on the hunt again. There was no sign, of course, of her mother, Penelope Bowen, or her mother's long-time lover, Peter Edwards. They wouldn't *dare* show their faces!

'Perhaps she just hasn't found the right guy yet,' said Jordan hopefully.

'Perhaps you're right,' Kate said doubtfully, watching Jordan as he headed in Melissa's direction.

She made her way back to the bar, where Angie was topping up her glass.

'Great party,' Kate said, 'and you never know who's going to come through the door next.'

'By the way, I invited Charlotte,' Angie said, '*and* her new man.'

'I didn't think you liked her that much,' Kate remarked, surprised.

'I didn't when she was grilling both Fergal and myself,' Angie agreed, 'but she was really nice when Fergal was in hospital, and she came in a couple of times to ask how he was, and brought some chocolates.'

'I wonder what brought *that* about?'

'She probably felt she'd been a bit hard on us both, which she had,' Angie replied, 'but I suppose she had her job to do. Anyway, I wanted to see this man of hers – a doctor, no less!'

It was only a couple of minutes later when Kate saw Charlotte and the doctor arrive. She pushed her way back to the bar and nudged her sister. 'Do you see who I see, Angie?'

'My God!' exclaimed Angie, laying her drink down on the counter. 'Will you look at *them*!'

Kate was indeed looking at them. As usual, the detective appeared to be immaculate and was wearing a very slinky black dress. Even more interesting was the man with her, who was impossibly good-looking, tall and dark-haired. Not only was he handsome, but he, too, was immaculate.

'*That's* the boyfriend?' Kate asked as the glamorous pair pushed their way through the throng.

'Barbie and Ken?' Angie suggested with a wicked grin. 'But I have to admit he's very tasty!'

Kate giggled. '*Suave* is what I'd call it! Such perfection!'

'You wouldn't want to be dropping crumbs on *their* carpet!' Angie added, taking a large slurp of her drink.

'We'd never get invited anyway!'

The immaculate pair had finally arrived at the bar. 'Congratulations!' Charlotte said to Angie. 'But where is your groom? Have you lost him already?'

'He's been swallowed up by the Connelly clan somewhere,' Angie replied, looking around vaguely.

Charlotte turned to her suave escort. 'These two lovely ladies, darling, are Angie, who just got married today, and her sister, Kate, who married my police predecessor. And this, ladies, is my fiancé, Giles.'

Giles positively exuded charm as he proffered a manicured hand to them both. 'My pleasure,' he said.

'Congratulations to you two as well,' said Kate, 'and when is your big day?'

'We haven't settled on an actual date yet,' Charlotte said, looking adoringly at her fiancé, 'but probably in the spring, in London.' Her hair was swept up in an elegant chignon, with not one wisp escaping. She had a rock to rival Gibraltar on her engagement finger.

'We're hoping for St Martin-in-the-Fields,' added Giles, 'and then The Savoy.'

'And both of you, and your husbands of course, will be invited,' said Charlotte.

'We'll look forward to that,' Kate said truthfully.

'Indeed we will,' echoed Angie. 'Now, what can I get you to drink?'

Kate, smiling, moved away while the happy couple were trying to decide whether they should have Veuve Cliquot or Laurent-Perrier, their choice simplified by the fact that The Old Locker only stocked Moët & Chandon.

Studying Giles from behind, Kate decided that, from the top of his beautifully coiffed dark hair, via his immaculately tailored suit, to the tips of his highly polished Italian shoes, this man was – without any doubt – the perfect partner for Charlotte Martin.

It was at this point that Angie and Fergal rang a bell, and the conversation lessened by about a decibel. Woody had joined them behind the bar and was bellowing for silence.

'Ladies and gentlemen!' he shouted. 'Not only has Fergal here come out of his recent trauma alive, if with a sore head' – here he paused for the cheering to subside – 'but, as you know, we're celebrating the fact that, this very morning, Kate and I accompanied these two to the registry office and finally witnessed them becoming legal. And then' – he waited for the cheers to subside again – 'we accompanied them to St Swithin's for a church blessing.' There was further applause and laughter. 'So raise your glasses, everyone, and let's drink a toast to Angie and Fergal!'

'Angie and Fergal!' everyone shouted in unison.

Fergal, a protective arm around his new wife, was waving his glass in the air. Kate wondered if he was actually holding her up, because she'd been on the gin all afternoon. At least they had the following day to recover on their way to London, prior to their flight to New York on the Sunday.

The following morning, Kate and Woody returned to The Old Locker to see Angie and Fergal off on their honeymoon. Angie had been anxious about leaving the place so soon after the party, but she needn't have worried – Emma and Carlos had done a great job of helping to run the bar last night, and a first-class job of tidying up afterwards.

'You wouldn't even think we'd *had* a party,' Angie remarked as she humped her suitcase downstairs and out to the car, 'particularly as we didn't wrap up until after two. There's bound to be someone complaining, I suppose, but I don't care. I've got such a bloody headache that I'm planning to sleep all the way to Heathrow.'

Fergal followed with his case and placed them both in the boot of the car.

Kate embraced her sister. 'Have a great time, Angie!'

'Oh, I intend to,' Angie replied, holding her tight for a moment. Then she gave Woody a quick peck on the cheek and got into the passenger seat.

'Drive carefully,' Woody advised Fergal, clapping him on

the back. 'We'll miss you both. Where are we going to get our daily dramas from?'

'Oh, I've no doubt you two will find some from somewhere,' Angie said blithely as she closed the door and wound down the window.

Fergal got into the driving seat. 'Watch out, Big Apple, here we come!' he shouted cheerfully as he slammed the door. He started the engine, they all waved, and then they were gone.

'I shall miss the silly cow,' Kate said sadly as, arm in arm, she and Woody walked up the lane to Lavender Cottage.

'I shall miss The Greedy Gull,' Woody said morosely as they passed the empty pub.

'Someone will take it over eventually,' Kate said. 'Life goes on.'

'Yeah,' Woody agreed with a smile, 'life goes on.'

A LETTER FROM DEE

Dear Reader,

I hope you've enjoyed *A Body in a Cornish Village*, which is the seventh in the Kate Palmer series. If you'd like to catch up on the other six, or any of my women's fiction novels, just sign up with the link below. Your email address will never be shared and you can unsubscribe at any time.

www.bookouture.com/dee-macdonald

If you enjoyed this book, I'd be grateful if you could write a review, because I love to know what my readers think, and it also helps new readers to discover my books for the first time.

This will be the final Kate Palmer book, as I do feel the poor woman needs to relax and enjoy the rest of her retirement, minus the murders! However, there is more women's fiction on the horizon and also more cosy crime with a Scottish setting.

You can get in touch with me at any time via my Facebook page or through Twitter.

With many thanks,

Dee

facebook.com/AuthorDeeMacDonald

twitter.com/DMacDonaldAuth

ACKNOWLEDGEMENTS

Huge thanks to my two brilliant editors at Bookouture, Lizzie Brien and Natasha Harding, who do such a great job at knocking my manuscripts into shape, and for being so positive and enthusiastic.

And thank you to my agent, Amanda Preston, and to everyone at LBA, for introducing me to Bookouture and for continuing to look after my interests.

I'm immeasurably grateful, as always, to my friend and mentor, Rosemary Brown, who insists I plot and plan before I go anywhere near my laptop, as otherwise readers would probably guess who the culprit is by Chapter Two!

Thanks to my husband, Stan, for putting up with these long writing sessions and providing the necessary refreshment, and to my son, Dan, and his family, for checking my reviews and sorting out my technical problems.

An enormous thank you to the team at Bookouture, who are the friendliest and loveliest publisher on earth! There's a large team who've helped to produce this book, including Ruth Tross, Alba Proko, Melissa Tran, Peta Nightingale, Mandy Kullar, Stephanie Straub and the brilliant marketing team. A special thanks to Kim Nash and Noelle Holden for all the promotional work they do on behalf of all the writers.

Last, but not least, thank you to you, the reader, for buying my books, and to all the book groups who kindly choose to read my women's fiction and take the trouble to contact me.

I am very grateful to you all.

Made in United States
Troutdale, OR
09/25/2024

23133526R00159